I0827643

Nashville

ISBN: 978-1-9194540-1-6

Cover Design: Chris Reilly (Deposit Photos/Canva)
Interior Format: Chris Reilly Author

NASHVILLE

BOOK 2 BLACKHAWK DISCIPLES MC

CHRIS REILLY

About The Series

The Blackhawk Disciples MC is a 10-book series. Each book focuses on a single couple who have their HEA within the book.

The overarching storyline will run through the full series and must be read in order. All the brothers of the MC appear in every book.

Trigger Warnings

This series has darker themes including, violence and death. In this book scenes of being held captive, forced prostitution and non consent drug use are a small part of the story. Trigger warnings for the series can be found on my website www.chrisauthorreilly.com

Chapter One

Nashville

Usually, when my phone rings, I'm quick to answer. It's never a social call, it's always work. Damn, I'm fucked, I can barely open my eyes, and where the fuck am I anyway? I peek open one eye and recognize my surroundings.

At least I'm in my own bed, and one glance behind me tells me I'm alone. So why do I feel like I've been clocked on the head instead of sleeping.

The phone stops ringing, giving me time to groan, wipe my eyes and stretch out like a starfish.

There is nothing like a good back crack when you wake up, even my toes pop. Rolling over, I pick up the phone and check the display, squinting again. With one tap on the base, the lamp comes on, it's on the lowest setting so I don't burn my retinas.

Last time I checked, it was Tuesday. Today is Thursday. Well, fuck me, I actually did sleep for two days. It's a miracle no one bothered me. Technically, I haven't slept the whole time, a man's gotta eat. But I do need a shower.

It's been a hell of a few weeks. And the problems the club is facing aren't fixed yet, so nothing is going to let up. The call was from Rebel, my VP at the Blackhawk Disciples MC. As an officer, I'm expected to be available at any time. Luckily, checking the call log, I've not missed any other calls.

Rolling onto my back and fussing with the pillow to get comfortable, I hit redial and try to sneak the yawn out before he picks up.

Rebel is a good guy, we get on, but he is super serious. Guess he has to be holding the role he does. Sometimes he's more of a hard ass than Nero, our president, and that guy is really something when he's out for blood.

After what happened with his son, who none of us knew existed till this week, and his new woman, he's shown a different side to himself.

Most of the officers at the club are good guys, given what we do. Occasionally there are some arguments, but we always have each other's backs. Then there is Stryker, our Reaper, the man who deals with the really fucked up shit no one else wants to.

We were at his farm outside of the city just a few nights ago, getting information from one of the assholes who attacked Nero's house. I'm just glad I left before the body was thrown to the pigs. I'm not as squeamish about it as Nero or some of the other guys, but I did watch them once. They don't even care they're eating clothes.

Enough of that shit.

"Need you at the clubhouse."

No preamble from Rebel as normal. "What's up?"

"The other issue Nero had us on, it's time."

"Give me fifteen."

Rebel hangs up. Fifteen minutes to shower, grab a pop tart and get to the clubhouse. Doable. Maybe. It actually takes twenty-five, but I'm only the fourth person to arrive, so I feel somewhat vindicated. At least I smell fresh as a daisy, even if my stomach is empty.

"This is that college kid?" Beast asks.

He's sitting at the table already, drinking a cup of coffee. Bastard. He's a big dude and he's been here a long time, but only became the Tail Gunner when Nero took over.

Some might say it's not one of the sexiest roles to have in an MC, but the tail gunner is really fucking important on runs. Anyone comes up behind you, trying to ambush or sneak attack, Beast is the first line of defense for the whole crew.

I sit next to him and lean over a little to sniff his coffee. He elbows me.

"Pots full over there, asshole."

He scowls at my grin. I go over to grab some and raise the pot at Blaze when he comes in. He nods, and I make him one too. He's the club secretary/treasurer, but also the guy who knows how to do all the technical stuff we use these days.

Like finding this college kid.

In all the hubbub with Storm, the ex-member who is causing us shit, dealing with this kid has been put on the back burner. Nero will never forget it. The dipshit attacked Taylor, Nero's woman. The stupid son of a bitch has been marked and doesn't know it yet.

We protect our own, and sometimes what we do is just mild retaliation, or a warning. Putting hands on a woman, especially the President's woman, well that is a fucked up offense.

The other man in the room is Fury, our enforcer, no need to explain his job. He beats the shit out of people. Although no one does that quite like Stryker who is nowhere to be seen.

"Sit down," Rebel says.

Razer, Nero and Stryker aren't here. We do as he says, Rebel standing at the head of the table. He won't take the chair, that is Nero's. His is to the right, but for whatever reason, he wants to stand today.

Shit, none of this is important. I do like to watch people though. Studying folk is a pastime I've had since childhood. My role here, sergeant-at-arms, means I'm in charge of dealing with any issues inside the club, if any brothers get out of line, anything I need to keep an eye on. Also, to make sure Nero is protected at all times.

That is kind of hard when he's avoiding me. Well, not avoiding me. He's spending time with his family after their ordeal. Would have thought he'd be here for this.

"You all know what this is about. Only two of the bastards got held over and charged with the attacks. The other three got off because of their rich parents, but they did what we wanted. They're pissed at Morris and think he turned them in. That little fucker has been hiding. Blaze."

We turn to him when he starts to talk about where Morris has been hiding out. Some fancy second home down in Severna Park.

Beast whistles. He's right too. That's an expensive neighborhood, with houses worth upward of five million. And not exactly easy for a group of guys on motorcycles to roll up on.

It has heavy security around it, given Morris is the son of a judge.

"Any way to lure him back?" I ask.

Blaze shakes his head. "This isn't a beatdown. Nero wants it to look like he's disappeared on his own to avoid his partners going after him. There are a lot of messages between the three assholes who got off. They're morons," he shakes his head. "It's a fucking miracle they managed to go undetected so long."

"They weren't expecting us," Fury smirks at Blaze.

These animals have been using motorcycles to rob unsuspecting pedestrians. Last few weeks, it has escalated from snatching phones and bags as they drive by, to attacking people. I've seen the video of what they did to Taylor. No woman should be punched in the face three times and knocked to the ground over a goddamn phone and purse.

The police hadn't been able to track them down, but Blaze knew who they were a couple of hours after Nero asked him to find the fuckers. It surprised me they went down the arrest route. Until it was explained they were setting Morris up by leaving him out of it.

Our contact at the Baltimore PD slipped the others some hints that they were turned in by one of their crew...

And of course, that would be the only one who wasn't brought in for questioning, or subsequently charged. His friends will believe his judge father pulled strings to keep him safe.

The rest is history. Another reason to admire the way Nero's mind works. This kid is a big deal, him disappearing for no good reason would have caused a shitstorm in the press.

We're setting up his so-called friends. No one is gonna come looking for us.

"So, field trip?" I finish off my coffee.

"Ronin and Ratchet are up there keeping an eye on him."

"We're gonna let them grab him?" I ask somewhat disappointed.

"No, you dumb fucker," Rebel smirks.

He doesn't mean it, so I wink, and he looks away with a heavy sigh.

"Nero wants this far away from us. He's not going to the farm."

That's news to all of us. The pig farm does a good job of making anyone disappear, so why would we take him somewhere else?

"It's what Nero wants."

Who are we to argue with that? Rebel tells us we'll be driving up close to Severna Park tomorrow night, we'll be keeping a low profile. Which means cages instead of our bikes. That doesn't bother me the way it does some of the other guys in the club. I like driving a car now and then.

We break up the meeting, and I go in search of food. The bar next door serves after midday, so I head through there. Raven is behind the bar on her phone, she smiles when I come in, then frowns when I let myself behind the bar and walk over.

She covers the end of the phone. "What?"

"I'm hungry."

"What do you want me to do about it?"

"Is Curly in yet?"

"No, stay out of my kitchen."

My grin stretches and she tries to grab me, but I hop out of reach and go through the door to the little kitchen. They don't serve big meals, just easy food. I help myself and make a giant sandwich then walk back through and sit at a booth in the corner.

Raven glares, but I smile back until she shakes her head and focuses on her phone call. She loves me really. A couple of the local community college students come in and sit a few tables away. They keep sneaking glances at me. Most likely because of the cut, but I like to think my mug is handsome enough to draw attention.

I'm not in the habit of flirting with girls that young though, so I finish up, then head to the kitchen to wash the dishes. They're still looking when I come back out, so I throw them a wink and disappear into the back. There is a short hallway through to the clubhouse that only the officers have the code for.

Until we head down to Severna Park tomorrow, there isn't much for me to do. Beast is just leaving, so I catch up and ask where he's headed.

"Elegance. There's an issue with one of the dancers."

"Sounds like you need a hand."

"Why are you suddenly so interested in hanging out at the strip club?"

"I wouldn't say I've been hanging out." I pull a bemused face at him. "I'm just bored."

"No blow jobs."

"Honey, I don't think you can handle me."

I get a punch in the gut for that, but laugh as he gets on his bike and rides off. I really am at a loss, and I know he doesn't mean to be a grump, so I get on my bike and catch up to him. He eyes me but says nothing.

When we arrive, I'm pretty sure he's glad I came along. Ellie is screaming at one of the other dancers, and three more are standing back watching. It's not like Ellie to get this angry, so it must be serious.

"You wanted to come with," Beast looks at me.

I hold up my hands. "Strip club is your business."

"Fucker."

"Oh, shit," I point and laugh.

The woman with the dark hair just tried to sneak attack Ellie with her bright red claw nails, but she bats her away and slaps her face so hard she spins around, loses her balance, and falls on her ass.

"Jesus fucking Christ."

While I watch him go into the fray, more of the girls come from the back. One of them is the new waitress. She's dressed in civilian clothes this time and is wide-eyed at the fight. Not in a scared way, more like she can't believe how stupid they're being.

She has the kind of face that is hard to look at, but difficult to look away from too. Her figure is slim but stacked, like a pin-up girl.

Damn, another woman who is close to Ellie has jumped in and grabbed the downed woman's hair. This shit isn't normal, Beast only hires the best here, and scrapping isn't something he has had to worry about before. Maybe it isn't so funny because this isn't your standard bitch fight, this is claws, feet and punches.

I wade in to help, and he gives me a grateful look.

"Bet you're glad I came now."

"Shut up, dickhead, just get her out of here."

"Why do I have to take the hellcat?"

"What's wrong, you can't handle it?"

For a second, I study how to go about it, getting in between all the flailing limbs and hair pulling.

Then a loud crash startles everyone. Including Beast. He's on his feet in seconds, his hand going for the holster under his cut. All the women stop, and I step around them, ready to take on whatever just walked in while we were occupied.

Well, shit.

It's the cute little waitress. I mean, it did the job.

She just smashed a three hundred dollar bottle of champagne on the floor.

Chapter Two

Charley

Everyone is looking at me. It might not have been the best idea, but it stopped the fighting. I can't stand fighting, and seeing women tearing at each other like that just brings back bad memories. It wasn't really a conscious thought to break a bottle, but I needed it to stop.

And the two bikers trying were doing a really bad job.

Only now I'm looking down at the mess and the label on the bottle. Oh God, this is going to come out of my pay. And that is a huge chunk of change.

I've dropped enough trays over the last week, I'm surprised they haven't already fired me. Ellie has been good about it, though another waitress has been helping me practice. She doesn't look as easygoing now. Hopefully, that has more to do with Stella starting a fight.

The interruption has given Beast and his friend opportunity to break up the fight and separate the girls. He has pushed Stella into the booth and is guarding her from getting up.

The other guy, the cute one who throws out winks like dollar bills, is watching me with a frown. He's probably pissed about the champagne too. My gaze goes back to Stella, there is blood on her face where Lily has raked her nails down it.

The fight has been brewing for a while. Ellie was trying to handle it, guess Stella lost her faculties for a minute if she tried to hit Ellie.

I've only known Ellie for five days, but I already like her. She's been nice to me, even if she's still refusing to let me dance. Which is why I came here in the first place.

I'm lucky to have the job they gave me. If they hadn't, my next stop was the club a few blocks over. I did my research, and although Elegance was my first choice, I was fully expecting to be refused a job here. The thought of dancing at a place called Fantasy Island made my skin crawl.

But I need money, and as much as I hate the thought of it, dancing at a place like this is a way to make it fast and easy.

If taking your clothes off in front of a room full of strangers is easy.

I'm still working up to it, which is crazy given I came here planning to do just that. Part of me is glad Beast won't let me dance.

I'm twenty years and nine months old, and he still refuses to let me dance. He really doesn't live up to that name. At least, from what I've seen of him, and the other girls all rave about how great he is.

Given he hasn't come over here and yelled at me or fired me for smashing that bottle, I have to agree.

There is still time. He needs to sort out Stella and Lily first.

Max comes out from behind the bar with a brush and shovel set. I take it from him, even though he offers to brush up the glass for me. This was on me, so I thank him but get on with it, he brings a garbage can out for me to dispose of the glass, then a mop and bucket to wipe up the alcohol.

Some of it got on my legs, and my shoes are soaked. They're the only pair of sneakers I have until payday. I've asked Ellie for an advance, she said I need to get through seven days before they consider it. Almost there.

If I don't get fired.

Like Stella just did. Ellie was going to do it anyway, but it's come from Beast, and she's not going to swing on him.

In the back of my mind, a small kernel of hope starts to build. They're down a dancer for tonight. It's too soon to go ask, right?

The hot biker escorts Stella back to the dressing room to get her things. Ellie is talking to Lily and doesn't look happy about it, but she rubs her arm at the end of their chat. I'm glad she didn't get fired too. I like Lily. Some of the other dancers haven't been as welcoming.

They think I'm entitled because I wasn't turned away when they said I couldn't dance. Beast gave me a server job. I'm not like that, it's not annoyance that I'm not getting what I want. It's disappointment and frustration.

The place I'm staying is loud, cramped and I barely get enough sleep, it was all I could afford when I got to Baltimore.

Luckily, I have access to this place early, so can sneak in for a shower before the others arrive for their shift.

It's been a long hard road getting here and I'm not out of the woods yet but for the first time, I feel like I've landed somewhere that is going to get me out of that apartment and into my own place, somewhere safe where I don't have to barricade the door before I go to sleep.

"It was good that you wanted to stop them fighting, but maybe grab one of the cheap bottles next time," Max says, taking the mop to wheel away from me.

"I'll try to remember that," I say with a sheepish shrug.

He's been nice to me too. I genuinely do feel lucky to have got a job here. Once he's gone and the other girls have gone in back, Ellie finishes up her talk with Beast and heads toward me. I wring my hands together behind my back, trying not to show any fear.

Ellie doesn't really appreciate anything but straightforwardness. She is no-nonsense, fair but easily irritated if someone is being dumb. I straighten my back and try to look like I'm not desperate. It's a look I've perfected recently.

She leans against the bar and looks where there are still a couple of upturned chairs. Beast is setting them straight, the rest of the girls have gone in back. The other hot biker is back there too. Probably getting a blow job.

Oh, I heard him make that comment the other night. Foolishly, it was the reason I tripped and dropped the tray, up until that point, I'd had no mishaps that night.

"Floor is still sticky," She taps it with the toe of her expensive shoes a few times.

"I'll get the mop and do it again," I tell her.

She blows out a heavy sigh and looks at me. Here it comes. There will be no tears. I'm not crying in front of anyone ever again. That can come when I get back to my shitty room where no one will hear me over the thumping music at all hours of the night.

"I know what you're thinking," she says, tilting her head to study me. "There is an empty slot for a dancer."

Well, I did think about that earlier, but not that she was going to raise it now.

"Beast won't let you take it. He's made that clear. And it's not just about our rules, Charley. It's state mandates for anyone performing in a club like this. You have to be twenty-one. He won't do anything to bring down sanctions or fines on Elegance. Before you ask, yes, you're not old enough to drink alcohol, but he has ways around you serving it, so that isn't the same thing."

"That's fair."

"However, I have watched you practice. You're very good at dancing. Don't look too excited," she cuts off what I was about to say. "Being a dancer and being a stripper are two different things. I know Beast makes everyone refer to us as dancers, but that is because he's too polite to call us what we are."

"If you think I won't be able to do it-"

"It's not that I think you won't be able to. I know you won't. I'm going to assume you're not a virgin?" A shake of my head answers that intrusive question. "So someone at least has seen your tits. In an intimate setting, that is all fine and dandy, but shaking them around on a stage, with men leering at you, is the total opposite.

"When you start out at Elegance, you do a couple of sets three times a week. You don't get to give private dances until you've been here a year. Anything that goes on outside of that is done on your own time," she gives me a pointed look.

And it's timely that she mentioned it, because the hot guy has come back into the room and gone to talk to Beast.

I'm still not sure she isn't going to fire me, but I don't think she would stand here telling me all of this just to ask me to leave.

There is no point arguing with her about whether I'd be a good stripper versus a dancer. The thought of it does terrify me, the problem is, I've had it in my head for over a year now that it is what I need to do to get where I want to be.

Dammit, I'm going to end up being a waitress. Unless I can prove myself. Well, I'm nothing if not determined.

"I've seen girls come and go over the years," Ellie continues, her eye on Beast. "Some good, some terrible, some far better than this place."

"Which one do I fall under?"

"Not sure yet. It's not terrible at least," she lets out another sigh. "You have what? Four months until you're legally able to dance?"

"I'll be twenty-one in December."

"Hmm," she fixes her hair and eyes me. "I'm going to give you the key to one of the back rooms. You can only use it out of hours and when there is someone else here to keep an eye on things."

It's on the tip of my tongue to ask if she is serious but that sounds like something a kid would say, so I nod instead, trying to look as if this is something I am very grateful for, rather than jumping up down and thanking her. Ellie wouldn't appreciate that.

"When you think you're ready, Beast and I will watch you."

That draws me up short. It's more that he's my boss rather than a man watching.

Ellie gives me a sad smile.

"It's fine. I can do it," I cut off anything she was going to say.

"We'll see. Get the mop and clean this again, we don't want anyone wearing two hundred dollar shoes feeling like they're in a college bar tonight."

Not even the thought of cleaning up can dull the excitement. I'm going to prove her wrong, and that she is right to put her faith in me.

After another long shift serving drinks to rich men and the occasional miserable looking woman, I head to the dressing rooms to change out of my uniform, if you could call it that.

It's one way to get used to people staring at my body. My ass practically hangs out the bottom of the shorts, and the apron does nothing to keep my boobs under control.

It's not exactly against the rules, but I have little satin covers over my nipples. To keep them from poking through the fabric if I get cold, not because I'm scared of anyone seeing them.

Lily is in the changing room when I come in, staring at her reflection. She is topless, wearing just a pair of denim shorts.

"Hey, break anything else tonight?"

I blow out a breath so hard my lips vibrate, then walk over and sit at the dressing table next to her. She's been nice to me from day one. I would have been really upset if she had lost her job over Stella.

"Beside the champagne bottle, no. I think I'm getting better."

She snorts a laugh and picks up some wet wipes to remove her makeup. The girls need to put on a lot of heavy makeup to wear under the lights. She is prettier as she removes it, and peels off her false eyelashes.

"Karin saw Ellie talking to you earlier," she looks at my reflection in the mirror beside hers.

"She was telling me that just because Stella is gone, doesn't mean her slot is open."

"That sucks."

"It's okay, I mean, I understand why. She says it's about making sure they don't break any laws."

That gets a real laugh out of her. She tosses her wipes into the trash can and stands to reach for her bra. I force myself not to turn away. Although seeing naked women in a setting like this isn't so bad.

"What's so funny?"

"You know who owns this place, right?"

"Beast?"

"And you've noticed what he wears?"

"Of course I have, I'm not blind. I know they're bikers."

"One percenter."

"Like Sons of Anarchy?"

She laughs again. "Yeah, like that. Only real life. Don't worry," she takes out her earrings and drops them into a tray on the table, it's just costume jewelry, so not worth anything. "There has never been any trouble here. But don't be under any illusions about these men. They're criminals, they do bad things. This place," she leans closer. "Either washes their dirty money, or it's one of the businesses they have that are clean, where their criminal dealings don't get involved. I've never figured out which."

Wow, that's interesting. I've worked in some shady places owned by unsavory people. This is nothing like any of those places.

"Like I said, they look after the dancers, the clientele is decent and if they're not, they get thrown out. And they pay really well. Which is why," she pauses to pull on her T-shirt. "I was an idiot for jumping into that fight. Beast doesn't tolerate violence."

"You were defending Ellie."

"I'm lucky they saw it that way. Plus, Stella is a bitch."

I have nothing to say about that. I didn't know her well enough, and she never made the effort to try with me.

"What are you up to tonight? Heading home?" she asks.

"I was going to go grab something to eat first, it's kinda hectic at my place, I prefer to wait till most of them have passed out."

"It's a little late, are you going with anyone?"

My throat gets tight. Her concern surprises me. People don't generally ask me questions like that, or care if I'm safe. No one needs to know my situation, so I wave her off and say one of my roommates works at the local twenty-four hour diner.

"Are you sure?" Lily asks, the look on her face saying she doesn't fully believe me.

"Scout's honor."

"Okay, well, be careful. And don't get too disheartened about dancing. I've seen you practicing on that pole, you're really good, Charley. When you're ready, you're going to drive them insane. And when that happens," she laughs and rubs her thumb and two fingers together, indicating that involves a lot of cash. "Have a good night, and I'll see you tomorrow."

She opens the door to find Walker waiting. He is one of the security guards, and he sees everyone out to their cars, even though it's all behind a high chain fence so people can't get in. He pops his head in and sees me.

"You heading out soon, Charley?"

"Two minutes," I tell him, jumping up to get my street clothes out of my locker. I did want to get in the shower, but I've spent too long talking to Lily. Although I have learned something I didn't know when I walked in here looking for a job.

Beast doesn't look like a criminal. I mean, he wears the leather vest and has tattoos, but he's kind of gentle, he talks softly, which makes his name really odd. Unless when he is away from here, he turns into some kind of beast.

Wonder what the other guy is called? It doesn't matter, that's not why I'm here, even if he is absolutely gorgeous, the kind of good looking you don't expect to meet in real life.

A knock at the door jolts me out of my thoughts, and I quickly throw my uniform into the bag and drag on my leggings and T-shirt.

Walker sees me out to the beat-up old car I bought on my travels a few states ago. It looks terrible and one of the rear windows has a bag taped over it to keep the wind and rain out but it gets me from A to B. Walker eyes it and waits until the engine turns over after a few tries of the key, then waves. The gates are automatic, so he goes back inside.

My stomach growls, but I'm tired, and it's late, and until I get that advance, I have to be careful with money. Decision made, I head towards home. If I can call a tiny room in an old four story house with the kind of people you wouldn't want to find yourself alone with, your home.

A few more months. That is all it's going to take. If I can convince Ellie to believe in me and not flake the first time I have to walk on a stage and strip.

Chapter Three

Nashville

"Have you ever thought about buying a house like this?"

Ronin is sitting next to me on a slope behind the Morris kids' house. The security around this place is insane, but we have at least established he's here alone. It's the kind of place where *one would have staff*, and the owner is rich enough to have a property like this sitting empty.

"You think I could afford this shit?"

"You know, if you had the money."

I like Ronin, he's one of the good guys in the MC, strong, reliable and knows how to get shit done. If there were an opening, Nero would give him a spot on the council. He does sometimes ask random questions when we're on a stakeout. It's a good job it's me he's talking to.

"Nah, not something like this. If I had that kind of money, I'd buy a yacht with a helicopter pad. Learn to sail and fly at the same time."

"I just think it's crazy that someone needs more than one house when there are so many people out there living in shit situations."

"Wow, I didn't know that was the way you were going with this. Now I feel kinda bad."

"It's all good, this guy's dad worked hard to make his money, to get this house, and his little shit of a kid is in there, hiding away with his 90-inch TV screen and gaming consoles and Rolex watches. I hate spoiled little bitches like him."

"Don't envy him too much. He's about to have a really bad night."

The security light at the back of the house goes on, and I sit forward a little. The door opens about twenty seconds after, and Dean Morris walks out onto the patio. He moves across the lawn to the swimming pool and pulls a pack of cigarettes from his pocket.

"How much do you want to bet he's so scared of his mommy he won't smoke in the house even when he's miles away from her?"

"Mommy will wish she hadn't been a bitch when her blue-eyed boy vanishes." I get up and turn on the comms receiver. "I love this shit," I tap the device in my ear. I've got no idea where Blaze got it all from, but I'm loving not having to use our cell phones to communicate.

"He's in the yard."

"I've got into the security system," Blaze's voice comes back.

He goes on to explain what he is doing. I'm not even going to pretend to know what he means, but I have the gist. The alarm system deactivated when Morris opened the door and came outside. Whatever Blaze has done has overridden the rest of the system so that all the doors and windows are knocked off the security alerts instead of just the back door that Morris opened.

We can sneak in without alerting Morris or their security company because he will have no idea it hasn't been rearmed after going back inside.

It takes the dumbass ages to finish because he takes out his phone and sits there doomscrolling. These kids and their fucking phones, he's supposed to be hiding out. Anyone with any tech knowhow could find him.

It's another twenty minutes of watching before he finishes and goes inside, then half an hour before all the lights finally go out. To be sure, Blaze tells us to wait a little longer for him to fall asleep. My ass is numb by the time we move. Everyone has their own part of the plan, Ronin and I are the ones who are going to grab him.

Ratchet will go inside and pack up some stuff, his phone and wallet, while Blaze gets into his bank accounts and transfers all the money out to an account no one will be able to trace.

Everything to make it look like he ran.

Ronin picks up the black duffle bag and we head down the hill. There are security cameras, but Blaze has disabled them. When we get into the back of the property, we pause and Blaze kills all the lights on the block. Ronin opens the door carefully and we step inside the house.

Any lights that were on before the blackout, come back on. People will report a power outage which will explain why the cameras went off if anyone decides to look into it. For the first few hours or a day or so, his parents will think something has happened to him and the police will be looking.

This whole operation has been planned down to the last detail, we've memorized the layout of the house and move silently up the stairs to the bedroom Morris has been sleeping in.

The TV is on and as carefully as I can, I push the door open an inch to see inside. He's laying on his back with one arm over his head and the other hand on his dick. Fortunately, he's asleep. I get it, sometimes the comfort of holding your junk makes you drift off easier.

The thought he jacked off crosses my mind and I hope he had some tissue to deal with the *fall out* of that. Indicating to Ronin that it's safe, he bends down and opens the bag, taking out the needle.

He manages to inject the sedative easily enough, but Morris wakes from the pinch of the needle. His eyes widen in fear when he sees us and just for fun, and for Taylor, I punch the fucker in the face. The point is not to leave any trace of him being taken but I have a solid right hook and with the quick acting sedative and the punch combination, he's out cold in seconds.

Ronin is busy unwrapping the body bag and we get him inside and zip it up. I radio Ratchet via the cool comms equipment, he comes in and looks at the body bag as we heft it up between us.

Morris is not a small guy. It always amuses me how these buff gym guys like to flex and pose in mirrors and take a million selfies, but when it comes down to it, they fall like a fucking felled oak tree.

When we reach the top of the stairs, I look at Ronin and he looks at me and without a word, we toss the fucker down the stairs. He doesn't make a peep, and hell it made our life easier.

Fury is waiting in the garage which he was breaking into while we were getting the fucker. We throw him in the back of Morris' own car and watch Fury drive away.

He's wearing a baseball cap to fool any cameras, but Blaze has mapped it all out and will make sure the driver is obscured in any images.

We meet Ratchet at the bottom of the stairs and sneak out the back. All in all, it took ten minutes max before we've made our exit back up the hill and a block over from the house.

Blaze is waiting for us in the van. We jump in and drive off to the meeting point.

"Nero is here," Blaze says.

That's a surprise but at the same time, not so much. I did think it was crazy he was going to leave us to this. With the whole Storm mess being on the back-burner while we track down the fucker, it's left him open to handle this.

It would surprise me even more if Nero went soft just cos he has a woman. Not many of the men with old lady's do, they become more secretive if anything.

Nero is waiting at a house in a less affluent neighborhood, and Fury has already carried the body bag in. We watch him tie the kid to a chair with zip ties at his ankles and his wrists behind his back. The others stayed in the van, so it's just the three of us now.

Nero nods at me, silently telling me we did a good job, then he takes out a rope and ties it around the kid's neck.

Once everything is set up, we wait for the drug to wear off. No one speaks, Nero sends a few texts, Fury stands over Morris with his arms folded.

Stuff like this bothered me initially when I joined the MC. It's a rite of passage, a tie in to the club every member had to take part in to prove their loyalty.

Since Nero took over, he's stopped all that hazing shit. Any necessary killing is usually done by the officers, away from the clubhouse. Sometimes he handpicks others to be a part of it but its rare, hence why Ronin and Ratchet are left outside for this part.

The kid hasn't got a clue where he is initially, all fucked up and disorientated. When he sees the three angry looking bikers standing over him he starts to struggle.

"What the fuck? Who are you, where am I?" he turns his head as far as he can, then dips his chin when he realizes there is a rope around his neck. "What is this? My parents have money, they'll pay you."

"We're not interested in your money," Nero tells him.

"Then what do you want? You've got the wrong person. I'm just a college kid, I'm not involved in anything. Please I won't say anything."

He keeps babbling and pleading, even though he doesn't appear to have a clue why he is here. That says a lot about the little fucker. He shuts up pretty quick when Fury takes out his knife.

His eyes go wide and in seconds the smell of piss fills the room. I'd feel bad if I hadn't watched the video of what this kid did to Taylor. He's a budding psychopath according to Blaze's research.

"Remember this?" Nero pulls out his phone and holds it up.

Nero can't see the screen and there is no sound but I watch it, see Taylor taking those punches to the face and falling to the ground. Nero doesn't want to watch it again and I get it. It hardens any doubts I had about this.

"I don't know what that is," he cries out. "That isn't me."

Nero nods to me and I walk behind him and grab the rope, jerking it hard so his back bows. For a good eight or so seconds I pull on it, making him thrash and try to fight it as his breath is stolen. Nero nods again and I loosen the slack on the rope.

Our Prez isn't big on torture, he usually leaves that to Stryker, or Fury. This is personal and before he ends things, he wants the kid to admit it. We go on for ten minutes, choking him and Fury cutting him in various parts of his body, before he is crying and admitting to it, begging for his life.

"You see that woman," Nero holds the phone up close to his face.

"I'm sorry, I'm sorry, please. It won't happen again. It won't, I will never do it again, I swear."

"The second you put your hands on her," Nero snarls at him. "Your life was fucking over. I want you to look at her, look at what you did."

He is crying in earnest now, squeezing his eyes shut. Nero looks at me over his head, a look of such profound disgust on his face as he lifts his chin. I loosen the rope and lift it over his head.

The kid looks up in surprise, his head swiveling between each of us, a look of hope in his eyes. Fury hands Nero the knife and any hope disappears as quickly as it came, the fear rippling through his body.

With quick precision, Nero slashes the knife across the kid's throat. An arc of blood sprays to the side. Nero had very thoughtfully placed a tarp beneath the chair prior to our arrival.

We watch as he gurgles and splutters and bleeds out. It happens pretty quick, the light dimming in his eyes.

The whole time, the video is playing, taunting him, showing him it was down to his own actions that he ended up here.

The clean-up isn't my favorite part but we get the dickhead back in his body bag, the tarp rolled and Ronin comes in to take the chair, zip ties and rope. Everything that was here when we arrived is gone. Not a speck of blood or a hint that anyone has been here by the time we leave.

"You know where you're going?" Nero asks Fury when the body is back in the trunk. He nods. "Razer is there with the bikes."

"See you at home, ladies," Fury heads around the car.

"Asshole," I call after him as Nero lets out a laugh.

Some might wonder how we make light of such a situation but we're used to it. It's our way of life and we only ever do things like this to people who deserve it.

In this case, you could say the punishment doesn't fit the crime, but Blaze believes the kid would move on to serious assault and likely murder if he was left to carry on.

With a dad who has pulled strings before to hide his son's abhorrent behavior from middle-school onwards, we did the world a favor. It's the only way to rationalize this.

Nero pats my shoulder and tells me he is going home. Taylor and Oscar are there with Jesse, his best friend. Jesse is richer than Morris' dad and lives in a penthouse apartment downtown but he's staying with them while he gets better.

I'm not sure it's necessary, he is pretty resilient and seems okay to me but they want him there. Guess when you go through an ordeal like what him and Taylor went through, it trauma bonds you.

We're quiet on the ride back to the clubhouse and go our separate ways once we're back. For a hot minute I think of going to the bar to decompress like the others but decide against it and head home.

After a night like this, a few episodes of Vampire Diaries, a guilty pleasure no one will ever hear about, and a couple of beers in my undies is what I need.

I'm sure tomorrow will bring a whole new set of shit to deal with. Right now, I'm going to enjoy my peace.

CHAPTER FOUR

Charley

THINGS ARE GETTING BETTER. I've had my advance payment so have been able to buy some new shoes and other items of clothes I found in a goodwill store. I've got the window fixed on my car, and I've spent the last two weeks using the room Ellie gave me access to, practicing as much as possible.

For the first time in months, the band around my chest loosens a little.

There have been no more mishaps at work, nothing broken and Beast has not been so tense when he sees me walking by anymore.

They replaced Stella which bummed me out but they did need a dancer to take over. I couldn't expect they'd wait around for me to be able to do it.

The only outstanding problem is where I live. I'm still not in a position to be able to change that so I'm not going to dwell on it. It's better than sleeping in the car.

As if to prove me wrong someone starts yelling outside my room, making me jump and almost burn my hand on the curling iron I'm using.

Another voice joins in, then some thumping and a crash. I get up and double check the dresser I've dragged in front of the door. It's heavy as hell, no one is moving that from the outside unless they're Hercules. It takes me enough time to drag it back and forth as it is.

I stand still watching the door with my fists clenched, and jump when something crashes against it. There is more yelling, then the sound of feet running down the stairs. Everything fades back to silence.

Maybe I shouldn't have bought new shoes and a window. I should have got a hotel room. But that requires a lot more money to keep up. At least here I just hand over a weekly cash payment. Chewing my lip I decide the risk isn't worth it. I'll find a motel somewhere when I get my next paycheck.

At least that way I have my own space and there is some element of security, even if there are shady types frequenting a motel.

It's not the same as living with a bunch of drug addicts, pimps and their girls and all the other dregs of society that have found themselves here.

It takes me another five minutes to finish my hair, grab my bag and put all my valuables in the lock box I carry around with me. I've made the mistake of hiding things under my mattress before.

The drive over to Elegance is busier than usual because of rush hour traffic, the less time I spend in that house the better, even if I just get a coffee and bagel and sit in the room Ellie said I could use.

Leo is there when I arrive today, Walker works the late shift. He's not as friendly as Walker and grunts more than talks, not that I want to hang around and make conversation. I grab a coffee from the break room by the offices, then head through to the private room.

Everything is so opulent here, the change in environments can be jarring. After breakfast I take a quick shower, careful not to mess up my hair and head back to practice.

I lose all track of time as I dance. It's been a dream of mine since I was a little girl to be up on stage dancing. My dance teacher when I was younger told me I had talent, she nurtured me, spent more time with me than her other students because she was sure I was going to make it.

Then mom died, dad re-married less than six months later to a woman with two daughters a little older than me and a son the same age. It felt like I became an unwanted visitor in my own house. Dad never stood up for me. He was the only thing I had left and he let me down.

I'm not sure professional dancing will ever happen for me. Being here at Elegance, fighting to be able to get up on the stage and dance isn't going to help. But I get to dance. It's the only thing that I have anymore. After my step-mother put an end to all of my dreams.

Then when the accident happened, everything changed.

Fighting those memories becomes impossible. The mangled metal, screams, the scent of gas and fire, melting flesh. I crumble to the floor clutching my chest as panic takes over. This is supposed to be getting easier, and it has been, but now and then the memory takes root and it's impossible to push it back into the recesses of my mind where it belongs.

I'm fucking horrified that tears are filling my eyes, and I lay down on the floor to catch my breath. If I thought I could, I'd go and make sure the door is locked but my legs have buckled, my heart feels like it is going to explode and my fingers have gone numb.

The medication I got when it first happened ran out months ago, I've had to deal with it the only way I can, letting it wash over me, until my body remembers that it's safe now. Until my mind quietens and the memories fade.

My skin is clammy when I eventually come back to myself. I've learned ways to control my mind, if not my body, when these attacks happen. If it happened when I'm at that house I know everything could fall apart. There is no way the people there wouldn't take advantage while I'm incapacitated.

It's not easy but I drag myself up and go over to the corner to get a drink of water. I need another shower but no one can see me yet. My eyes are still a little wild, my hair a mess and it will be impossible to hide there is something wrong.

Something wrong with *me*.

That's all I heard for years. So much so, I started to believe it.

"You're not there anymore," I whisper, closing my eyes. "No one can hurt you."

After a few deep breaths I turn back to the small stage with two poles. It's a private room but there is space for a small group to watch. Lily says it's usually bachelor parties or businessmen who use these rooms, two dancers work in tandem, routines have to be practiced.

That sounds like something I'd be happy to do.

Swallowing down the fear, panic and anger, I stomp back over to the stage and grab the heels from my bag. It's time to get out of my usual mind set and into that of a stripper. Like Ellie said, they're called dancers, but that isn't what they are, not really.

All the girls here have talent but at the end of the day they do it without their clothes. And if I ever want to be there, I need to practice. On my own, able to look at myself in a mirror and watch as I take off all my clothes, imagining having the eyes of a lot of men on me as I do.

Cranking up the music, I tug off my t-shirt but leave the shorts and bra. For now. I've watched a lot of routines on the internet, and seen the girls here, worked out how the moves are slightly nuanced and different to what I'm used to, how to sway in a certain way, arch my body to maximize the effect.

Some of the girls bump and grind but I don't think that is something I'm capable of. I have been practicing a certain routine though and I start to do it, working around the pole before jumping up and swinging.

There is nothing clumsy about me when I'm up here and I start to lose myself again, but pull back from the edge, long enough to let my feet hit the floor, twirl around the pole with my back to the seats and unhook my bra.

My throat swells but I cast it aside, with a sexy flick that I've seen the other girls do, then I turn around, grabbing the pole and leaning my upper body back, my back arched, boobs thrust up to the ceiling. I'm spinning, twirling and using the pole like it's an anchor when I spot my reflection in the glass.

It makes me stall and gasp to see my naked breasts. Get used to it, Charley. This is what you need to do. There is a place in my mind I can go to, muscle memory taking over when I dance. I just need to avoid the mirrors.

"Why did you stop?"

The voice startles me. I grab my boobs and look over at the door. Relief floods me when I see it's Ellie. She must have crept inside while I was lost in the music, standing back in the shadows.

"Just overthinking." I decide not to lie.

"You need to get out of your own head," she tells me.

She looks gorgeous in designer jeans, knee-high boots and a tight sweater. Her hair is pulled back in a sleek pony tail and her make-up is perfection.

"It hasn't gone unnoticed that you're working hard, Charley but you still have some sort of mental block."

"I'm working on it."

"If you want to dance here, prove to Beast you're worthy of a place on that stage, you need to do more than work on it. You will have to audition. It's not just a given that you will get a spot."

I didn't know that. That's a whole other layer of shit on top of the ever-growing pile.

"Come outside," she says and leaves.

I put on my bra, and shirt and follow her, leaving everything else. Ellie has walked over to the main stage and is waiting for me. There is no one else around which I'm grateful for when she tells me to get up on the stage.

This stage is big, it has enough room for whole dance routines as well as the poles, and there are booths right up to the edge of the stage. These are the expensive seats, with higher backs than the rest of the booths to give the people who purchase them a bit more privacy.

The stage is high enough that people behind them can still see, but now I'm up here, it's jarring how close those booths are.

Lily said they're the men you want to dance for. Not just the owners who frequent them, but the men who have subscriptions here, who hand over hundreds instead of tens and twenties. It's the Holy Grail to dance this stage.

"Do that routine," Ellie said, leaning a hip against the booth. "All of it, from the beginning and then go onto the pole like you did back there."

I touch my top and pinch my bra strap.

"You can leave that all on for now," she waves a hand.

She reminds me of my old dance teacher, a little tougher and intense maybe, she's very intimidating but if she didn't think I could do it, she wouldn't be helping me, right?

Sucking up the nerves, I move to the center of the stage. If I fuck this up, I don't think Ellie will let me take it any further.

Think of the money, think of getting your own place, finally feeling safe, you can stop running, never look back, live a better life.

There is no music, but I hear it inside my head, counting down and starting to move. I don't look at Ellie, I don't worry about anything except getting this right, proving I have what it takes.

I've been used to dancing in bare feet or dance shoes but luckily with my practice over the last week I've gotten better in the killer heels and I nail every step and move, every twirl and bend.

When I move over the pole, I leap up and wrap my legs around it, spinning and arching upwards, then stretching out my legs and slowly dropping my feet so my back is pressed against it, my hand gripping at the top of my ass. I bend my knees, roll forward and simulate taking off my bra, then I step around the pole and look down at her.

Her face is unreadable but I focus on catching my breath, breathing in and out. She is quiet so long I'm starting to think I fucked it up.

"You're too good."

"I'm sorry, what?"

Ellie shakes her head, looking perplexed.

"Why are you here, Charley?"

"I want to dance."

"You've already said that. And I understand that. What you did there, and what we do here, are two completely different things."

"I thought I did what you wanted."

"You did, and so much more. You should be doing this on a professional stage, not here."

"But... I..."

Ellie holds up her hand to stop me stuttering at her. "You move beautifully, like you were born to do it and before you get excited, that isn't a compliment. At least, not here. I could watch you dance for hours but the men who come here, that isn't why they pay hundreds of dollars."

"I can work on the routines."

"I'm sure you can. Before you go any further with what you're practicing, you need to stop and focus on a different style. Watch the girls, see how they do just enough to look like amazing dancers, but they pull back and add in what these men want to see."

I nod, I can definitely do that.

"Then you need to practice more with no clothes, Charley. What I saw in there was a girl who is unsure of herself. Embrace your sexuality, let it empower you, not scare you. These men are here to watch you, maybe to get off on seeing naked ladies, but at the end of the day, we're the ones with the power Charley. You can't forget that. If you don't project that confidence, you'll fumble, drop a tray of drinks," she smirks.

I half smile at the analogy. With a determined look I nod at her. She stares at me for a good long while but I force myself not to look away, not to wilt. She is testing me and I will not fail.

"In two weeks, I want a different routine, I want you topless, and able to dance with people watching. I'm not a dance teacher, Charley. I'm not going to pat you on the back for a job well done. I am going to assess you. If you can't do it, then I'm going to recommend that you don't even try."

"Thank you."

"Don't thank me yet. Go get ready, we'll be opening soon. Eat something, I can hear your stomach from over here."

I'd laugh if she wasn't right. I'm hungry. I watch her walk away and look around the room. The heels are hurting my feet, so I sit down to untie the buckles. Some of the girls might talk about her behind her back, but Ellie didn't get to where she is now by being super nice to everyone. She isn't horrible at all, but she is exacting and wants everyone to perform to their best ability.

I never thought I would be disappointed in someone telling me the way I dance is *too good*. How insane is that?

Someone speaks and my stomach drops so fast, I almost throw my shoe into the shadows where it came from.

"What the fuck?" I cry out.

Chapter Five

Nashville

"Ellie's right."

My voice in the quiet room startles her as she searches the darker area at the back to see where it came from, she lifts her shoe and shouts out a very unsavory word for such a pretty little thing.

I walk around the column I'd been watching her from while she was dancing, then talking to Ellie. I didn't exactly ask around but I know her name is Charley and that she spends a lot of time here when the club isn't open.

Not that I've been hanging around here too much or anything. Things have been quiet, no sightings of Storm or anyone messing with our business or warehouses. When Nero said he'd go to ground, he was right.

Blaze is doing everything he can to try to dig the worm back up.

I was wrong about Charley being like Bambi, when she gets to her feet, there is nothing wobbly or disjointed about her, she's more like a panther, graceful, lithe.

Beautiful.

"Right about what?" she asks, a scowl on her face.

It's more from fear at me freaking her out than genuine anger. I'm not sure she is capable of anger.

I move a little closer, not enough to freak her out even more. We've never talked, or been alone, just the two of us. She is dressed like a dancer at a rehearsal, not in her underwear, but the fabric is skintight, clinging to every inch of her perfect body.

"You're too good to dance here."

She rolls her neck, looking away from me. It makes me smirk but when she looks back my face is carefully neutral.

"Do you know how many times I've heard that?"

"Probably a lot. It might have more to do with you trying to dance at all the wrong places."

"How am I supposed to get the experience I need if no one will let me dance?"

"For the kind of dancing you want to do, you think they'd accept this as your experience?" I indicate around us.

Elegance is a high-end place, but there is no getting away from the fact that the women who dance here, though extremely talented, do it with their tits and ass, and occasionally their pussies on display.

Something tells me this little beauty couldn't handle that. She's picked a good place to try. Some other strip joints would have had her up on stage the second she walked through the door.

I don't know much about professional dancing, but I do know those chicks are a lot skinnier than her.

She has a beautiful body, no doubt she's kept herself fit with all the dancing she does, but her tits are more than a handful. And from the way they move when she dances, even all bound in those tight tops, they're real.

Beast tries not to take anyone on who has fake tits, but it happens a lot in this industry.

Everything about this girl is real, pure, and that is why it's dangerous for her to be in this business.

Well fuck, now I know why Beast is letting her work here. A few blocks away there is a club I've heard a lot of bad shit about. The strippers there are hardcore and dance because they have to. Here, the women dance because they love it, they feel safe and we pay them well.

Beast is worried about her so he's doing what he can to keep her here, even though she is one of the clumsiest people I've ever seen. Except when she is on stage.

"It pays well," she answers.

"You'd sacrifice your chance at professional dancing for money?"

"That isn't what I'm doing," she takes a step toward the edge of the stage, a little fight in her tone.

It's fucking hot, more so than how she looks. "Forgive me if I'm being naïve but aren't those dance types all hoity toity about where someone learned to dance?"

She licks her lips, not in a sexy way, she's trying to think of a response. My guess, she knows I'm right. Dancing here will hurt her chances of ever doing anything better. Of following her dream to be a professional dancer.

No woman ever dreams of being a stripper, I'm pretty sure of that. And even if they do, this girl isn't one of them.

"Servers here are paid well, you'd be best off sticking to that."

"Right," she mutters and reaches down to grab her shoes, muttering to herself.

She doesn't realize I have exceptional hearing.

"If Beast thought you were that bad, he would have let you go weeks ago. We've all seen you dropping a tray full at least once," I laugh.

Her back straightens and she bites her lip. Fuck, this girl. She's killing me.

"I didn't mean... I can't lose this job. I'm..." she blinks and looks as if she is trying to force the words out. "I'm practicing."

It's hard not to snort a laugh out. "Hey, no one is saying Beast is gonna fire you. And practicing will help," I wink and she frowns, like I'm making fun of her and she doesn't like it. "Stick to doing that. You get good tips."

"Not as good as the dancers," she sighs, then walks to the steps that lead down off the stage.

I watch how she moves, she carries herself like someone of a higher standing and I wonder where she came from, but it's none of my business. *She* is none of my business. It would have been best had I not stepped out of the shadows and butted into whatever was going on up there in her head.

People say I've always been a sucker for those down on their luck. That isn't what this is, but she is sad about something. Defeated was the way she looked when Ellie walked away and left her sitting next to that stripper pole.

"Well, maybe in three months you'll get your shot."

Her head comes up, a hopeful expression on her pretty face.

"Not up to me," I hold up my hands. "Buttering up Ellie or Beast won't work. They see what I see."

"What's that?" she asks, her voice quieter.

"Someone who doesn't belong here."

The little frown is back, indignant and sexy as fuck. Before she can say anything in response, or I get drawn even deeper into everything she has got going on, I turn and walk away.

With very great restraint on my part, which I have to congratulate myself for, I don't look back as I push out through the back exit which leads to the dressing rooms, offices and bathrooms. It's also the way out to the back parking lot only staff can access.

I've really got to stop hanging out here, especially when it's closed. The door opens to the outside before I reach it and a woman comes in, juggling her purse and some outfit bags. She glances up, surprised to see someone here and for a second, fear etches her face, but it passes when she sees my cut.

That's a fucking insane thought. She's less scared of me in a cut than a man in a suit. I dip my chin and hold the door open for her. She shuffles through with a quiet thanks. For a moment, I watch her as she walks down the hallway, pausing when the door to the club opens and Charley comes through. Something like relief passes over her face as a smile brightens Charley's.

They start to talk and Charley helps her with her things.

Damn. I let the door go and step outside. I really need to get the fuck out of here before my dick starts getting ideas that are going to get me in a whole world of shit.

It happens, quite a bit, regardless of what Beast wants. Hell, even Nero has been with some of the dancers. For a while, him and Ellie had a semi-exclusive mutual arrangement. Not a lot of people know about it, and I'm sure he would like to forget it now he's with Taylor. They're never likely to meet.

I can't imagine Taylor would be happy knowing her guy has slept with a stripper who everyone likes and respects, looks like an iconic movie star who does outstanding burlesque shows, and gets secrets out of men by fucking them until their brains melt and their lips start flapping.

Or maybe she wouldn't care, don't know her well enough.

Rebel texts as I'm leaving to say Nero is calling Church and I should get back to the club. It will have gone out to all the officers, and means drop everything, especially when it hasn't been scheduled.

I make good time but am still one of the last to arrive. Nero wants to let us know that nothing has come back on us from the Morris disappearance and any police investigations going haven't connected us in any way.

He runs through some other business then gets to what he really wanted to talk about.

"You remember Cannon's club got raided a few weeks ago?" he asks.

"Yeah," Razer laughs. "That was a shame."

A couple of the others laugh. Nero orchestrated it after the owner, who we'd been working with for years, decided to go get his product from Storm, another way that piece of shit was trying to undercut us. Whole thing went to shit and now he's facing jail time.

"They're having to sell the club to pay for legal fees and other shit."

"Serves the fuckers right," Beast leans back in his chair.

"Where would we stand if I wanted to buy it?" Nero looks at Blaze.

"It's in a good location, has a fairly decent reputation and handled the right way, it can make a pretty decent turnover. We'd want to change things up and relaunch though. After the raid people are going to be wary."

Nero waves his hand like that is all something we can think about later.

"Are you thinking legit business?" Rebel asks.

"Yeah, what we put into it we'll make back within a few months?" he looks to Blaze to answer that, and he nods.

"Once it's up and running, we can bring in some in house dealers, take a cut," Razer says.

"Blaze run the numbers, if it's doable, Razer work on the purchase. Once we have it, we'll figure out next steps from there."

Razer nods. He studied law in community college before he joined the club. He never passed the bar, but he understands it better than the rest of us and it's the kind of shit he likes to do.

"Everyone in agreement?" Nero asks.

No one disputes it.

"Okay. Anyone have anything they want to bring up?"

"Where are we with Storm," Stryker asks.

"Still can't nail down a location," Blaze says in annoyance. "But I've got a few ideas I'm working on."

"What ideas?" Nero asks.

"Nothing I want to go into yet, Prez, if that's okay? I'm trying to think outside the box."

Nero frowns but after a moment he nods and tells him to keep him up to date. No one else has any further information on Storm but we're all working with our contacts to find out what we can.

"Things have got heavy the last few weeks, we've had to deal with some bad shit that I know none of us ever like to do, so I was going to suggest we arrange a cookout. Invite the community."

"You sure it's the right time?" Rebel asks.

Nero scrubs a hand over his chin. "Yeah. We're not going to go on the back foot and hide until we flush that little prick out. And I think everyone could do with letting off some steam. Rebel, can you get Raven to set something up?"

He nods, checking his phone which makes Nero frown but they have one of their weird silent conversations so no one questions them.

Nero asks me to hang back when everyone else heads out. Once it's just the two of us, he gets up and goes to the fridge, grabbing two beers. I take one, waiting for him to say what he wants me for.

"I need your help to find someone."

"Okay," I nod, popping the cap off my beer and taking a swallow. "Who?"

"You know Speedway has a sister, Sheridan?"

"Think so, she came round a bit a few years ago, didn't get on with Raven."

"Yeah, that's the one," he says, his voice dripping with sarcasm.

Fought with Raven is what we really mean. No one ever did find out what went down that caused the usually unflappable Raven to lose her shit and throw a drink at Speedway's sister. Pretty much everyone in the bar was stunned when she grabbed Sheridan by the hair and threw her out of the bar.

"She in trouble?"

"Not sure. She originally went to Alexandria, but he tracked her to Kentucky."

"That's kind of a hard left on the highway."

He doesn't acknowledge my analogy of the two places being massively far apart. He's used to me by now.

"You got people back home could help?"

"Nashville is close to the state line with Kentucky but it's a big state."

"We can track her to a particular city but not where she's gone from there. Your brother is still a bounty hunter?"

"Yeah. He's expanded the business they're doing so well."

"Think he'll help."

"No doubt. You got a picture, any other information?"

He explains Speedway will get it all to me. I drink some more beer and watch Nero. If this was a Speedway problem, he would have come to me himself to ask for help. I'm the guy the brothers come to when they have issues.

Nero chews on his cheek and his eyes come back up to me.

"This doesn't leave the room."

"Of course."

"She's Oscar's mom."

My brows lift but I keep the real surprise of that statement to myself.

"She's been a good mom the last two years, we shared custody. She came to me saying she needed a break and went to Alexandria for what was supposed to be a couple of weeks. Then she stopped contacting me. I sent Speedway to find her." His face darkens. "She said she met someone and wasn't coming back."

"That's cold."

"It would be if she was someone else. It was one night, and she kept it a secret until Oscar was born but she's always done right by him."

"Do you think something more is going on?" I sit forward.

"I'm not sure. I don't want to ask Speedway to go looking too deep in case there is something."

"To do with Storm?" I surmise.

He grits his jaw and takes a second before he nods. "I can't be certain. I wasn't convinced he knew about Oscar when he sent those men to my house, but now I'm not so sure. I think it was Taylor he didn't know about. He was using Jesse to get to Oscar. He didn't count on Taylor being there."

Despite the shitty topic of conversation, the pride is clear on his face when he talks about her. She is still something of a mystery to most of the club, but we all know if she wasn't there that night, Jesse would be dead and Oscar probably taken.

"I'll speak to Camden," I say, sensing he doesn't want to go any further into this.

"I'll get you all her info. Keep it between us."

"No problem, Prez."

We finish our beers and chat a while, then head downstairs just in time to see Beast lose his shit and storm out of the clubhouse.

"What the fuck now?" Nero asks, then pauses, seeing a girl who doesn't belong standing by the couch, her arms folded over her chest with that teenage, *I hate everyone*, attitude radiating off her.

She's tall, slim and has blonde hair down to her ass. There is a suitcase at her feet and she is glaring at Ratchet who is staring at her like his fantasy just came to life. I walk over and slap the back of his head. She's clearly underage, even if she is wearing a lot of make-up and is dressed in designer clothes.

"What are you doing here kid?" I ask her.

"Yeah, I think you might be lost," Ratchet smirks.

I glare at him till he gets the idea I'm about to lose my shit and he shuffles around the couch and walks away.

"I'm here to see my father."

"You sure you're in the right place? I doubt your daddy is anywhere around here."

"Oh really?" She juts out her hip and looks at me like I'm the shit on her shoe.

This kid has attitude I'll give her that, but this isn't the right place to be throwing that attitude around. Especially not with Nero staring at her.

"Well that's funny," she accentuates the f in a way I'm not sure I could replicate. "Because he just took one look at me, lost his shit, and ran away."

"Wait... Are you saying you think the man who just left is your dad?"

"I don't think it, I know it," she drops her arms and reaches inside her coat.

Everyone reacts and for the first time the girl actually looks her age and she takes a few steps back like she is about to be attacked. That attitude disappeared faster than Beast did. I hold out my arm behind me for everyone to cool their shit.

"Be careful, kiddo, you're in a room you really shouldn't be in, where movements like that can cause a whole heap of trouble."

"I was just getting this picture." She holds out a polaroid. "When I showed it to him, he freaked, didn't even say a word. Just ran away."

Taking the photograph, I glance at Nero, who is watching us, letting me handle it. It's a picture of Beast and the girl. No wait, it's not her. It's someone who looks like her. And Beast is probably about fifteen years younger in the picture. Definitely before I knew him.

"Who is this?" I point to the woman.

"My mom," she says it like I'm stupid.

"I'm trying to help you here kid, drop the attitude."

"I don't understand why people don't believe the words I'm saying. It's not like I'm talking French or some shit."

"Watch your mouth."

Someone laughs behind me. And sure, maybe that did sound crazy and even a little hypocritical but she is young.

"That is my mom," she points at the doppelgänger of her in the picture. "And that is my dad. And I came to find him, to tell him that I need help. And just like he did to my mom, he ran the fuck away."

I ask her to take a seat. She eyes the couch then gives me a look that says I'm crazy if I think she is sitting there. Looking around, I spot Rookie, one of the prospects and call him over.

"Take... What's your name?"

"Isabella. But everyone calls me Tink," she looks at Rookie, her eyes holding a little too long.

Fucking hell. "Okay take Tink next door, get Raven to look after her, and stay with her."

"I don't need a babysitter."

"Did you want our help with your dad?" I try not to show my amusement.

"Uh, fine." She picks up the suitcase and thrusts it at Rookie. He almost falls over but follows her outside.

"What the fuck is going on?" Razer asks. "Another fucking kid we didn't know about?" he laughs.

Nero gives him a dirty look, but Razer doesn't lose the smirk just cos Nero is offended. I show them both the photograph as the other brothers who were in here talk and laugh about what just happened.

"Shit, they look like the same person," Razer says, peering at the picture. "You think Beast's her dad?"

"I think this girl might believe he's her dad, doesn't make it the truth," Nero says.

"What are we supposed to do with her?"

"Raven can handle that for now," Nero blows out a heavy breath. "Go find Beast. He wouldn't have run out of here like his ass was on fire if there wasn't something to this. Jesus fucking Christ, does the shit never end around here."

"Doesn't seem like it."

I snatch the picture back out of Razer's hand and head out to find the latest father of the year at the Blackhawk Disciples.

CHAPTER SIX

Charley

LOUD VOICES OUT IN the hallway startle me awake. It's nothing new, except I'm at Elegance, and I fell asleep on the couch in my practice room, which I've come to start calling it. The lights are dim so it looks like no one is in here.

The male voice is loud and angry and the female voice is placating but as always not taking any shit. It's Beast and Ellie. They don't usually talk to one another like this. What on earth is wrong? I don't think I've ever heard Beast raise his voice.

The door is ajar and I peer through. There is another room opposite this one but the door is further down the hall. The shouting dies down but they're still talking. Has something else happened? Like what happened with Stella.

I step out into the hall, wondering if I should check on Ellie. It seems impossible to believe Beast would hurt her but I haven't forgotten who these men are, they can be dangerous. It's a bad idea but my feet don't listen and I move along the hallway.

Something scrapes on the floor and Beast grunts. What the hell? I get level with the doorway and my mouth drops open. It's some kind of games room and Ellie is lying back on the pool table, her skirt hiked up around her waist, her legs wrapped around Beast's waist and his naked ass is clenching as he thrusts into her. He's doing it so hard the pool table is moving.

For a second I wonder if he is hurting her, but she starts to moan and reaches out, clawing at the felt on the table. Her eyes are closed, she is clearly into it. Beast is like an animal, this is the first time I've ever understood his name.

Someone grabs my arm and drags me away from the doorway and I come face to face with Nashville. He doesn't look happy, but he doesn't say a word as he pulls me away from where the fucking is starting to get louder. Neither one of them seems too concerned about keeping quiet.

Nashville guides me back into my room and closes the door. "You get off on watching people?" he lifts a brow.

"No!"

Oh God, I was just standing there watching them. My hand goes over my mouth at that realization and I'm mortified Nashville saw me. I haven't gotten over his comments the other day about me not belonging. In fact, I was pissed about it for far too long to be normal.

"I thought he was... They sounded like they were arguing and I wanted to make sure she was alright."

"Ellie can hold her own."

"I know that." I drop my hand. "I didn't expect that they would be doing *that* when I went to look."

"But you figured you would stay and watch?"

"Will you please stop saying that? It was like seeing your mom and dad screwing. I froze."

Nashville laughs and when I ask what's so funny, he says nothing and puts his hands on his hips, glancing back at the door. The laughter fades and he gets a concerned look on his face. He can't deny it, there is something odd about this.

"Sometimes it happens," he breaks the silence. "It doesn't mean anything. They're both consenting adults."

Lily has mentioned some of the girls give extras. I can't help but wonder if it's expected that they're available when these guys want them. And they don't pay...

"It doesn't mean you have to do it," Nashville says, like he can read my mind.

"I know that. And I wouldn't..." I trail off, remembering the first time I laid eyes on him. He'd been in the back room getting blown by someone.

That shouldn't make me squirm, squeezing my thighs together. It should gross me out.

"Don't read too much into it. Ellie and Beast have a long relationship, they understand one another and sometimes, when one of them needs something, they're there for each other."

"He needs rough sex?"

Nashville laughs again. "It's not unheard of, I don't particularly want to see one of my friends' asses, you know. And I won't judge if it's your thing, but you gotta ask if it's okay first."

"Oh my God, stop," I turn away and grab my bag.

"I'm kidding," he takes a step closer. "I'm sorry, it's just been a weird day, and this wasn't what I planned on seeing, I'm sure you're the same." He scrapes a hand through his hair, ruffling it up. "Let's not speak of it again, let them think they were alone."

"Oh, don't worry, I have no intention of letting them know. I'm embarrassed enough that you know."

"I won't tell anyone." Nashville makes a key locking gesture by his mouth then fake throws it over his shoulder. "What are you doing in here anyway?"

I've kept it to myself that I'm practicing a different kind of dance, Ellie told me not to say anything about coming in here but he is looking around like he suspects I'm up to no good.

"I dance in here, out of the way."

"Like what you were doing the other day?"

"Yeah, but... different."

"You're not much of a straight talker are you?"

"Around people I don't know, not really."

"Ah, you know me."

"Do I though?"

He grins. "We've had a couple of conversations, I've watched you dance, which was incredibly impressive by the way, and I felt bad about what I said to you."

"You don't have to feel bad. It wasn't anything I haven't heard before, like you said. It's just hard to wrap my head around getting a compliment, but feeling like I'm letting people down at the same time."

"That does seem like it would suck."

A flush burns through my chest at that word coming from his lips. I clear my throat and check my watch. There is still a while before opening time.

"Sounds like they're finished." He's right, it has gone quiet out there. "Might be safe to leave."

Right, leave. Not stand here getting all flustered because a man said 'suck'. A gorgeous man, with a beautiful smile and kind hazel eyes that always seem to be laughing.

My gaze lowers to the vest and the patch over his chest. Sergeant-at-arms. I'm not sure what it means but Lily said most of the bikers who come in are high up in the club. Before I make an ass of myself I grab my rucksack and sneakers and walk past him to the door.

When I pull it back, Ellie is walking along the hallway and pauses, surprised to see me. She looks beyond me and sees Nashville. I'm not sure what she is thinking but her eyes narrow minutely, then she walks on. Then Beast comes out of the room and sees me standing there.

"What are you doing here?" he asks, his voice gruff.

"She was helping me with something," Nashville says, coming out of the room.

"What?" his attention goes off me.

"Yeah, a lightbulb blew out, she helped."

"A lightbulb?" Beast clearly doesn't believe him.

"Yeah, we fixed it. Charley was just going to get ready for work. And you and I need a chat."

"Not now."

"Yeah now," he says. "Nero asked me to come see you about a package you got."

Beast glares, turning his head away. "I don't have time for this."

"Sure you do."

I don't know what is going on, but it's none of my business. While they continue their weird stare off, I walk away and head to the dressing rooms.

Weird stuff happens here all the time. It's crazy. Whatever that whole situation was, I'm not going to bring it up, to anyone. Especially not to Ellie.

Who is waiting in the dressing room when I walk in, making me draw up short.

"You're in early."

"I was getting some practice in."

She stares, and I blink but keep my mouth shut. After a few moments she nods and leaves the room. I really need to find somewhere else to hang out during the day. Or just lock myself in the dance room and not come out till I absolutely have to.

My shift goes by fast, I don't see Ellie or Beast again for the rest of the night, and I'm even more disappointed that Nashville isn't around either. It's dumb of me to attach to anyone, I've learned that the hard way. Lily has been a good friend which has helped.

When all the patrons have gone and the doors are locked, the lights come on and the cleaners come in to do what needs to be done. One by one the girls leave too, Walker seeing them out as usual. I decide to take advantage of the shower after all the dancing and the long shift.

Walker isn't around when I leave the dressing room, which is fine because I feel safe in the car park with all the security. It's starting to get cold, so I pull my wool cardigan tighter around me, reminding myself I need to get a warmer coat. At least the window in the car is fixed. The heater is slow to start, but it's not a long drive.

In the car, I turn the key and all I get in response is a click. Shit. I try it again a few times, with the same outcome. "Damn it," I groan and put my forehead on the steering wheel. Why does this keep happening? Just when I start to get on an even keel something else goes wrong.

I could open the hood and look inside but that would be pointless, I know nothing about cars. A frustrated cry spills out of me as I keep trying to turn the engine over but it's just not starting.

A knock at the window startles me and I clutch my chest. It's Walker. He steps back as I open the door and offers to see what he can do. I stand back, shivering as he tries to get it started but nothing is happening. He looks under the hood after it takes us a while to get the lever to work to open it.

I've never been more embarrassed.

"It's your starter motor."

"What does that mean?"

"A mechanic will have to fix it, sorry Charley this car isn't going anywhere tonight. I can arrange a ride for you."

"Ah, that's okay, I can Uber," I say quickly. Anyone giving me a ride will see where I live and I can't let that happen.

"You're not getting an Uber at this time of night."

I'm startled again by the new voice and turn to see Nashville strolling towards us.

"It's fine, I do it all the time." Lies. I can't afford to get an Uber.

Walker tells him what's wrong with the car and shuts the hood. He eyes Nashville who tells him all is good and he can head back inside.

"Come on," Nashville says and walks away towards the rear of the lot. When he realizes I'm not following he stops and turns back to me. "You're not getting an Uber Charley, I can give you a ride."

"But, I'm really fine..."

"I'm really not fine with you getting into a strangers car. Let's go."

It takes me a second to move but I follow him, then come up short when he stops at his bike. "You're kidding, right? You want me to get on that over an Uber."

"It's more exciting," he laughs. "Don't you think?"

"Uh dangerous you mean?"

"Nah, it'll be quicker too and I'm done arguing, so here," he grabs a helmet and hands it to me. I stare at it like it's some kind of alien item. "I'll help," he steps up close and takes it back, then raises the helmet.

I'm about to protest again when he pushes it down and everything goes dark for a moment, he flicks open the visor and grins, tipping my head up by shifting the helmet. He tightens it and clips me in, then takes my purse and stows it in the little bags on the side of the bike.

"What's the address?"

Shit. I can give him a fake one nearby and walk the rest of the way. I tell him the name of the street, he frowns but nods and gets on the bike, then helps me on behind him. It feels super weird and I'm also more than a little terrified.

Nashville grabs my hands and pulls them around his middle. I'm not stupid, I know I need to hold on but I figured I'd grab his shoulders.

Nope, he warns me to hold on tight, then starts the bike. I jolt a little when he moves and grab at his clothes.

"Relax," he says. "You're squeezing the shit out of my thighs."

Oh Jesus, I loosen my grip on his legs.

"You'll be fine. Just keep hold and lean when I lean."

Easy, yeah. Right. We set off and go through the security gate. As he picks up speed, I cling to him, put my head down and keep my eyes shut the whole way. It doesn't take too long and when we stop, I all but fall off the bike, only that he catches my arm I don't land on my ass.

He helps me with the helmet and I thank him.

"We'll get your car fixed up tomorrow."

"You don't have to do that."

"Don't worry about it, I'll sort it for you."

"Nashville-"

"Stop arguing, and get inside, it's late, and it's cold. Where is your coat?"

"I didn't realize it was going to be this cold," I lie. He nods and tells me to go. Shit, I pick a house and run towards the door, pretending to take out my keys. I wave for him to leave and after a moment, he does. "Fucking hell," I lean against the wall and count to fifteen, until I can no longer hear the bike.

When I'm sure he's gone, I hurry down the block and around the corner to my actual home. Thank God he left. I'm embarrassed enough.

And not just about where I live. Being pressed up against his back, feeling the hardness in his abdomen muscles as he turned the bike and the thickness of his thighs against mine scrambled my brain. I let myself in and hurry up the stairs as usual. There are two men hanging out on the corridor just past my door.

Avoiding eye contact, I push my shoulders back and try to look unaffected, but my heart is hammering. I don't know about embarrassment, I'm likely to die of heart failure first.

My hand shakes as I get the key in the lock, the two men are watching me and one shifts as the door opens. I practically fall inside, close and lock the door. Then quickly drop everything and run to the dresser and start pushing.

The door handle rattles and my panic ratchets up as the stupid dresser moves a couple of inches, nowhere near enough to stop anyone coming in if they decide to break down the door.

"Hey sweetheart," a dark voices says from outside. "Want some company."

My instincts tell me not to respond and I continue pushing the dresser, moving it a little more.

"Come on, let us in, we can have some fun."

My eyes start to water and my arms and legs strain as I put all my weight behind moving the dresser. A bang on the door makes me yelp. I'm not going to get it across in time.

Then a voice interrupts the two men and the rattling stops. I strain to hear and instantly recognize the voice. Shit even more on all the other shits.

"I'll give you to the count of three to get away from that door before I fuck you up."

Chapter Seven

Nashville

I KNEW THE SECOND she walked away from the bike that wasn't where she lived. This isn't a nice neighborhood, I know people from around here, the kind a woman on her own should never be around, especially a woman like Charley.

To not make her any more uncomfortable, I rode away, but I didn't go far, leaving the bike and walking back, just in time to see her go into the worst fucking place she could be entering. I didn't want to risk losing her, or for something to happen so I ran up the steps and into the building.

Fuck it doesn't even have security doors, any asshole could walk in. And they do. There are people at this address that have worked with the club. Charley is just round the second floor staircase as I hurry up behind her. I can't miss which apartment she goes into. I'll bang on doors if I have to.

I'm not scared, people here are scared of me.

When I reach the second floor, Charley is gone but there are two scumbags trying to get into a door further down the hallway and the shit they're saying makes me see red.

When they start trying to break the door open, I walk up behind them. There is no doubt this is the room Charley went into.

I'm so pissed right now, anyone who crosses me may end up shot or thrown over the fucking railing to the ground floor.

"I'll give you to the count of three to get away from that door before I fuck you up."

"Who the fuck do you think-" the man standing back starts to say, but he's seen my cut.

The other one is still banging on the door. His friend drags him and he's about to say something about stopping when he sees me.

"Nashville," he takes a step away from the door.

"Don't ask me who the fuck I think I am," I walk closer. "I don't have to tell you shit."

"No, no, sorry I didn't realize it was you."

"And you think that makes it okay? If I was someone else you'd be fine to break into a woman's apartment?"

"It's not that, we know her. She uh, she's a friend."

I cock my head. "One who doesn't want to open the door to you? Does that sound reasonable?"

Both men shrink a little at the way I'm looking at them. I might be a jovial happy kind of guy but when I smile like this, people know they're in trouble.

"Seriously, Nashville, we know her."

"We don't want any trouble."

They speak over each other. The one who said the sensible thing is backing off. The other one is standing his ground. They dealt drugs for us in the past, it's been a while since we've had anything to do with them because they use what they're supposed to sell.

Before the dickhead can even open his mouth to argue, I am on him, my forearm on his throat, ramming him into the wall.

"You want to rethink what you're about to say?" I snarl at him.

He splutters and tries to push me off but I punch him in the gut. He can't bend or get away because of how I'm holding him. The other guy has moved further away. Fucking smart. If he tries anything, I really will shoot them. They won't, they know the wrath of the club will come down on them if they lay a finger on me.

"What were you planning on doing? You were going to hurt her?"

He tries to shake his head but his face is turning red.

"That's not what it sounded like to me. Sounded like you were planning to take something you had no right to take." My voice is low, close to him because I'm sure Charley can hear through these walls.

My anger spikes again, this time at her, for living in a shit hole like this. I release the idiot and take out my gun anyway, when he drops to the ground trying to catch his breath, I press it against his temple. He stops moving instantly.

"You ever try anything like this again, and I'll send Stryker round here to deal with you."

The man shakes and promises he won't. I don't believe him, but the only person I give a shit about is not spending a single night more here.

"Both of you get the fuck out of here. All the way out. I hear about you coming back around here, you're not getting a second warning."

For good measure, I pistol whip the back of his head, making him fall forward. When I step back his friend drags him to his feet and they run away like the punk ass cowards they are.

Now to deal with this little pain in my ass. I knock on the door but there is nothing from inside.

"Charley, open the door."

Still nothing.

"If you think I'm going away, you're wrong. I'll stand out here all night if I have to."

After a moment, there is a dragging sound then the lock turns, and she opens the door. Before she has time to say anything, I open it wider and go inside, closing the door behind me. It's one room with a bed, a fridge a tiny bathroom and, fuck is that a dresser she is dragging over to the door.

The marks in the threadbare carpet tell me exactly what that is. She comes in here and barricades herself enough to feel safe.

Now I'm really pissed. She's staring at me with wide-eyes, not moving or saying a word. Good, she knows she's in trouble.

"Pack up your things, you're coming with me."

"I can't do that, this is where I live, you can't just walk in here and make me leave."

"Wanna bet," I go to the dresser that is askew by the wall and start opening drawers. There isn't much in here but what there is, I start taking out and tossing on the bed.

"Stop that," she comes towards me.

"No, get a bag, Charley. You're not staying here."

She looks at my hand and her cheeks flush. I follow her gaze and see a handful of panties and bras. I tighten my fist around them and her eyes get bigger again.

"Bag, now. Don't make me even more annoyed than I already am." That sounded like a threat and I don't want to scare her, but I'm still shocked that she has been staying here. "Do you have any idea about the people who live in this place?"

"Of course I do."

"And you're okay with filthy fucking men trying to break in here?"

"No, that's why I..." She waves a hand at a dresser.

"That thing is fucking heavy, Charley. They could have broken that door down before you got it across. Then what?"

She looks away from me. Shit, I hate frightening her, but she needs to see the reality of the situation she has put herself in. If I hadn't come back...

Darkness descends over my mind. I'd fucking rip the head clear from the neck of any asshole who hurt her.

"Pack," I say.

Her chest heaves up and down as she breathes. Before I can say anything else, she grabs a beat up suitcase from behind the dresser and does as she's told. I fold my arms and watch, guarding the door. It doesn't take long, she doesn't have a lot of stuff.

I grab the case and open the door, going outside to check the hallway. There had been people milling around before but word must have spread that a Blackhawk Disciple was here and everyone has left or gone back to their apartments.

We walk the few blocks to my bike and after some screwing around with a bungy rope, I get the case secured to the back of the bike, leaving enough room for her to get on behind me. She hasn't spoken since we left her apartment.

Now that we're on the bike, I haven't really thought about my next move. There is only one thing I can do this late in the evening. It's not ideal, but it doesn't have to be long term, just until I find somewhere else for her to go.

The garage door on my house starts to rise before we pull up because I have a controller on my bike, so I'm able to drive straight inside.

Charley gets off the bike and takes off the helmet herself, looking around as the garage door goes back down.

"Where are we?"

"My house." I don't say anything else as I detach her case.

I may have joked around to Ronin about having an expensive house, truth is my house wasn't cheap at all. It has a front and rear yard, the garage holds three cars and it's set over two stories, there are three bedrooms, a gym and office. Not that I use most of them, I just like having the space.

Where I grew up there were four boys, really close in age, in a three-bedroom house with our parents. As a teenager, sharing a room was bad enough, two teenage boys who almost topped six feet sharing a room was horrendous.

I like having space and I'm earning more than enough money to be able to have that. I'm not a foolish person who squanders money. When I get it, I invest it and I've made some good choices that have kept my little pot of gold growing.

Charley is looking around and her gaze pauses on my 1969 Shelby Mustang, it's parked in front of the BMW X5 that I use when I need a cage. The Shelby is a rich dark green with two white stripes over the hood and roof. It rarely leaves the garage but sometimes I like to take her for a spin.

"Is that yours?"

"You like classic cars?" I ask, putting the helmets on the hooks over a work bench.

"It's unusual to see one, and it's in really good condition."

"I can't take any of the credit for that, I bought it that way. Come on."

Carrying her case, I lead her inside, pointing out rooms as we go. She doesn't say anything and follows me up the stairs to the spare bedroom. For some reason, I'm not quite sure of, I point out my bedroom, then take her a couple of doors down to one of the spares.

It's the only one that has furniture in and the bed is made. Occasionally one of my siblings will visit so I make sure there is a room ready. It's been a while since I saw any of them. With this task Nero has set me, I'll be seeing my eldest brother soon enough.

Charley enters the room cautiously and looks around. I lean against the door frame after setting her case down and letting her in.

"Bathrooms there, you have your own, but if you need it, the main bathroom is just opposite."

"Thanks," she turns again, so she is facing me. "You didn't need to do this. I was fine, I've lived there for weeks."

"And you're lucky nothing has happened to you. Don't even think about going back there, Charley."

Her fists clench and she takes a few breaths. "It's the only place I can afford."

"That isn't somewhere that a person who isn't a criminal, a junkie, or a hooker lives, Charley. I won't let you go back there."

"What am I supposed to do? I can't stay here."

It's on the tip of my tongue to ask why not, but I guess she is right about that. "We'll figure something out, but you're not going back there. Don't argue," I cut her off before she can get her words out. "There are places you can stay, and we can sort out rent and shit with you. It's not like we don't trust you, Charley."

She still wants to argue but after another look around and seeing my expression she agrees.

"Until then, you're welcome to stay here, there is no one else in the house and I'm out a lot of the time so just treat it like your own."

"I can't do that."

"Okay," I say it in a way that means I absolutely do not agree with what she just said and she gives me a look that says she's not entirely happy with me. "Door has a lock," I tell her, she chews on the inside of her cheek but doesn't say anything. "It's late, I don't know about you but it's been a shit of a day. Everything you need is in the bathroom. Help yourself to food and whatever in the kitchen. I'll sort out your car in the morning."

"Nashville, you have done enough."

"Not enough if you ask me."

"What?"

"Charley, you were dragging a heavy dresser in front of the door to keep yourself safe. And I nearly had to kick the shit out of the two pricks who were trying to get in. This is the least I can do."

For a moment she looks like she is going to say something but I guess she is overwhelmed so just says she is tired and thanks me in a quiet voice.

It's probably best not to tell her I'll be giving her the keys to the SUV until her car is fixed. Instead I say goodnight and head to my room for a shower. It really has been a long fucking day. And one I never thought was going to end with a hot blonde under my roof.

Get your head out of the fucking gutter. She just went through something traumatic, and God knows how long she has been living on edge going in and out of that hellhole. How the fuck did Beast not recognize that address when they took her on? The Disciples know it all too well.

Which reminds me, I fire off a text to Rebel telling him what happened. Word might get back I was down there and I don't want anyone getting any surprises. I don't tell him why but at least I've filled him in.

I try not to think about her while I shower, wondering what she is doing down there, whether she's taking her own shower or is plotting how to escape. Not like I've kidnapped her or anything but I get the sense her pride his hurt. Why else would she pretend she doesn't live there. No one wants to admit things are that bad.

Makes sense why she wants to dance so bad. Beast pays all the staff well, but no one gets what the dancers get, on top of what Elegance pays them, they get to keep all their tips.

I'm caught in this weird feeling of anger at her for thinking it was okay to live there, to awe that she has managed to make it there this long, and semi-arousal at the thought of her sleeping in my house. That last one makes me feel a touch of disgust for myself so instead of dwelling on it, I go downstairs and grab a glass of juice and a left over taco, set the security system and go back to bed.

If she tries to sneak out, she'll set off the alarm. Charley isn't stupid, she knows better than to do that. Even if she is pissed about it, she knows this is a better deal.

There is no sound from her room as I pass so I'm assuming she is asleep or in bed at least. While I eat, I think about what happened with Beast earlier.

Despite telling Charley it's nothing unusual, it really fucking is. I'm not sure Beast has ever fucked Ellie before. We all know she does it, and Nero uses her a lot to get information out of people, like a honey trap, Ellie is happy to do it, no one coerces her into anything.

Fucking Beast is a weird one. Of course I didn't let on I'd seen him fucking her, or that I caught Charley spying on them. We talked about Tink. Or I asked a lot of questions he refused to answer. Fuck knows what Raven did with the kid after I left. That's a problem for another day. Or someone else.

I've currently got my own unexpected house guest to deal with. I'm just glad she isn't a surprise daughter I knew fuck all about.

Yeah, I'm really glad she's not related to me. The thoughts I'm having about her would be a whole lot of wrong if that was the case.

Chapter Eight

Charley

It's after eleven when I wake up, which is really late for me. I'm usually at Elegance by now. Rolling over onto my back, I stare up at a ceiling that isn't covered in mildew and cobwebs, there are no mysterious stains on the walls or curtains that might as well not be there they're so thin.

The mattress is comfortable and the sheets smell like fresh air, which sounds like the biggest cliché ever but considering I've been sleeping on cheap sheets that I was washing and rotating every few days, this is like heaven. Snuggling in under the duvet just a little longer, I close my eyes and wish this wasn't just one night.

One day. Soon. I'll get my own place. I haven't slept so well in ages. It has a lot to do with not falling asleep praying no one gets into my room and robs me, or worse. Waking up feeling so rested and safe is something that hasn't happened to me for a very long time.

And the reason for that is a six-foot biker whose smile is as dangerous as his reaction to the men trying to hurt me. I couldn't hear everything he said, but the men knew who he was and they were scared of him.

It should worry me, but just like with Beast, I'm not afraid of him. He's said some things that bothered me, and there is the whole getting a blow job in the back room that irked me, which I have no right or reason to be thinking about.

How the hell am I supposed to deal with Nashville? Last night, I was so relieved to hear him outside my room, chasing those men away, I could have kissed him. Which brought all manner of thoughts that rendered me speechless, until he demanded I pack so he could take me away from there.

If I'd had my wits about me, I would have argued more, but at the same time, what he did for me probably saved my life.

Who would have thought he'd whisk me away to this beautiful house? It was not what I was expecting at all.

After a shower, I creep out of the bedroom. I've procrastinated as long as possible, worrying about how I'm going to pay to get my car fixed and where I am going to sleep tonight.

His bedroom door is wide open, and I peer inside, but he's not there and the bed is made. Short of walking right up to the door, I can't see much more than the bed. Which means he is up already.

I'm not sure how to face him. I was too stunned to react properly last night. It was only after I had locked the door and was lying in bed that I let my mind think about what could have happened.

That was the first time anyone had tried to get into my room. I'd thought about it happening more than once and I was prepared for it in a way, with two knives hidden under my pillow and in the dresser.

Both of which are still there. They're easily replaceable, hopefully the next place I go is somewhere I won't need them.

The house is quiet and for a second, I wonder if Nashville has left already but he is standing in the kitchen with a steaming mug of coffee reading something on a laptop he has set up on the counter.

What the hell do I say? This is the first time I've seen him in normal clothes, as in a Black Keys T-shirt and dark sweatpants, without the leather vest. I mean, why would he wear that in his own house? You never see him or any of the other bikers who frequent Elegance without them.

"Morning."

My eyes jump up to his face instead of ogling his chest. I was admiring the T-shirt, nothing more, I love The Black Keys.

"Sleep well?"

"I did, thank you."

"Coffee? Fresh pot just brewed."

"Thanks, I can make it."

I walk to the coffee pot and grab a mug from a metal stand, keeping my back to him. How do I tell him thank you, but I need to leave and not come back, and let's not talk about what happened last night ever again? That's not too much to ask.

The burn of his eyes makes me almost overfill the coffee mug. I take a good gulp before I turn around. He's watching me intently and isn't even trying to hide it. Holy shit.

"If you're hungry, I can throw something together." He exits out of the window on his laptop and closes the lid. "You okay?"

"I'm… fine," I rub at my brows then lean back against the counter.

"If this is about you staying here, don't sweat it."

"Don't sweat it," I laugh. "I'm not staying here."

"If you think you're going back to that crack house you're wrong."

"You don't get to tell me what to do."

"I'm not telling you what to do, I'm telling you what is not going happen."

"What?"

"It's not happening."

"Staying here is what is not happening."

"Fine, we'll figure something else out but going back there isn't one of the options. I know what happens in that building and I cannot stand the thought of you being there. You don't belong in a place like that Charley."

"It's…" I clear my throat, feeling stupid. How do I say it's all I can afford and no matter how shitty it is, no one will ever go looking there for me? Same as at Elegance.

Shame burns through me at everything I'm hiding and the real reason why I want to dance at Elegance.

"There is no harm in asking for help."

"Who was I supposed to ask?"

"Anybody at Elegance, they all would have helped."

"I'm not asking for charity, Nashville."

"Callum."

"What?"

"My name. It feels weird you calling me Nashville. You're thinking I don't look like a Callum?" he raises an amused brow. "Funny story, my dad is Scottish, he came over to the US in his early twenties, met and married my mom and they had four sons."

"There are four of you?"

"Yep and all our names are Scottish and begin with the letter C. Dad always said if they had a girl mom would get to name her and it didn't need to be Scottish or begin with a C."

"And that never happened."

"Nope, she kept on having boys. Camden, he's the eldest, then me, then they had Craig and Cameron is the baby."

"Camden and Cameron."

"Cam and Ronnie, keeps things easier."

Wait, how did he divert the conversation so easily? By giving me a small piece of information that led me in a completely different direction. He grins, knowing exactly what he just did.

"I have to be somewhere in about twenty minutes," he looks at his watch. "You're going to have to get yourself to work."

"I'll call an-"

He slides a set of keys across the counter, there is a BMW logo on them. There was a giant BMW in the garage behind the amazing Mustang that I would love to drive.

"Stop dreaming about the Shelby," he says with a knowing look. "No one drives my baby but me."

"Your baby?" I smirk.

"Correct. There is a fob to the garage that will let you in and out inside the car."

"Nash... er Callum," I quickly amend when he gives me a look.

"I'm in a hurry so can we argue about this later. I'll see what I can do about your car and we can figure something out about where you're going to live but for now, you come here. I mean it Charley. I'm hardly here so you'll have the place to yourself."

"You don't even know me, how do you know you can trust me?"

"I'm an excellent judge of character." He walks around the island, picks up the keys and puts them in my hand, then leans in closer. "And I know when someone needs help but is too proud to ask for it. Take this for what it is Charley, a temporary arrangement until you get on your feet. And think about those people back in that crack den."

"What? I don't understand."

"I'll have to burn the place down, with them all in it, if you even consider going back there."

"Are you serious?"

"Deadly. You should get to work, there is a key to the house on the ring. I'm not sure when I'll be back so help yourself to anything. Within reason," he winks. "Although I got to touch your underwear, so if you want to go rooting around in mine."

"Holy shit," I mutter the burn in my face coming back.

"Don't leave."

"But I can't impose."

"Not imposing. I really have to go. If you pull any stunts, don't forget, I know where you work."

I'm still standing there, staring at the empty doorway long after he's walked out. "What the hell just happened?"

And oh my God, how could he bring up that he had a handful of my underwear last night.

"He's crazy," I look down at the keys in my hand.

How am I going to explain to everyone when I show up at Elegance driving this thing? There is no way I can stay here with him but he is right about one thing, I can't go back to that place, not after those two men tried to get into my room.

They might have been afraid of Nashville, but he won't always be around to protect me. I'll just have to do what I was planning, find a cheap motel. I can do that but right now, I need to get to work.

Sleeping so late means I'm behind schedule, and there is no time to fit in any dance practice. I can worry about everything else later.

Lily is the only person I'm getting closer to at Elegance but telling her about last night isn't happening. I hate the thought of her finding out I've been lying. The only thing I can do is keep it to myself. Along with the fact I'm staying at one of the Blackhawk Disciples houses.

Beast isn't around the whole night, none of the Disciples are and I can't help but be disappointed that Callum didn't show. It's weird to think of him as Callum. It's easier than calling him Nashville and I kind of like the idea of knowing his real identity, which in turn makes it easier to go back to his house, in his car.

This isn't something I can get used to. I've had the big house, the fancy cars, my life isn't like that anymore, I'll find somewhere else and tell him I'm going, tomorrow, because he isn't here.

I'm oddly disappointed, it's not like he didn't tell me he wouldn't be around much. It never entered my head that he meant it literally.

Three days pass of me coming and going and hardly any sign of him ever having been here, except for a cup in the drainer or a fresh batch of laundry being done, including my clothes, which I'm not overly thrilled about but it's nice having fresh clothes to wear.

Then last night he brought home takeout, and we watched re-runs of Vampire Diaries together. I've never seen it before, but he confessed it was a favorite and if I told anyone he would never speak to me again.

That was nice. Apart from the threat, which I know he didn't mean but I won't tell anyone. Even if we didn't chat a lot, it was just nice having company. He is fun to be around, laid back and likes to crack jokes.

I can't forget that I've seen him angry though, how he can switch from the guy eating pizza on the floor talking about who his favorite vampire is, and the one who threatens to kill people. And they listen because they know he means it.

After a week of staying in his house, and while driving to work in his BMW, I'm shocked to realize not only have I got used to this, I haven't looked for anywhere else to live.

When I get to work, Ellie is sitting in a booth and the dancers are all gathered around. Jealousy sweeps over me and I curse not getting a fake ID when I first came here. I didn't think they wouldn't allow me to dance because I'm a few months younger than the legal age.

"Charley!"

I stop on my way to the staff room and look at Ellie. She waves me over to join everyone. Whatever has happened, it's put everyone in a somber mood.

"Thanks everyone, I'll arrange for some flowers and figure things out. Extra shifts are going to be paid at double time, just for a short period."

The girls all thank her and head off. What the hell is going on?

"Jessica was in a car accident last night."

My throat starts to tighten and white flashes behind my eyelids when I shut them. Stop it. Be normal. "Is she okay?"

Ellie is watching me, trying to figure out that reaction. I'm not exactly close to Jessica, she is nice enough, but she keeps to herself.

"She's going to be fine, but she broke a couple of ribs, her collarbone and ankle."

"That's awful, I'll chip in for flowers."

"This isn't about putting towards her gift. Karin also quit this morning."

"Oh my God."

"We could have coped with losing Jessica for a few months, Karin going as well is a problem. There is only going to be so long the girls we have can cover all of those extra hours. For reasons I won't go into Beast isn't going to be around much."

"What are you going to do?"

"We've advertised for dancers so will wait and see what comes of it, but it takes time."

My heart starts to pound. They've been adamant about keeping me off the stage but they're in dire straits right now.

"You're two months away from turning twenty-one, right?"

"Yes." It's the only thing I can muster up because I might puke. This is what I've wanted since I got here.

"I'm not sure you're ready. You'll need to be able to dance in front of people, Charley, on stage. Not just in front of the mirror in an empty room. We have a private party on Saturday night, the whole club has been bought out for this. You've seen the girls doing their routine."

I have, I didn't know it was for a private party but I've seen them all dancing, even stopped to watch.

"This wouldn't be happening if Beast was around but I'm in charge of the dancers and I know that getting someone new in and having them learn this routine is going to be a disaster. The routine needs eight girls."

"What about the other spot?"

"I'm going to do it."

My eyes widen. Ellie doesn't dance anymore, at least, not out on the main floor.

"It's a big deal that we can't afford to fuck up. Do you think you can do it?"

"If I spend time working with the girls to get it right, I'll be able to do the dance."

"You have to take off your clothes, Charley. There will be twenty plus men here that night. Important men. If you're going to flake, I can't put you up there."

"I won't."

"Maybe we should practice another routine," Ellie shakes her head, the frustration clear.

"Ellie, I promise I can do this. I'm not going to let you down. You and Beast and everyone else here have been amazing to me. You can trust me."

"We have four days."

"I'll be ready."

"Rehearsals are every morning from now until Saturday, ten till twelve."

"I'll be there."

"Between now and then, dance for someone. Have the girls watch, anything to get you used to being on stage in nothing but a G-string and heels. I don't often do this, Charley but I'm putting my trust in you."

All I can do is nod. I'm not going to let her down. I've spent the last two weeks getting ready for this, without even knowing it was going to happen. But she is right, I need an audience.

My attention is dragged away from those thoughts by male laughter and I turn to see Max walking in with two of the Disciples I don't recognize. Could I ask them?

Shit, just watching the three giant men scares me. Panic starts to set in. How am I going to do this? I'm going to let Ellie and the girls and everyone else at Elegance down.

"Charley? You okay?"

The sound of his voice snaps me out of it and I look up into his beautiful hazel eyes. The concern is written all over his face. He might not have been around much but I trust him.

Is this something I can ask him to do for me? He'll say no, and then I'll feel like an idiot. I should just ask the girls.

"What's going on in that head of yours?" he asks.

The other men have all disappeared into the back, so it's just me and him. I'm not going to let anyone down.

Squaring my shoulders I tilt my chin so I can look him in the eye. “I need a favor.”

Chapter Nine

Nashville

Beast is out of action while he gets his head around the fact he has a seventeen-year-old daughter he didn't know about. She had nowhere to go for reasons he is refusing to talk about so is currently at Raven's apartment. Nero gave him a few days to get his head straight but expects him to take ownership of his responsibilities.

It's not because he's a father himself now, Nero is a hard man, but he has a heart, even if he hides it really deep down where you need a flashlight and a pickaxe to find it. He won't see the kid out on the streets. Which reminded me of Charley being at my place.

I haven't told anyone else she's there, and know she hasn't mentioned it to anyone, because Ellie would have been on my ass about it.

She keeps to herself around the house, like she is trying not to bother me. I have no intention of kicking her out. And truth be told, I've not been looking for somewhere else for her to stay either.

I've been out of the house a lot partly because Nero has needed me with this whole mess with Beast, and because I don't want to crowd her or give her the wrong idea about why I'm doing it which is getting harder for me to ignore.

I've never lived with a woman before, the house smells different with her there. It's not like she is doing anything out of the ordinary, or spraying perfume and what not around, it's just her scent. And my dick is getting the wrong idea. So I've stayed away.

I brought takeout home a couple of nights ago, and she watched my guilty pleasure TV show with me, surprised as hell by it.

Shocking people is one of my favorite things to do, though it's not usually about my enjoyment of teenage vampire shows. We couldn't talk much because we were eating and watching but it was nice. Different.

I'm not sure what it says about me that I still haven't done anything to find her some place else to go, or get her car fixed.

There is going to come a point when she asks, or maybe she is happy staying with me. It's safe there, she doesn't need to worry about anyone breaking into her room.

It's time to stop thinking about Charley and handle what I've got to get done. First, taking a delivery at Elegance, which needs to be done while Beast is examining his feelings or some shit.

My phone rings so I tell the others to go inside, Ratchet and Wheeler have come with me, to help they said, but I figure it's more about having time to chat with the dancers. Not that they're disrespectful, and if they were, I'd beat their asses.

No one messes with our dancers. Unless they initiate it. Nero laid down the law when we first opened the club. The women are to be looked after and protected.

It's not about the money we make here, it's about keeping them safe. We have very strict rules and aren't afraid to enforce them, even with our own men.

It's my brother calling.

"Hey," he greets me. "We're closing in on your target."

"Do you have to talk like some special forces secret agent, it's just me dipshit."

"You want my help or not?"

"All you gotta say is we have found Sheridan and we're gonna go talk to her."

"What do you not understand about us closing in?"

"Something obviously because it doesn't sound like we're on the same page."

"Jesus, I forgot what a pain in the ass you are."

"Just speak layman to me, Camy."

"You're a fucking idiot. We haven't found her yet, but we've tracked down some people who know where she's been."

"So you've got nothing?"

The phone goes quiet and I can picture him holding it away from his ear so he can call me names, or count to ten like he used to do when we were kids.

Shit, I need to take this seriously, this is about the mother of Nero's kid.

"Cam... Camden...Hey."

"You done being a dick?"

"It's out of my system. Dazzle me."

"Jesus, can I deal with someone else in the club."

"I'm done. So you found someone who has seen her?"

"Yeah, in Elizabethtown in Kentucky. We're heading over there tomorrow. Once we've got more news, I'll give you a call. Did you want to be here when we grab her?"

"Yeah, Nero will want that. And less of the grabbing. We're not arresting her, we just need to talk to her, find out why she disappeared on her kid."

"Leave the fucking attitude at the clubhouse Callum. I'm not having you on a job with us if you're going to be an idiot."

"It's a sibling thing, I promise I'll remember you're the boss and behave. Just keep me posted and as soon as you need me, I'll be there."

Cam hangs up. Pissing off my older brother is like second nature to me. Sometimes I forget he is an ex-marine, scary as shit bounty hunter now, and in a fight he'd likely beat my ass.

Nero will want to know about this but I push it out of my head for now. I've got to get shit done here and make sure the club is okay without its leader.

Inside the lighting is dim as usual and it takes my eyes some time to adjust. Ratchet and Wheeler are talking to Max, strolling through to the back. They give a cursory glance to the woman standing by the private booths but don't stop.

Charley is watching them like a hawk, something ticking over in her brain. I'm not sure I like the way she is looking at them, I can't figure out what it is.

"Charley, everything okay?" I ask stopping behind her. She jumps and whirls around.

Why is she such a bag of nerves? I hate that I scared her. I really want to know what it is that keeps her up at night, or had her staying in that shit hole, and why she so desperately wants to dance at Elegance.

"What's going on?" I ask.

It's taking a lot for her to speak, that much is obvious. I've been watching her these last few days, not when she is sleeping or anything, that would be creepy as shit. She projects this persona of being strong, but there is a vulnerability to her too.

"I need a favor," she says.

She's proud, and doesn't like asking for help. Yet here she is, asking me for something. And I don't mind helping. Which is why I answer without waiting to hear the favor first.

"Just let me handle this delivery them I'm all yours."

"Okay," she bites her lip. "I'll be in the room where-"

"You dance, got it. I'll be there as soon as I can. And don't worry, whatever it is we can figure it out."

Her face blanches a little, but she turns and hurries away before I can ask why. It means I get the delivery and storage sorted in record time, then tell the others to fuck off back to the clubhouse or their own jobs. The dancers are out on stage practicing some routine and having these assholes ogling them wouldn't be tolerated by Beast, so I'm not having it either.

Once all that is done, I go find Charley.

She turns when I knock and open the door. My heart almost falls out my ass when I see her. She's wearing a thong, so her whole ass is on show, and a complicated looking sparkly top that wraps around her tits with a tie between them, it has long sleeves that almost cover her hands and dips low into her cleavage.

I'm about to excuse myself and leave but she calls my name. My real name. And that makes this a whole hell of a lot more dangerous.

"Could you close the door?" she asks.

I do as she asks and step inside. The lighting is down low and there is music playing that I hadn't noticed when I first came in, far too fixated on her perfectly round ass.

"Ellie is down two dancers, and there is a big private party here on Saturday."

I know all about that. It's something Nero has been working on and is looking to secure a business deal with these guys. Having a private party at Elegance is one way of getting them on our side.

"She's asked me to fill in. Which is great, I can do the routine no problem but Ellie is concerned."

"About what?" I take a few steps closer, then notice the chair in the center of the room.

"That I'll freak out and ruin everything."

"Why would you do that?"

"Because I've never danced in front of an audience."

"I've seen you do it," I say, confused as fuck.

"Yeah, but not..."

"Oh."

It dawns on me what she means. This is her first dance out on the stage. Things must be desperate if Ellie has asked Charley. Beast has been adamant she can't do it till she turns twenty-one.

Another reminder to me how young she is. I mean, I'm twenty-nine, it's not like I could be her dad or anything. Fuck, not the time.

"Ellie wants me to dance for someone."

"Naked?" My eyes widen.

"Well, yeah," she smiles, it's a little nervous, but she's amused at my reaction. "I trust you. I need to nail this Callum, not just for Ellie. If I mess this up, I'll lose my job and the only chance I have."

"Charley, if you're so scared to take your clothes off and dance, how can you ever do this job?"

"That's why I need you."

Oh hell, don't say that shit. Not when you're half naked and begging to take the rest of your clothes off in front of me.

"Please, Callum. I know I can do this, but Ellie wants me to prove it."

"She probably means with the other girls."

"I could do it in front of the girls with my eyes closed and Ellie will see right through that. She wants me to prove I can do it for a man. Men."

This is a bad idea. I've been attracted to her from the get-go but having got to know her a little, to see some of the things she has been hiding, it's a whole lot more complicated. I've fucking jacked off to thoughts of her, and felt like the world's biggest dickhead afterwards.

She looks at me with such pleading in her eyes, and a touch of disappointment because she is expecting me to say no. Fuck. I can do this for her. I mean, it's no hardship. And all I have to do is just watch and let her prove to herself and Ellie that she can do this.

I scratch the back of my head and look around. For a split second, I think about having her ask one of the other guys, but a burning rage fills me at that thought. Her dancing out there, with the other girls, and the men not able to get near her, is all good and well.

In a private room, where I know what goes on. Shit, no one is getting to see her like that. Not if I can help it. And not for her first time. That thought gets me more excited than it should.

"What do you need me to do?" I ask.

"Just sit down, and watch."

"Easy peasy," I smirk.

"Exactly." She smiles.

"Okay then."

"You'll do it."

"Sure. I'll do anything to help you out."

"Thank you."

"You're welcome."

"Great."

"Charley?"

"Yeah?"

"You want to get started?"

"Oh, yeah, right. Take a seat. I'll set up the music."

She turns around and Jesus, that ass. What the fuck am I doing? I turn away and move the chair back a little, then take a seat, in time for the music to start and Charley to turn and face me.

The music doesn't even register when she gets up on the stage and starts dancing. My eyes trace every inch of her body from the top of her head to the tips of those pointy and high as shit heels she is wearing.

Her body moves in fluid motion, never stopping, never hesitating as she nails every move, spin and undulation of her body. I can't take my eyes off her as she grabs the pole, arching forward and dragging her breasts up it, popping her ass out.

Then she spins around it so her back is to me, gliding down a little and back up again. Her elbows go out to the side and the sparkly top is in her hands, opened.

My mouth goes dry when she spins around, throwing her head back, allowing the fabric to fall down her arms and pool on the floor behind her.

My cock starts to get hard and I shift on the seat. It's impossible to hide it, but what the hell am I supposed to do when she is practically naked in front of me?

Oh hell, this was a bad idea.

She straightens up and grips the pole her eyes opening. When she sees me, she falters and loses a step but keeps going, spinning around the pole and getting back into the rhythm.

I'm transfixed, my eyes greedily eating up every ounce of her body, the subtle sheen of her skin, the tightness of her ass, and the outline of her pussy, which is hidden from view but the hint of it is giving me all kinds of crazy ideas.

Then there are those tits. Perfect, bouncing slightly in a natural way, her nipples are rock hard, a dark rosy pink and the urge to go over and bite them takes over enough that I move forward in the chair, only catching myself when she turns her back to me and bends over.

Her long legs are crossed, presenting that perfectly peachy ass as she touches the floor with her fingertips.

The music ends, my cock is so painfully hard I need to fucking touch it, or her. Or... Shit.

Charley straightens up and turns around. Her arms are fidgeting like she wants to cup her tits and hide them, but she forces them at her sides. She is breathing heavily enough that they're rising and falling and I picture that happening while she is riding my cock.

"Callum?"

A weird sound comes from the back of my throat, some high pitched, throat clearing sound. "Yeah."

"Was that okay?"

I almost say no. Because if I said no, she'd think she was bad and she wouldn't do this and no one else would get to see her like this. How much of an asshole would I be to do that? It would break her heart.

"Yeah, it was, good, great. You were..." I stutter over the words.

"Are you okay? It was bad wasn't it."

"Jesus no, there was nothing bad about that."

I stay seated because getting up would show her just how bad it *wasn't*. Get it together asshole, she doesn't need to see me freaking out.

"Charley, if you dance like that, you're not going to ruin anything. It's kind of weird that I've seen your tits now."

"What?" Her eyes widen.

"Shit, did I say that out loud?"

She covers her mouth with her hand to hide a laugh. "Are you blushing, Callum?"

"I mean," I grab the back of my neck. "That was hot. I'm not going to lie."

Her smile grows, but it's no longer amusement, she is happy.

"You did falter once, when you turned around."

I hate to break that happiness, but she did ask me to make sure she got it right. I can at least give her better feedback than what I have up until this point.

Charley nods. "It was that split second of knowing I was about to turn around. Was it that obvious?"

"If the pole hadn't been there, you might have fallen, but if you keep practicing, it'll get easier."

"With you?" She lifts a brow.

"Don't say shit like that to me."

"Why?"

Words leave my head. Thoughts dance across my vision of an entirely different scenario with a naked Charley standing in front of me. She is still naked. That realization seems to hit her at the same time. She goes and picks up the top, not helping matters where my cock is concerned because her ass is pointed at me again.

At least when she turns back around her tits are covered. Not the slope of her waist and the flare of her hips, or that sweet spot between her thighs.

"I should go," I stand up and turn away. "I have work to do." I move quickly to the door, willing my cock to behave. Before I run out, I look over my shoulder. "You'll be amazing Charley. Believe in yourself, you'll knock everyone dead."

Thank fuck Beast's office is empty. I go inside, slam the door and lock it. It's fucking obscene getting my dick out in here, but I need relief and the image of her tits bouncing up and down does me in. Cum spurts all over my hand as I lose it in record time. My chest is heaving as I try to catch my breath. When my heart rate finally slows and I tuck myself away, guilt pours through me.

It's a really fucking weird feeling, being attracted to someone and feeling guilty about it. She isn't a child, she is just a few years younger than I am.

How many times have I watched the dancers here? I've had lap dances, I've had girls go down on me, sit naked in my lap and feed fucking appetizers to me.

No one has ever made me feel the way Charley just did. And I don't know what the fuck to do with that.

Chapter Ten

Charley

He was hard.

That thought hasn't stopped running through my mind for my whole shift. Not only was he hard, but he was flummoxed too, he didn't know what to say. I can't believe I had that much of an effect on him. The Nashville everyone knows is never lost for words.

It makes me feel powerful, it gives me confidence that what I did back there was enough. Even his comment about seeing my tits didn't upset or embarrass me. The more I think about it, the more I understand what Lily has been telling me about how dancing makes her feel.

Okay, she says it feels like she is holding their balls in her hand, that she could do or say anything and they'd give her whatever it was she wanted.

Having that kind of power over anyone isn't something I want but I do understand it.

While I wait for Max to fill a tray with drinks for me, I think back on the interaction. He agreed, no questions asked, to help me tonight. He took me home not caring that it was out of his way, and he rescued me from that house, letting me into his home.

No one has ever been so selfless toward me before. He's always been respectful, but occasionally I've caught him watching me, he always tries to blow it off with flirty joking banter. I may be younger than he is, but I'm not blind, or dumb. Or immune to his charms.

He is a gorgeous man, his hazel eyes are so expressive, and his smile could melt ice caps off the mountains. And his body... I caught him coming out of his home gym a few nights ago, shirtless, covered in sweat and trying to catch his breath.

Instead of facing him all hot and bothered I hid in the shadows and waited until he had gone upstairs, then imagined him in the shower.

It's been a really long time since I had sex. And honestly, I wish I could forget every second of it. I'm not looking to get close to anyone. It isn't worth it. You always end up being hurt in the long run, that's the way things have been for me since I was nine years old.

Even the one person I thought could never turn their back on me, did it without a second thought. All because he was too weak to fight back against *her.* The woman who ruined my life.

How did I go from thinking about Callum having a very hard, very large bulge in his pants, to remembering the horrible place my step-mother turned my home into?

I've got more important things to worry about than the past, or a crush on the guy who would probably enjoy a few nights with me but isn't looking to get into anything serious.

Like I am. Shit.

The drinks are ready to go and I lift the tray as someone slams into me from behind, hard enough that my hip hits the bar. I scramble not to drop the tray but my wrist twists and the tray goes over, all the drinks falling off the tray.

Alcohol spills all over the floor, my legs and the suit pants of the idiot who ran into me, and glass is shattered all around us.

"Jesus, Charley, I thought you'd got over that?" Max comes back along the bar, not looking happy.

My instinct is to say it wasn't my fault, the asshole ran into me, but we don't blame the clientele for anything and given my history who would ever believe me? Having Max think I'm back to being a klutz is annoying as hell.

I apologize to the man who glares at me.

"Look at my pants," he snaps.

"It was an accident," I say, through gritted teeth because it was caused by him. Not me.

"An accident, do you know how much this suit cost, you dumb bitch?"

"Excuse me?" How fucking dare he call me a bitch.

"You heard me, what kind of fucking idiots do they have working here? One word from me, and you'll be fired."

He is so angry I take a step back, bumping into the bar. I've come across men like this before, men who never take responsibility for their actions, who think nothing of belittling women. Or hurting them.

I don't know who he is, haven't seen him here before and have no idea if what he just said is true.

I hate groveling to anyone but losing my job can't happen.

"I'm very sorry that we bumped into each other."

"We bumped into each other?" He takes another step toward me but there is nowhere left for me to go so he is in my face when he shouts. "What the fuck-"

"Mr. Cantrell."

We both turn to Ellie, looking gorgeous as ever in a nude colored dress with sequins over her breasts and down between her legs, everything else is see-through. Her beauty stops *Mr. Cantrell* in his tracks.

"I can only apologize on behalf of our wait staff, she's new and still learning. Please allow me to get your table some complimentary champagne and we will of course pay for any dry cleaning."

It's hard not to let my mouth fall open, or be hurt that Ellie could say something like that about me.

"Max, three bottles of our best champagne please."

"So long as she doesn't bring it over."

"Of course not," Ellie turns to me. "Please go in back and wait for me."

"I hope you're going to fire her ass."

Ellie just smiles and links her arm through his walking him away. Max is busy getting the champagne and calling over one of the other girls.

I've never felt so stupid. And not because of what happened with that bastard, I never thought Ellie would treat me like that. So stupid that my heart hurts.

Instead of standing here waiting for people to ask questions, I turn and head to the back, dodging around people so I don't bump into anyone else.

Damn it, I can't believe I'm going to lose everything, when I was so damn close, because some idiot can't admit that he was in the wrong. Or that I ever thought anyone was going to have my back.

Just the way it has been for the last decade. Dumb, he's right. I really am.

Instead of going to the office to wait, I head to the dressing room to get my things. I'm not hanging around to be fired. My hand hurts when I pull my bag out of the locker and I wince, only just noticing a cut and blood running down my fingers.

"Charley? I told you to wait in the office."

Ellie's tone is sharp. I quickly hide my hand and she eyes my bag and frowns.

"What are you doing?"

"Getting my things."

"Why?"

"You said..."

"I said what I needed to. I didn't want that fucking twat causing a scene. Do you really think I would fire you?"

"I... You were very convincing."

"Something I've learned over the years. If you think I would take his side over yours, then you don't know me very well."

"You're kind of hard to read sometimes," I tell her honestly.

"His father is important. The Cantrell's are working with the club." When I frown she shakes her head. "The Disciples, not Elegance. That means we don't rock the boat. Sometimes, the best way to diffuse a situation like that is to give the man child what he wants. In this case, to feel important. He wanted you fired, I let him think it would happen."

"That's smart."

Now I feel even more stupid. This isn't my world though, I'm still not used to it.

"Is that blood?" she looks at my wrist and pulls a face like she might get sick. "That fucking asshole."

She takes out her phone and texts someone while I set my bag down and go to one of the tables to grab a tissue and clean up the blood. There is a lot of it. Shit, the wound is deeper than I thought.

A few minutes later, Walker comes into the room and Ellie tells him to look at my hand It's throbbing now, I guess the adrenalin of feeling like no one gives a shit about me, and I was about to lose my job is wearing off.

"Jesus, Charley." Walker guides me to a chair to sit down. He grabs a towel from the chair behind me and places it under my arm. "Ellie do you have any tweezers?"

"There should be some on one of the tables. If you're about to do something gross, I'm leaving. Do I need to call an ambulance?"

"No," I protest. "I'm fine, don't worry about it."

"There is glass in the cut, Charley."

"Okay, I'm leaving and I'm putting in a call about this. No one hurts a member of our staff and gets away with it. I don't give a fuck who their daddy is."

She disappears while Walker gets the tweezers. I'm not squeamish. I've learned to deal with injuries over the years. Still, it hurts when he pulls out the small glass shards. He's so good at it, he must be used to this kind of thing.

"Walker?" I ask, as he cleans off the blood.

"Yeah?"

"Who is Mr. Cantrell?"

He frowns and looks up at me. "That's who did this?"

"It was an accident," I say with a note of sarcasm in my tone.

"His father is connected."

"To what?" Walker laughs and I realize what he means. "Oh God. Like that."

"Yeah, like that. They're not good people but then again, who is? You don't need stitches but I'm going to put some of these on to keep it together before I bandage it. You're lucky," he smiles. "It won't need amputating."

"Good to know," I smile back. "Thank you."

He sets the butterfly stitches on after cleaning the blood and wraps a bandage around it. Lily has come in by the time he's finished which I'm glad about because she didn't have to see Walker fixing me up, but her eyes widen in horror at the mess around us. Walker starts gathering it up.

"Jesus, Charley, what happened?"

"Nothing, I just dropped a tray and cut myself." Walker lifts his eyes to mine but keeps his head down. "I'm fine."

"Does it hurt? That's a stupid question. Here, I have some pain pills that will help."

"I don't like taking pills."

"Relax, its over-the-counter stuff, it's not strong but it will take the edge off. Do you need a hospital?"

"She's fine, Lily." Walker stands and looks over at her. She stops talking. "The pills will help, Charley, that is gonna hurt."

I guess that means I'm taking the pills, I read the box when she hands it to me. It's not that I don't trust her but I don't like the idea of not being in control of myself. This brand is non-drowsy, so I follow the directions and take two.

Walker offers to take me home, but I have Callum's car so I tell him I'm fine.

"Can you let Ellie know and... tell her I said thank you."

Walker nods and heads out. Lily chuckles about my being clumsy again and I let her run with it.

As I drive back to Callum's house, I'm not sure whether I want him to be there or not. This would be one way to break the tension, but I doubt it would be in a good way. I've heard enough times that the Disciples protect the girls. Or maybe he wouldn't care...

That isn't true, he's already proven that in the way he treats me now.

None of it matters, because he isn't here when I get home.

It's hard to fall asleep. Despite the pain relief the cut is throbbing, and I'm too scared to take a shower because I'll never be able to re-wrap it the way Walker did. And for a long time, I listen out for Callum coming home.

But he never does.

Chapter Eleven

Nashville

Everyone is looking at Beast while he stares at the wall. So far no one has asked him anything and my tongue is itching to be the first but Nero comes in before I can, which is probably a good thing. He looks at Beast too but doesn't make a big deal of it.

Nero gets down to business asking Blaze if we're anywhere on finding Storm. He gets the same response, following leads, tracking men we believe he worked with, but still no sign. Nero's frustration is obvious, but he doesn't take it out on Blaze. He is doing his best, working night and day on this.

"Beast, you good?" Nero asks.

"Yeah."

"You want to try that with a little less lie in your answer."

"Fuck," he sits back and puts his hands behind his head. "She's... I had a paternity test rushed through. And its ninety-nine point nine what the fuck ever she's mine."

Everyone is quiet, no one wants to make fun of this the way they have with Nero but that's a different kind of situation. Nero knew about and had been raising his kid without telling anyone. This is very different. This is a whole ass teenager showing up out of nowhere.

"You don't need to tell us everything, but I do want to know where it goes from here, how it affects you as an officer."

"It won't affect anything," he drops his hands. "I'm figuring shit out. Her mom was someone I knew in high school. Shit was rough for me back then and as soon as I could, I got the fuck out. Didn't know I'd got her pregnant."

That explains why Beast has a seventeen-year-old at his age. He was the same age as her when she was conceived.

"They kicked her out when she got pregnant, she raised the kid alone."

"Damn," Fury says from beside him.

"Yeah, she's had a tough life. Her mom died, she has no one else. Not gonna get much better with me as a father."

"You'll figure it out," Nero tells him.

He's not leaving room for arguments. No matter how it goes, this kid is part of the Blackhawk family, she'll be taken care of.

"Where is she?" Razer asks.

"Staying with Raven," Rebel speaks up. He eyes us all after our reaction to that. "Surprised me too, but she didn't want the kid left here, or out on the street."

Beast clenches his fists.

"Okay, so long as she is somewhere safe, and not being corrupted by Raven," Nero adds, which gets a laugh from a few of us. "We had a situation at Elegance last night."

My head whips up to Beast. His eyes meet mine and he shakes his head, he doesn't know what Nero means.

"It involved Cantrell junior. The dickhead hurt one of the wait staff. Ellie and Walker dealt with it, but I want someone watching the fucker on Saturday."

"Who did he hurt and how?" Beast takes the words right out of my mouth.

"Charley."

My seat flies back and I start to get up. Everyone looks at me. Shit.

"What's wrong with you?" Rebel asks.

I can't let them know she's living with me. Or that I am full on infatuated with her. Jesus Christ how did I not know she got hurt? Because I avoided going home last night like a fucking child.

"Something bit me."

"What?"

"Nothing, go on, what did he do to her?"

"Bumped into her, knocked over some glasses on her tray and wanted her fired."

Fired? Fuck.

"Ellie stroked the idiot's ego and sent the girl home, but she didn't fire her."

"Doesn't seem too bad to me," Fury states.

"She cut her hand, pretty bad Walker said. Glass sliced through her palm, but she is okay, he dealt with it. It was *all* dealt with," Nero eyes Beast. "But we can't afford for any shit like that to happen again."

"I'll be back there tonight," Beast says, his expression troubled. He's the one who kept giving Charley chances, so it stands to reason he's worried. "Did Ellie say if she told Charley to stay off a couple of nights?"

"Does he look like a messenger? Speak to Ellie," Rebel cuts in.

The whole time they're talking my blood is boiling, the rage growing. He fucking made her bleed? Now I know what Nero felt when he saw that video of Taylor being attacked.

I'm not even in a relationship with Charley and I want to break Cantrell's fucking neck. Something I can't do given the negotiations he is into with the club over distribution of weapons.

God dammit. My leg starts to bounce as the meeting goes on. I can't go running home to make sure she is okay and stupidly, I don't have her cell number.

When the meeting finally breaks up, I'm the first to head for the door, trying to figure out how I can check on Charley without letting on to anyone, but Nero calls me back. Shit, I can't say no. This is about Sheridan and my brother.

Before he can ask, I give him the lowdown on what Cam told me and that as soon as he is close, he'll call me.

"You'll go down there?"

"Yeah, I'll bring her back."

"Okay," he leans an elbow on the arm rest of his chair. "Everything else okay?"

"Fine."

"Why do you look like you want to get out of here?"

"Just some stuff going on, it's not important."

"You sure about that?"

"Positive."

Nero knows I'm lying, but he doesn't probe. If it was an issue for the club, he trusts that I would raise it, but since Chains turned traitor on us a few months ago, he's more watchful. Not that I think he doesn't trust me.

"Then let's go get a drink next door. I could do with a break."

"A break?" I ask in surprise.

"Taylor and Jesse are suddenly like siblings who can't stop pecking at each other."

"Sounds fun."

"They're worse than Oscar," he rolls his eyes.

"Is Jesse not ready to go back to his place?"

"He's been ready for a week but Taylor wants him to stay longer." He laughs at my expression. "Exactly, figure that out. So yeah, I need a drink."

We head over to the bar, the whole time I'm there I fake a smile and barely finish one drink, just long enough to get away with not looking like I'm running out on everyone when I say I have to go.

It takes a fucking age to get home and when I pull into the garage I'm relieved to see the BMW there.

Charley is in the laundry room emptying the drier and I almost snatch the basket out of her hands, making her squeal. When she sees it's me, she hits me. Not hard, and not on purpose, it was a reaction to me walking in and scaring the shit out of her.

"What the hell?" she pants.

"Sorry," I hold up my hands. "I didn't mean to do that."

"Jesus, Callum." She puts both hands on the top of the drier and leans forward, but winces and pulls her hand away, then she turns to me, her eyes wide. "It's nothing."

"It's not nothing, I know what it is."

"I just dropped a tray."

"You expect me to believe that."

"I'm clumsy."

"You were, you haven't dropped anything in weeks. What did he do?"

"Nothing," she can tell I'm fully up to speed with what happened. "He actually did only bump into me, it was a complete accident that didn't need to turn out the way it did. Alcohol spilled all over his pants and shoes and he wanted to blame me."

"Fucking asshole."

"Ellie handled it and my hand is fine."

"Let me see."

"No, it's bandaged, I'm not untying it to show you a cut."

"What if there is glass still in it?"

"There isn't."

I open my mouth to argue some more but she walks around me and leaves the room, and the laundry. I glance down and see a pair of tiny white lace panties sitting on top and my head scrambles for a moment.

"Charley," I drag my eyes away and follow her.

"I promise, I'm fine," she stops at the bottom of the stairs.

She doesn't look fine, but I don't want to make her feel any worse than she clearly already does. If she thought Ellie was going to fire her last night and told her to stay off work a few days, she could have done with having someone to talk to when she got home.

Home, shit. This isn't her home. This is temporary, albeit a little longer than the one night I first said when I got her out of the crack house. But that is beside the point.

"Callum," she touches my forearm with her good hand and I swear sparks jolt up it and go straight to my dick. "I'm good. I've even been in to Elegance this morning to practice with the other girls."

Right, the dance for the special party on Saturday. The one for the fucking Cantrell's. He'll see her there and know she didn't get fired but with the entire council and more of our brothers there, he won't try anything. He'd be seriously fucking stupid to.

Doesn't mean I won't be watching Charley like a hawk.

"How did it go?" I ask, to divert from asking any more questions about that fucking shitbag.

"Good, well, I didn't mess up. But it's a dress rehearsal so..."

"You'll be great," I reassure her. "You're an expert now."

"Doing one dance for one guy makes me an expert?"

"When I'm the guy," I wink at her. "I decide, and I say you're going to be great."

"You're full of shit, but thank you," she smiles.

"Do you want to grab a drink?" I blurt out.

"What, go out?"

"No, I mean, I have drinks here, I just thought we could hang out."

"Hang out?"

"Is there a parrot in here?" I grin. "Come on, have a drink with me," I tug her sleeve and step back. It's not hard enough to drag her, if she doesn't want to, she doesn't have to, but shit, my smile gets wider when she agrees.

I get her a bottle of wine and glass, and grab a six-pack so I don't have to keep getting up and we go into the living room. Using my phone, I start up a playlist of alternative rock music.

"No Vampire Diaries," she smiles, sitting down and folding her legs underneath her butt.

"Nah, I've had enough of Damon and Stefan for a little while. Besides, we can't talk if we're watching TV, right?"

She brushes some hair behind her ear. I love it when she wears it all loose like that, spilling over her shoulder, kind of like it was when she was dancing and her nipples were peeking through all that golden hair.

"So where are you from?" I ask, sucking down some beer.

"Originally? A little town in California."

"That's specific," I laugh. "North, South?"

"In the bay area. Woodside."

"Expensive round there."

"Kinda," she takes a healthy gulp of her wine.

"Any siblings?"

"Nope."

"That's a shame, although sometimes when I was a kid I did wish I was an only child."

"Three brothers will do that," she laughs. "So with an accent like that I'm guessing you're not a native to Baltimore."

"Nothing gets past you." She laughs again. "I'm from Nashville."

"Seriously," she twists around and draws her knees up, her bare feet are close to my thigh. "Is that where the name comes from?"

"Right again."

"Is that how you get your names, like where you're from?"

"Sometimes. Mostly it's about personality, or attitude, or something that just fits."

"If that is the case Beast seems like his name is all wrong."

"Why do you say that?"

"He's more of a bear than a beast, he's nice and genuine and doesn't raise his voice. He's the least beastly person I've ever met."

"Maybe it's just when he's in the sack," I grin. "We saw how... vigorous he can be."

Her cheeks turn pink and she hides her face behind her wine glass. "Stop it."

"Don't pretend you don't agree," I poke her ankle.

"Okay fine. But, I'm going to choose to believe he got the wrong name."

She hasn't seen him doing what he does for the club so I'm not going to change her opinion on that.

"Okay," she says after taking another sip of wine. "If you could choose your name, instead of it being Nashville, what would you have picked?"

"Shit, I've never really thought about that. We don't choose our own road names, they're given to us, like we're born into the club."

"So, if you were given the name," she rubs her lips together and looks up at the ceiling, thinking of a name. "Sprinkles! You would have been happy with that?"

A loud laugh bursts out of me. "I mean, I think I could pull that off."

"Your bikes exhaust could fire out glitter," she chuckles.

"And I'd have to have a pink helmet with a unicorn horn."

"I would love to see that," she tilts her head back and rests it on the back of the couch.

"You think I could look tough in that get-up?"

"It takes a strong man to be confident enough to wear a pink unicorn horn helmet."

"Damn straight."

"But I wouldn't want to see you getting your ass kicked so maybe stick to Nashville."

"I think you're right. But now we've talked about it, I do kinda feel a little let down. Does it make me unoriginal, Charley?"

She raises her head and looks at me. “Honestly,” she nudges my thigh with her toes. “I don’t think there is anything unoriginal about you. I’ve never met anyone like you.”

“How do you mean?” I turn to face her.

“I’ve been really crap at trying to find somewhere else to live. I told myself one or two nights max and I’d leave you alone and, every time I thought about looking I got distracted. You could have kicked me out ages ago.”

“I wasn’t about to do that. And to be fair, I haven’t exactly looked either.”

“It’s on my list. I can’t keep imposing on you.”

“Funny thing is, it’s been nice, having someone around.”

“Someone to watch cheesy vampire shows with and not judge you?”

“Exactly,” I lean forward and tap my beer bottle against her glass. “In all seriousness Charley, I’m not planning on kicking you out. The last thing I want is for you to go from one bad situation to a slightly better one when you can get what you actually want if you wait a little longer.”

Her head dips and she stares into her wine. “At least let me pay rent.”

“You don’t have to do that.” She is about to protest and I understand that it’s not just about paying me for being here, it’s about pride. “How about you pay for the groceries, and gassing up the SUV?”

“That sounds like I’m getting off easy.”

“Yeah well, it’s not going to be forever, right?”

She frowns into her wine and nods. When she looks up at me, it’s hard to read her expression. Is she disappointed by that statement, or looking forward to the day she gets out of here?

It’s really hard to tell and when she finishes her wine and says she needs an early start at Elegance, I don’t ask her to stay, instead telling her I’ll handle the clean up.

“Goodnight, *Nashville*,” she smiles as she walks around the couch.

“Hey, that’s Sprinkles to you.”

Her laugh is sweet and kind of throaty and it makes my gut clench. When she’s gone, I face the giant screen TV and study my reflection. My cut is hanging on the back of the chair in the corner, I’m wearing a dark shirt and jeans, but kicked off my boots when I came in. My hair is a little on the scruffy side and my face could do with a shave.

I've never had a woman turn me down and I'll admit, in my younger years I played up to that shit. I can't help but sit here and wonder what a woman like Charley could ever see in a guy like me.

The way she has been living, and the desperation to dance and earn money tells me one thing about her. Coming from Woodside, that tells me a whole lot more and intrigues me.

I've always been a geography buff. That shit enthralled me when I was a kid. I loved reading maps. I kinda hate GPS systems, they've taken away the fun of reading a map.

Woodside is in the Bay Area and is one of, if not right up there, as one of the most expensive places to live on the west coast. I met a guy once who came from Woodside, he was fucking loaded, like serious money.

How did she go from that, to this? Obviously she didn't want to tell me and I won't ask. I could easily get Blaze to look into her for me, I'm not going to do that either. All I can do is hope she finds what she is looking for.

I've never felt any real connection with a woman before, never really wanted to get to know one, or been worried about them.

As fun and light as I kept things tonight, my eye never went too far from that bandage on her hand. This odd sense of protectiveness is growing for her, and I don't have a clue how to deal with that.

Charley is different to other women I've been around. She isn't trying to impress me, or anyone else, she hid the fact she was in a bad place and was doing her best to make it work. She doesn't like taking help... And yet, she hasn't left my place.

Maybe I make her feel safe. That scares me and thrills me in equal measures.

There are a lot of reasons to back off and leave her be. Stupidly, I don't want to.

Chapter Twelve

Charley

The last three days have been hard work but I've loved every second of it. When I'm not working my shifts, I'm practicing in the private room, or doing the routine for the big private party with the others.

Ellie came in to watch me do a dance where I stripped. She could have brought someone else, but she didn't. It oddly felt like I was dancing for my life dancing for Ellie. She's been working alongside us all in the rehearsals as she's taking a part and I'm in awe of her.

She told me I was too good to dance here, I'm not sure she realizes she is even better. I would love to get to know more about her, find out how she ended up here, but that would open myself up to questions and I don't want to get caught in that trap.

It takes a lot to impress her and my heart soared when she said I'd exceeded her expectations but she still had me dance for a bigger audience first. I had a set last night, one dance, on one of the smaller stages.

Even though my heart was pounding, I got up and did the dance, took off my top and imagined it was Callum watching and no one else. Which probably wasn't a good idea, but it worked.

Both Ellie and Beast were watching. Ellie didn't go into too much detail, but she did have to talk Beast around.

Every time I see him now, all I can think about is me saying he is like a bear and Callum saying he's a beast in the sack. Whatever Ellie did, it worked and he let me dance, he even told me in not so many words, that I did a good job.

"Are you nervous?" Lily asks, watching me dust some of the highlighter the girls all wear over my collar bones.

"I'm excited."

She beams a smile. "Good. These private parties usually are a blast and the men are so rich, they literally give you hundreds in tips."

That's good to know. The more money I can save, the easier it will be when I have to move out of Callum's place. He might say I can stay indefinitely but he isn't always going to want me around.

What if he wants to bring a woman home? That thought makes me feel sick to my stomach. I will never admit it, either to myself or anyone else, I really like him and imagining him with some other girl hurts.

He's never given any indication he sees me as anything more than a friend, or employee, or house guest. Well, except for when he got hard when I was dancing, that's biology though and it's not like he acted on it.

"Okay ladies, ten minutes," Tami shouts. "Everyone is here, having drinks, enjoying themselves and ready for the show."

The girls cheer. It's nice to see them happy about it. Not a lot of people would understand, they look down on strippers, but most of these women have a story. Lily has shared some of hers and she does tend to gossip a little so I know about some of the others, like Karin had to quit because she found out she was pregnant.

Standing in front of the mirror, I adjust the red, three quarter length blazer I'm wearing. It about skims to the center of my ass. It has embroidered flowers all down the lapel to the waist line where a sash is tied holding the two sides together. There is a small clasp to stop it from opening too soon when we're dancing because we're naked from the waist up underneath.

"Your straps aren't straight," Lily bends down to adjust the straps on the garter belt so they're lined up straight at the front of my thigh. They're holding up the sheer black stockings with lacy top and match the sheer black thong. It will be the only thing we have on once the jacket comes off.

And the killer sparkly heels with studs on the back seam of the heel. The whole outfit has to cost at least a grand. Wonder if Ellie will let me keep the shoes?

Speaking of, she walks in the room and I stop and stare. Lily nudges me with a laugh, it's hard to drag my eyes away. She's wearing the same outfit as the rest of us but she pulls it off effortlessly. She looks like a 1940s movie star, or burlesque dancer.

"We all want to be Ellie when we grow up," Lily laughs.

"Is everyone ready?" Ellie asks.

She pauses on me and I dip my chin once. I'm not going to try to convince her anymore.

"Let's go knock these pricks on their asses then," she smirks and turns around.

We all file out after her. The lights are down and there is a low pulsing beat playing through the sound system as we take the stage. The chatter of the men dies down as we take our places.

I'm on the back row, which is fine, I understand they don't want me front and center, just in case. I've nailed the routine on every practice, even the dress rehearsal.

Facing the back wall, I spread my ankles and bow my head. It seems like there are more people than Ellie said but I guess they are the men from the MC. Callum never explicitly said he'd be here but he is an officer in the club, it makes sense he will.

The beat of the music changes and the lights move, pointing towards the stage. Someone whistles and a few men cheer and laugh. Ellie told me to always ignore anything that comes out of their mouths, especially when they're being pigs.

If they're overheard by any of the staff being disgusting, they get kicked out. It doesn't happen often given the clientele but these aren't the usual people who come here.

This is all about getting this Cantrell guy to work with the MC.

I flex my hand and look at the cut, it has healed up enough not to be bandaged, but it's a stark reminder that the asshole who caused it is somewhere in the audience. I won't let him get in my head.

Instead, I count down the beat and turn when the music kicks in. The two rows in front of us do their turn one after another and then we start the dance. Centering my mind and body, I let the music take over, flowing through my body, moving to the beat.

All around me the others do the same and we're so in sync it's perfect. The lights make it hard to see the audience but there are lots of silhouettes and occasional flashes of faces. When we rotate and I am at the front for a brief moment, the booth in front of me lights up.

There are a lot of Blackhawk Disciple cuts but not the one I was hoping to see. One man sitting in the center of the group isn't watching the dance, he's chatting with another MC member beside him.

Wow, he is really good looking. I twirl away towards a pole. Eight of them are lined up in a diagonal pattern on each side, the closer to the front of the stage, the wider apart they are.

It's almost the moment. We're going to rip open the jackets two by two getting closer to the front, then step around the side of the pole, drop them and carry out the rest of the dance wearing nothing but our stockings, panties and heels.

Lily said that was classy, which initially made me laugh but the alternative is fully naked, so I was happy to agree.

The two girls behind me rip open their jackets. After a count of three I do mine and when the music changes we all turn around and throw the jackets to the side. The men cheer and clap but I shut out the noise and carry on dancing.

As I work the pole and bend down so I can see the audience between my legs, I spot Callum. He is staring right at me.

From that moment on, my eyes keep going back to him, he never takes his off me. It's odd how his intense focus gives me confidence. He isn't staring at my breasts like most of the other men, his gaze is on my face.

Everything around me becomes instinct as I keep my attention on him too. Before I know it, the dance is over and we're all breathing hard. Some of the men get up and come to the front, handing out cash. No one throws money here.

Except for one guy, who tosses a hand full of bills at my feet. I raise my eyes and try not to snarl at the idiot who cut my hand. He sneers at me and walks away.

"Leave it," Ellie says, moving close to me, her lips barely move. "Do not show any reaction."

It takes a lot to do as she says because there is at least three hundred dollars on the floor, but I have more pride than to bend down when the rest of the girls are having money handed to them. Someone else presses money into the string of my underwear and I smile at him. He's wearing one of the MC vests, but I don't recognize him.

When I look at Callum, he is no longer watching me, his face is thunderous, and he is staring at Cantrell. For a moment, it looks like he is going to go after him but he leans back and drinks some of his beer, his brow creased.

I appreciate the sentiment, but I wouldn't want him to get into any trouble.

After the money giving has died down, we file off the stage and head to the back. The others will do a quick change then head back out to dance some more but they will just be background, the men will be doing business.

My time is done. Ellie only wanted me for that dance. Slipping my sleeves back into the jacket I go into the private room instead of the dressing room. I need a minute to get my head around everything.

Dancing up there was amazing. I loved the routine, the stripping part didn't bother me as much as I thought it would. Everything Ellie has done has really helped my mindset.

Staring at myself in the mirror I smile. I did it. Something I set out to do by myself I've finally achieved. If only they could see me now.

My step-sister, Adeline would lose her shit and call me all kinds of names, but that is nothing new, she has done that from the moment I met her.

I don't want to think about Stephen, and close my eyes to push memories of him away. My step-mother can't say or do anything anymore, given she is dead.

The door opens and I turn around to tell whoever it is that I'll get out of their way. It's Cantrell, and he's glaring at me as he steps inside.

Shit. I've allowed myself to be cornered in a room where no one knows I am. And there is so much noise outside and everyone is distracted, they're probably not going to miss me.

"You're not supposed to be back here," I say, sounding a lot more confident than I feel.

"I thought you were fired." He closes the door. "Instead they just moved you up on the stage. Makes sense, with tits like that."

I breathe through the anger at his words. Ellie is right, not reacting is the best thing I can do.

"You think you're too good for my money?"

"I'm not supposed to pick money up from the floor."

He laughs. "Don't whores always scoop up whatever people throw at them."

"I'm not a whore."

My nostrils flare as my words come out emotionless. He doesn't like it. From being in here a lot over the last few weeks I know there isn't really anything I can use to protect myself. A wooden chair maybe.

There are always my heels, with the pointy studs. It will be a shame to damage them but if I have to, I will. This snake is not getting his hands anywhere near me.

"Working in a place like this, don't kid yourself. And I think I'm owed something seen as how I tossed you three hundred bucks. What does that get me?"

"Nothing."

"Bullshit, I think it gets me bending your ass over that chair and fucking it, hard. And no one is going to stop me." He moves towards me.

My throat swells and pinpricks start to swirl at the edges of my vision. Shit, I cannot have a panic attack, not now.

I'm so lost that I don't notice light spilling into the room behind him. He's so focused on hurting me, he doesn't either.

Until something rams into his back and sends him sprawling face first into the floor.

CHAPTER THIRTEEN

Nashville

"THAT FUCKER IS GETTING on my last nerve," I snarl at Razer.

"The dickhead who threw cash on the floor?" he answers, drinking from his glass of vodka. "They're fucking idiots all of them."

"Keep that shit to yourself," Rebel boots him. "You want to fuck this up?"

Razer holds up a hand to say sorry but we all know he only means sorry for saying it out loud, not that he is sorry for actually saying it.

"At least she didn't pick it up," he says.

No, but I did. I wasn't letting that fucker take it back. Charley earned that fair and square, he was just being a prick because he thought it made him look good. Every single Disciple in here saw that and instantly hated him.

Even Nero shifted in his seat. We all know what this deal means, and no one wants to cause shit. Ellie handled it, the way she handles everything else, getting Charley to do the same, with decorum and grace. I watched him as they walked away, saw the rage brewing.

"Nero is working the old man," Fury says from beside me. "He doesn't give a shit about the younger one. Only person that ass cares about, is himself."

"He needs to learn some fucking respect."

We stop talking when Nero comes over with the older Cantrell. He can tell instantly there is something up, but he's made a move to bring the guy over to the officer's table and can't take it back. We make space for them and Cantrell starts talking about the show.

Beast grimaces when he mentions the hot brunette at the front of the stage. Ellie. I'm not sure if it's protective of one of his staff or something more. Hell, I'd been as shocked as Charley was to find him fucking her the other week. I never knew that was a thing. Whatever their situation is, he doesn't like the insinuation or Cantrell asking if Ellie takes dates.

She takes *dates* all right, but it's usually when Nero needs her to get information out of someone. Without her working over Chains a few months ago, we never would have found out half of what we did about Storm.

"She makes her own rules," Nero says, not giving away her name.

Cantrell laughs and Nero smiles back but it's not a real smile. Part of me wonders if he is regretting having this here. His eyes flick to the door that leads to the back, and he turns to Beast. What was that about? I look too just as the door is closing behind a man.

A quick search of the room says that Cantrell junior isn't where he was before. Most of the men in here are either chatting or watching the dancers that have come back out.

My gaze flicks back to Nero, his jaw is tight, but he's talking with the older guy as if nothing is amiss. A slight move of his hand gives me the go ahead.

After excusing myself, I walk through the booths and tables and head for the door no one other than employees should be using. And given it's a limited staff tonight, there is someone back here who shouldn't be.

And I'm itching to fucking knock the shit out of him. A couple of the dancers hurry out of the room and I ask if they've seen anyone back here but they say they were in the dressing room.

I duck my head in and search around, getting an eyeful of bare tits and a pussy. Tami sees me and straightens up, fully naked and smiles.

"Anyone seen Charley?"

Her smile slips, and she shakes her head. “I think she went to the bathroom.”

I don’t give a fuck if she isn’t happy with me. After the last few weeks I regret getting that blow job off her. The bathroom is empty. As I’m walking back, I eye the door of the room Charley has used to practice.

She’s struggled a lot with the stripping side of things, even though she did a fucking amazing job tonight. I couldn’t take my eyes off her.

Knowing her now, it makes sense that she wants to be alone after something like that. And that fucker throwing money at her like she was some hooker.

When I open the door and hear the filth coming out of his mouth, I don’t even hesitate, or think about the consequences. He goes sprawling when I slam into him, his face hitting the hard wood floor. Good, the trail of blood left behind when I grab him by the hair and pull him up gives me a sense of satisfaction.

Taking hold of his shirt and tie at his neck, I push him back, mostly holding him up too as he’s shorter than me and I’m moving fast. I slam his back into the wall and punch him in the side so hard he loses his breath.

“What the fuck did you just say to her.”

He’s disorientated and there is blood all over his face. In my peripheral I see Charley moving, she is clutching the little red blazer closed over her chest.

Rage fills me all over again and I pull him forward and slam him back again so his head cracks against the wall.

Someone says something in the hallway but I don’t hear them as I hit the fucker again, this time in the face. He’d fall if I wasn’t holding him up. He gets his hands up to try to fend me off but I’m fucking livid. Nothing can stop me.

“Nashville.”

I pause, but I don’t stop choking the little fucker.

Beast walks into my line of sight. He stares at me, then Cantrell, finally his eyes fall to Charley. He understands exactly what is going on and any move to stop me leaves him and he takes a pace back.

It’s Nero I need to worry about but he tells Beast to shut the door, which he does.

Now it's the three of us with him. And one of the dancers. I'm not sure of her name. Nero says something, and she hurries over to Charley and pulls her away.

Our reflections catch in the mirror. It is hard to read her expression, but she does pause and I'm pretty sure she isn't mad I'm beating the shit out of this guy.

"My father is going to fuck you up."

Lucky for him, Charley and the other dancer had left before he said that.

"Let him go."

It takes a few moments for Nero's order to register. His hand coming down on my shoulder is what makes me release the fucker. He drops like a lead balloon and grabs his throat.

The urge to kick him in the head is so strong. Nero reads me and uses the hand on my shoulder to move me back.

"What did he do?" he asks me in a low voice.

"Threatened to rape her."

His jaw clenches and he looks back at Cantrell. I know this deal means a lot for the club but even Nero won't stand for that. My eyes widen when he kicks him in the face. Cantrell flops to the side, out cold.

"Fuck," Nero turns away from him. "Did he touch her?"

"No, I got here before he could. Heard him telling her what he was going to do."

"She's the one he threw money at?" he asks. I nod. Nero grimaces and looks down at Cantrell, his mind working. "Beast, go get his father."

"Are you sure?"

Nero doesn't say anything. We wouldn't normally question his orders but this is probably not the best of ideas. Cantrell is connected, he's not a big player, but he is also someone you don't mess with.

Good thing we're scarier than he is and don't give a fuck.

Nero eyes me as I start to pace. Charley better be okay.

"Fuck," I curse out. "Five minutes later..."

"It didn't happen."

"It could have."

"It didn't and it won't and he isn't getting away with it."

The door opens and Beast comes back with Cantrell and Fury. He is smirking like he thinks he is getting a present until he sees his son out cold and covered in blood.

"What the fuck?" he steps forward, going toward his son, but Nero sidesteps and blocks him. "What the hell is this? Do you have any fucking idea what you've done?"

"He threatened one of my employees," Nero says.

"What? One of the girls? He didn't mean it. He may be my son but he's an idiot who runs his mouth."

"I'm glad we agree he is an idiot."

Cantrell turns his head to Nero his face a mask, but Nero doesn't falter as he stares him down.

"No one threatens my staff. If you're happy to have a rapist as a son, then this deal is off."

"A what?"

"Don't bullshit us."

Nero eyes me and my mouth snaps shut. There is no way this guy hasn't hurt women before. He's gonna fucking regret trying to hurt Charley.

Cantrell looks at his son, then back to Nero. Whatever he sees on my President's face makes his shoulders drop. "I don't want to fuck up the deal."

"Then deal with that," he points at his son. "I don't want to see his face in my city."

"You can't..." He trails off.

He is standing in a dark room with four of the most dangerous men in the city and he knows trying anything with us is only going to end with him getting hurt, shunned or worse, losing money.

"I'll send him to California tomorrow, to work with my brother."

"Do it tonight," Nero says. "Take him out the back."

Cantrell makes a call and two men come in to help carry the fucker out of the room. When it's done, he focuses on Nero again.

"Things can go ahead as discussed?"

"If you hold up your end," Nero tells him and Cantrell leaves without another word. "Fucking hell."

"You know I wouldn't have done it if it wasn't necessary."

"I'm not pissed at you," Nero says. "I'm sick and tired of filth like that wandering this city. If I could have got away with it, he'd be at the farm."

Beast glances at me and Fury grins. Shame we can't.

"Someone check on the girl, make sure she gets home okay."

"I'll do it," I say before Beast can. All eyes turn to me. "What?"

"You're getting close to her."

"I'm looking out for her. And she is probably shaken the fuck up so I'm gonna go do it now."

Before Beast says anything else, Nero tells me to go sort it out. I'm assuming he just wants to get back to the club but knowing Nero, he's seen right through me and I'll be hearing from him.

Charley is in the dressing room, fully clothed and promising everyone in there that she is okay. Her eyes meet mine when I open the door and she glances at my fist, which is swollen and will bruise after how hard I hit that dickhead in the face.

"Come on," I say to her. Ellie watches her walk to me but I don't spare anyone a glance, just hold the door for Charley. "You have the keys to the beamer?" She hands them to me. My bike will be fine here overnight.

"What's going to happen to him?" she asks as we drive out of the gate. "Has it wrecked everything?"

"No, don't worry about that. Nero knows what he is doing. And forget about that asshole, he's leaving the city tonight."

"You have that kind of power?" she asks.

"Yeah." There is no point in lying. "Are you okay?"

"He didn't touch me."

"That's not the point, he cornered you and threatened you."

"It was bad, but I had my shoes."

"Your shoes," I look over at her.

She takes one out of her bag and shows me. "One of those to the eyeball and he's out of commission."

"Jesus Charley," I laugh. "And here I was thinking I'd upset you my smashing his face into the floor."

"He deserved it."

"Damn right he did."

We drive the rest of the way in silence and walk into the house.

"I'm going to take a shower," she pauses at the bottom of the stairs. "I have this glitter all over me.

"Sure," I tell her, looking down on her now that she wearing flats. "Give me a shout if you need anything... After the shower," I add. "Not during. Unless you want to."

"Jesus Callum," she pokes me in the stomach and laughs.

Funny thing is, I wasn't joking.

Chapter Fourteen

Charley

THE HOT WATER IS going to run out if I don't get out of this shower soon. It took a long time to get the shimmery cream off and I've washed my hair twice, and scrubbed myself red. It's easy to tell yourself you're okay and you can deal with something like this when it happens. Or that nothing did happen, you're safe and weren't hurt.

None of it makes the terror you felt in the moment go away.

The bathroom here is amazing, so much better than what I've been used to the last two years. Even the really nice ones at Elegance can't beat this. And the towels. Callum spared no expense. He's definitely a conundrum, but one I'm more than happy to be around.

The violence doesn't scare me. If he was attacking people for no reason I'd hate it, but every time I've seen him when the rage changes him, it's to defend someone. Well, me.

Drying off and slipping on a camisole and shorts, I come into the bedroom, drying my hair. I stop short when I see Callum in the doorway. Did I leave that door open?

His eyes trail all the way down to my toes and back up again, pausing on my breasts which makes my nipples go hard, pushing at the silky fabric. He's taken off his cut but is still wearing the clothes he wore to the party.

My first thought is to ask what he is doing but breaking the silence would mean breaking this spell.

For a long time, I've thought about what it would be like, to touch him, to feel him against me. I never dared to believe he felt the same.

His throat works as he swallows, not taking a step inside, just watching. Almost waiting for me to tell him it's okay.

Turning so I'm fully facing him, I drop the towel on the floor and in a moment of insanity but complete desire, I move the strap of the camisole off my shoulder.

It falls to my elbow and the fabric, which is low cut anyway, drapes over my breast, hanging off my nipple for a moment before falling as far is can with the other strap still on my shoulder.

"Fuck," he groans under his breath.

It's like he's fighting with himself. I'm not sure why. This is an invitation, maybe it wasn't enough. I lower the other strap, so the whole thing falls to my waist, baring me to him.

This isn't the same as when I did it in the room at Elegance, or on the stage where he was watching me.

He takes a step into the room. I push the camisole over my hips and step out of it so I don't get tangled and fall on my ass. His chest is heaving as he watches me push my hands into the waistband of the shorts.

"Don't," he speaks.

I pause and look at him. Really? I'm here offering myself and...

He moves towards me and takes my wrists, gently moving them away. He is so close I can smell the scent of his skin, the warmth of his hands makes fire burn up my arms and shoulders and my throat tightens.

"Let me," he whispers and releases my arms to push his hands under the fabric at my hips. I watch his face as he pushes it over my ass, holding it as long as he can before it drops down between our feet. Now I'm completely naked and he is staring into my eyes.

No man has ever looked at me like this before. Like I'm the only thing he wants to stare at, captivated is the word that springs to mind.

It's heady and my mind is spinning as he raises a hand, ghosting it over my breast but not touching it, until his palm cups my jaw.

It's almost reverent how he is holding my face. How can a man go from the violence of just an hour ago, to treating me like spun glass? I'm not complaining because the way he is looking at me is making me feel powerful and beautiful and wanted.

But it is also driving me crazy. I push up on my toes and bring my mouth closer to his. He shifts his hand so that his thumb is on my lower lip, the rest of his fingers holding my chin. In the split second before his head lowers, our eyes lock again, until mine sweep shut and I lift higher.

Our lips join and his kiss is delicate, hesitant almost so I push further into him, letting him know I'm not breakable, he doesn't need to treat me like I'm delicate, or worry about what happened at the club.

Once he gets that signal, he pushes back and kisses me, pulling me against him, the scratch of his jeans against my bare skin makes me shiver. He wraps an arm around my waist and tilts my head so he can deepen the kiss.

I want to open my eyes to watch him but I also want to feel every moment of this.

He pulls back and stares into my eyes, something possessive comes over them. I stand still as he drags his T-shirt over his head and drops it on the floor, then he leans around, grabs the back of my thighs and picks me up, my legs going around his waist.

He groans and his eyes close for a second. I'm not sure why until he presses his lips to my ear.

"I can feel how wet your pussy is against my abs."

Oh...That's kind of hot. Hot enough to make my chest flush and my cheeks burn.

He turns and walks out of the room, heading along the hallway to his. When he sees my frown, he smirks. "I'm fucking you in my bed, Charley."

He kicks his door shut which is pointless given we're alone but that thought falls from my head when he sets me down and moves back, his eyes eating me up again. His fingers trail up my thigh to my hip then dip between my legs.

"Need to touch you," he murmurs.

"Please," I put a hand on his chest and move closer.

His traces my inner thigh and over my pubic bone.

"Are you a tease, Nashville?"

He growls. "Callum. And I'm just savoring the moment before..." he pushes two fingers inside of me, making me go up on my toes and grab onto his arm. "Damn, your tight," he frowns.

"Not what you think," I squeeze his arm. "It's just been a long time."

"Good," he pulls back his fingers and lifts me, setting me on the bed, I push up on my elbows and watch him unbutton his jeans and lower them, dragging his underwear with it.

My mouth waters at the sight of his cock. It's bigger than what I've seen before and a small bead of pre-cum glistens on the head. I chew on my lip and he takes it with his thumb, pulling it away with a smirk.

"Move into the middle of the bed."

I do as he asks, and he opens a drawer on the table beside us, taking out a strip of condoms. He sets it beside me, then climbs onto the bed, nudging my thighs apart so he is kneeling up between them.

He eats me up with his eyes again and I clench, desperately wanting him to fill me, to ease the empty ache inside of me.

Instead he lowers himself so his face is level with my breasts and tugs a nipple between his teeth. My back arches at the contact, like I've been hit by a lightning bolt.

He cups the other breast as he sucks and nips the sensitive skin around it. Then he moves higher, kissing up my throat and neck, nuzzling into the gap beneath my ear. I'm just trying to get my senses straight from that when his fingers fill me again and I cry out.

"That's it," he whispers. "This is only the beginning Charley."

That is a promise I am whole-heartedly behind. I spread my thighs wider, and he presses his knees into my ass, pushing in and out of me faster then slower. Teasing me to the point I want to yell at him, but he takes my mouth with his before I can do anything.

He finger fucks me and rolls his tongue around mine in rhythm with each other and it feels like I'm going to fly off the bed the way everything tightens inside of me. It's too fast, I want to enjoy it.

"Yes," he says against my lips. "Come for me, Charley, show me how you're going to treat my cock once it's inside you."

A whimper escapes.

"Don't hold back," he orders. "I want to hear every single second of your pleasure while I feel it."

It's like the dam breaks and I let out a cry as my back bows and I bear down on his fingers. He doesn't stop moving them as he bites the side of my shoulder making me cry out again.

When I snap back down onto the bed, my mouth is open, trying to catch my breath.

Callum strokes my hair back and smiles at me. "You look beautiful when you come."

I'm lost for words. Even when he has me breaking in mere minutes, he is gentle and sweet. I lay still as he grabs the strip and tears off a condom. I'd offer to help but I'm still reeling from the aftershocks of that orgasm. It's only the second I've ever had with a man. Something tells me it won't be the last.

Callum settles between my legs, our hips pressing together, his chest against mine. He cups my face and kisses me deeply, pouring everything into it, then one hand slides down my body as he grips his cock, holding it steady, stroking it up and down my pussy, nudging at my clit, then he lets go and pushes inside.

My instant response is to squeeze, and he grits his teeth, pushing further and further until I'm so full it feels like heaven and the relief at having something inside makes me clutch his shoulders and encourage him to move.

He makes a few tentative thrusts until I open my eyes to tell him he doesn't need to be so gentle but he is grinning at me when I do and before I can ask why he thrusts even further into me, pushing me up the bed. My breath, my brain, my heart, it's all gone with that one push.

All I can do is hold on to his hips as he moves, the drag and push of him inside of me driving me into a frenzy.

He slows down again and kisses my breasts, my shoulder and then my mouth as he rams in hard. The slow and fast of it is making me insane.

"I knew you would feel like this," he says.

"Like what?"

"Perfect, wrapped so tight around my cock, I can barely fucking hold back."

"Don't."

"Be careful what you wish for Charley."

"I won't break. At least not in a bad way."

He lets out a laugh. "Is that a challenge?"

For the first time in a long time I feel bold, asking for something I really want has never come easy, because I've always been denied, or made to feel stupid for asking. Callum isn't like that.

"Fuck me," I grip him at his nape, my nails scratching through his hair.

He lifts my thigh and wraps it over his hip and back, my foot presses against his ass as he moves faster, his hips rising and falling instead of pushing in and out. It somehow makes him go deeper and hits a spot inside of me that makes my vision blur.

"Yes," he groans. "That's it, fucking hell Charley. Fuck."

He moves faster and I grip him harder with my thighs and arms, tilting my head back on the pillow. He bites my neck and thrusts faster, groaning loudly as his dick pulses inside of me.

"Oh yes, yes. Fuck!" I cry out as my whole body shatters, a million times more powerful than the first time. I've never sworn out loud like this during sex either. I barely recognize myself.

He is talking, telling me how good I feel, how he wants to fuck me over an over until we both break. It's like a dream voice, breaking through the ecstasy.

His forehead drops onto my shoulder as I lower my head. His weight is on me but not fully, he is keeping himself from crushing me. For a moment we stay like that, our gasping breaths the only noise in the room.

He lifts his head and looks at me. "Are you okay?"

All I can do is nod. He holds my chin and kisses me, rolling his tongue with mine, and he groans when I squeeze my walls around him, unintentionally, he is just that good of a kisser.

"That was amazing," he says, as he lifts up slightly. "Wish I could stay cocooned in here forever."

But we can't. And he eventually pulls out and flops onto his back beside me. My eyes roam his body, taking it in for the first time, the golden tan, the ridges, his tattoos, a couple of scars on his abdomen. My brow furrows at one that looks like a small circle.

He sees me looking and rolls up, taking off the condom. "We're not going to discuss that right now," he gets to his feet and walks around the bed. "Come on," he holds out a hand.

"Where are we going?"

"Bathroom. You have to take care of yourself after sex."

How is he real? How does the big bad biker turn into this sweet, caring guy? I'm still too stunned to argue when he disposes of the condom and steps outside to give me privacy. I use the toilet and wash my hands then come back into his room, a little unsure.

He's lying in bed and sets his phone down when he sees me. "Come here."

That answers my unasked question. I walk over and climb onto the bed. He shifts around and gets me under the covers beside him.

"I want you right here," he says, putting his arm up so I can duck under and rest my head against his chest. "So if I wake up and need to fuck you again, you're right where I want you to be."

"You have a way with words, you know that?"

"I only speak the truth," he places his chin on the top of my head and strokes a hand up and down my arm. "Are you sure you're okay, after everything tonight?" he asks after a short silence.

"I never thanked you," I say against his chest.

"You don't need to."

I tilt my head. "Yes I do, it's the second time you've saved me."

He laughs softly and stokes some hair behind my ear. "I'll always save you."

My nose stings and I close my eyes, ducking my head under his chin again. He holds me tighter against him. I wish I could believe his words. I want to. Callum isn't like anyone I've ever met.

It's my own cynicism that keeps me from believing I'm worthy of that promise.

After everything I've been through tonight, my body crashes faster than I expected and I drift off to sleep to the rise and fall of his chest as he breathes, and the beat of Callum's heart.

Chapter Fifteen

Nashville

FUCK SHE IS LIKE a furnace, in a good way.

Last night was a dream come true. She was everything I thought she would be, even if for a moment I panicked that she may not have done it before. That just made me mad because she said she had. But, we all have our pasts.

At some point, soon, I'm going to try to get her to talk about hers. I want to know everything there is to know about her.

I wasn't lying last night, my protective instincts over this woman I barely know have taken over rational thought. It could have fucked up everything for Nero last night. Even if he did stand by me, everything could have gone to shit.

Nothing was planned when I went upstairs last night. I was going to bed, or to get into bed and think about ways to murder Cantrell, involving getting on a plane and following the asshole. Until I saw her door was ajar.

Was it a mistake, or an invitation?

For the first time in ages, I knew what I wanted. Fuck the age difference, fuck what anyone thinks. I wanted to feel her, to take away some of her pain.

And here we are, me cuddled up against her back, her hot supple body making mine stir into something less protective, more possessive. My cock is rigid against her ass. I carefully reach over behind me and grab the condom strip. Charley barely stirs as I get it on, then shuffle down a bit and lift her thigh, pushing mine between them.

She moans and shifts as I reach forward and slide two fingers between her lips. Naughty girl must be dreaming because she is soaked enough that I don't even need to think about warming her up. I shift and nudge my cock to her opening, lifting my hip a little to spread her wider.

Charley moans and shifts, pushing down as I push in and groan into her neck. I move slowly thrusting in shallow pulses until she lifts her head, awake finally. Then I push all the way inside, making her cry out.

I grab her hip and move faster, forcing her body to move with mine. Her hand comes around and cups the back of my head, hers twisting to get closer. Our lips meet and I glide my fingers between her legs, catching her clit between my thumb and forefinger.

She cries into my mouth and tightens around me. This is fucking intense and I'm already dreaming about how many ways, and how many times I can fuck her.

Charley must have the same idea because she grabs my hand and shifts away, my dick falling out of her and onto the sheets. It doesn't take long for me to swallow a protest, because she turns, pushes me onto my back and straddles my hips, taking me back inside of her before I can even say her name.

She rides my cock like a pro, placing my hands over her tits and holding them there as she undulates over me, pushing her chest out and tipping her head back so her hair tickles my thighs.

Watching her use my cock to get her pleasure is a mind fuck I don't want to come out of. She's fucking beautiful. I allow that for a while, then take my hands away and sit up, wrapping an arm around her waist so I can lift her up and down over me. She leans forward and kisses me as I thrust upwards, starting to lose myself to her.

Her climax takes me by surprise but I'm not one to miss an opportunity. I hook a leg over her and spin us so she is on her back and fuck her through it, pushing hard and fast until my own orgasm rocks through me.

Jesus, I don't think I'm ever letting her go. Even if I have to lock her in here. Shit, *that* was a thought.

We lay still for a while, getting a grip on ourselves, then I tell her to take a shower while I make breakfast. After all that I'm fucking starving.

I'm pretty sure I've got it out of my system and can behave like a normal human until she walks in wearing just a T-shirt. She lets out a surprised cry when I scoop her up and set her on the counter.

There is one thing I haven't done yet. Her legs spread as I bend down and push my face in between them, licking a path up her pussy.

"Callum," she sighs.

And I really fucking like that. Want to hear her say it as she comes more though, so I tongue fuck her till she is almost there, then grab a condom from the living room while she is still calling me names for edging her. She shuts up when I come back, tugging the condom on then push into her.

I feel like a fucking teenager, like I'm never going to get enough of her perfect body. The gates have opened and I'm well and truly inside of them.

We sit on the floor by the counter afterwards and eat bagels and drink coffee. It's uncomfortable as fuck, but neither of us makes a move to get up. We eat, and talk, and laugh, until the doorbell rings.

Charley rolls onto her knees and grips the counter. You can't see the door from here so I'm not sure what she is doing which makes me laugh.

She is right to be a little concerned, no one knows she's staying here. It's probably salesmen or something. I help her up and tell her I'll get rid of whoever it is.

When I pull the door back and see Nero standing there, I know that isn't going to be possible. He eyes my half naked state and messy hair and lifts a brow.

"You reek of sex. Wanna make yourself decent so you and I can talk?"

"Uh... Sure. Come in, there," I point to the living room. He does as I ask and I pull the door over.

Charley is clearing up the mess on the floor when I come back.

"So," I rub a hand over my hair. "The Prez is here."

"The... from the MC? He's here? What does he want?"

"Yep, he wants to talk."

"To me?" her eyes widen comically.

"Relax, no, just me. Go upstairs, take a shower, I'll call you when he's gone."

"Will he be mad?"

"About what?"

"This, us..."

"It's none of his business. Or anyone else's for that matter. Stop freaking out, it's fine."

I kiss her until her body relaxes then walk her to the stairs. She hurries up them without looking back.

"Fuck," I sigh, then grab a T-shirt from the laundry room, fix my hair in the mirror in the hallway and go to face Nero.

If he has a problem with me smelling like I just got through fucking my girl, he shouldn't have shown up unannounced. *My girl...?*

Nero is sitting down checking his phone when I come in. "Thanks for making an effort," he says.

I shrug and sit on the chair on the opposite side of the room. "I won't subject you to it if I'm all the way over here."

He laughs under his breath, then sighs. "It's the girl from last night?" I nod. "How is she?"

"Fine. She's stronger than she looks."

"I don't care what you get up to or who you fuck, but Beast might have a problem with it."

"He won't fire her over it."

"I know, doesn't mean he won't be on your ass about it. It serious?"

"Not sure," I eye the door, not that I think she would be eavesdropping. Nero doesn't miss it.

"It wasn't too long ago I felt the same way."

A few seconds pass before I understand what he's getting at. I go to protest but what would be the point. Nero has this uncanny ability to see inside people's heads. Sometimes, it's like he knows what other people are thinking before they do.

Well, jokes on him, cos I haven't got a fucking clue how to feel about what is going on with Charley.

"Shit sneaks up on you. And next thing you know-"

"Do not say what I think you're going to say."

Just because he got himself an Old Lady doesn't mean that is what this is. I'm still fully aware that I'm almost a decade older than her. We can have fun, see how things go, it doesn't mean she's going to become that big of a fixture.

Shit, that feels bad just thinking it. Nero is watching me with one of those looks of his that makes me want to rip out my own eyeballs for seeing it.

"Cantrell is gone," he changes the subject, kind of.

At least he's not giving me shit about having an Old Lady anymore.

"I've got one of the guys from the Sacramento chapter on his ass. He'll keep an eye on him."

"Thanks."

He nods his head in acknowledgement. "I called Camden this morning."

That makes me sit up a little taller. Nero wouldn't usually do something like that. He's tasked me with finding Sheridan, that means he stays out of it.

"He has a lead. He said he was going to call you."

Well, I haven't looked at my phone yet today. Nero sees that too. Fucking psychic.

"If he needs you to go down there."

"Absolutely, not an issue."

"Blaze will book you a flight."

That means Camden has more than Nero is letting on. We both get up and Nero tosses something to me, I catch it with one hand. It's the keys to my bike.

"Razer found these in the back room last night. Must have fallen out in the scuffle. I guess it's lucky she had the keys to your SUV."

"Fucking hell."

He laughs. Asshole. "I'll get Taylor to come round if you're gone a while."

"Nope, don't do that."

"She'll love it, meeting a new friend."

"Fuck, Prez come on," I hold out my hands. Meeting his Old Lady means something more than either of us are ready for.

"Rebel told me you got her out of the Pembroke House, Nashville. And everyone knows she's been driving your car."

I shake my head. "All this time?"

"I deduced," he grins but it fades. "Now get your ass to Kentucky and find what I'm looking for."

It's not like I can ask Charley to leave, and I don't want to, but she doesn't need to hear this call. She doesn't seem too concerned when I tell her I'm going into the gym for a bit but she is far more intelligent and knowing that most people give her credit for.

My brother picks up after what feels like twenty-seven rings.

"I'm in the middle of something."

"So why did you answer?"

"Because you wouldn't fucking hang up. Guess your Prez got hold of you. We've got a confirmed sighting on the woman, holding off until you get here. When will that be?"

"Blaze can get me a flight today."

"Good, I gotta go."

A woman's seductive voice in the background makes me cackle. Cam calls me a fucking wanker, a favorite insult of dad's, and hangs up on me.

Charley is on the phone when I come back out and she frowns, clearly I've not been working out. When she hangs up, she doesn't question me.

"That was Lily, she wants to grab coffee before my shift."

"Are you good with it?"

"Yeah. You said he was gone."

"You've got nothing to worry about."

"Okay," she chews on her lip and stares at my chest.

"Jesus woman," I go over and grab her ass, pulling her in so I can kiss her. "I've unleashed a beast," I waggle my brows, and she laughs while simultaneously looking grossed out. "Go, have fun. I have to go out of town."

She pulls back and looks at me.

"Just a couple of days. I'm going to see my brother back home."

"Oh, is he okay?"

It's not a lie, technically. Plus, even if she were my Old Lady, which she isn't, I wouldn't be able to talk about this shit with her. Remembering Nero throwing my bike keys reminds me that I gave Charley a ride to that house on the back of my bike.

I didn't think anything of it at the time but shit... Now it's gonna play on my mind.

Did I make some kind of statement doing that? That is the way it will be seen if anyone finds out.

"He's fine, just haven't seen him in a while."

Charley nods. "I guess I'll see you when you get back."

"What time are you meeting Lily?"

"An hour," she runs a hand through her damp hair.

My smirk has her eyes widening. "What are your feelings on simultaneous oral?"

"Is that the polite way of saying a sixty-nine?" she arches her beautiful brow at me.

"See, you get me, Charley."

"Now who is the beast?"

"Shit, please don't say that when we're in bed. I'll end up picturing his face."

"It's okay, my mouth will be too busy."

"Fuck, I think I like cheeky Charlie."

Chapter Sixteen

Nashville

I'm not in the least bit surprised when my brother is waiting outside the airport in a G-Wagon with tinted windows and red trim on the alloy wheels. It's so shiny I need sunglasses to look at it.

He's leaning back against the side of the hood with his arms crossed in dark fatigues and a tight black T-shirt that his muscles are practically bursting through. There is a holster strapped to his thigh but there is no gun in it. Which makes sense given we're at an airport.

"Subtle," I stop beside the monster truck.

"Get in the car."

"I might need a stepladder."

"Cos you're a short-ass."

"Fuck you."

Camden slaps my shoulder and grins. It's been a couple of years since I saw him in person so this is nice. The banter never changes but we have each other's backs and would die for one another, no questions asked.

"You gonna go to Nashville and see mom while you're here."

"It's not exactly a social call."

"That's why I didn't mention it," Camden starts the car and pulls away from the collection point. "You need to come see her soon though."

"Yeah, just with everything going on, it's hard to get back."

Technically I'm not supposed to tell anyone about club business, but Camden is different, I know I can trust him. It also helped him when he was looking into finding Sheridan and Nero gave his blessing, so long as I didn't give him too much information.

"Ronnie wants to throw her a sixtieth birthday party, so be prepared for an invitation."

I could say something stupid here but don't because mom deserves to be treated to a party. She should receive an award for raising us four boys and not tearing every hair out of her head.

"Okay. How's dad?"

"Same old," he shrugs. "Getting on mom's last nerve but god forbid you tell her he needs a kick up the ass."

"They're set in their ways," I watch the dark road ahead as we make the forty-minute drive to Elizabethtown. "I don't think it would be normal if they weren't communing through shouts and exaggerated hand gestures."

"Truth. I've left Martinez watching the house where she's at," he looks over at me quickly, the seriousness in his expression is a stark change to the grinning idiot. "It's not pretty, Cal."

I nod but don't say anything.

"We haven't seen her but have solid intel she is inside."

"Any way of knowing her condition?"

"No, but I'd say be prepared for the worst."

"Fuck," I lean an elbow on the bottom of the window and rest my head against my palm.

I haven't told Nero all the details yet, because I need to be sure. If I thought the house where Charley was staying is bad, this place is a million times worse. I'm also not sure of Nero's relationship to Sheridan. She might be his kid's mom, but they were never together.

She *is* Speedway's sister and I'm not looking forward to telling him what has been going on.

"I figured you'd want to go straight there."

Camden dips his chin toward the glove compartment. Inside are two Glock 17s.

"Martinez called in the crew when I picked you up. There will be eight of them, plus you and me."

"Jesus Cam, is it that bad?"

"Better to be safe than sorry. Not to mention this isn't going to be clean, so we'll need clean up before we call in the cops."

"How many of them are there?"

"We've sat on it for a few days and watched comings and goings and figure at any one time there are four of them inside."

"This is fucking horrible."

"Tell me about it." His jaw clenches and he drives in silence for a while.

It's funny, in a none 'ha ha' way that both me and Camden have turned out the way we are. We have morals and there are things neither of us would ever do, but at the same time, we're not afraid to do what needs to be done, and we've made choices and done things most people would object to.

"What about the cops?" I ask after we've gone a good ten miles.

"I have a relationship with a Detective in Narcotics, she's good people, she'll take them down," he glances at me again. "We don't need to worry about what happens until we call them in. You traveled on the ID Blaze got you?"

"Yeah."

"No one will know you were here. I've got medics lined up too."

My stomach is sinking the more he talks. I'm glad I decided not to visit my parents, this shit is going to be hard to deal with and I won't be the best person to be around afterwards.

"Keep your cool in there, Callum."

"You don't need to tell me that, Camden."

"Martinez has years of experience with this shit and even he reacted."

"I guess we wouldn't be normal people if we didn't."

Camden gives a tight nod, and we drive the rest of the way in silence, each lost in our own thoughts, each preparing for what is about to happen.

When we reach his men, there aren't involved introductions, just names so we know who I am talking or listening to on the comms.

Martinez eyeballs me enough that I want to square up to him but Camden stares his man down and tells him I can handle this and wouldn't be here if he didn't believe that.

It's almost eleven at night and the street the house is on is quiet. It's run down, a lot of the surrounding properties are boarded up.

Camden told me people started moving out of the area years ago when drugs started moving in. The cops know about what goes on down here, but they rarely do anything, which is why I'm still skeptical about Camden's detective.

We don't have a chapter in Kentucky but there is one in Nashville. Nero decided to keep them out of it, which means my cut is back home.

It's weird to not to have it on. The less identifiable we are here, the better. There is no need to ask about cameras, this is the kind of place the people who run it wouldn't want anything being recorded.

If he was worried, Camden will have already dealt with it. He has a woman who does his tech that Blaze would be impressed by. Once we've run down everything we know is inside, and Martinez has shared how to react if there are any variables, we surround the house.

Out of experience, I'm at a different entrance to my brother. He can't help but try to keep an eye on me and that compromises both of us.

Turns out they over planned the attack because the three men guarding the house are taken out before I even get inside. I step over the first dead body without a second glance.

Three more of Camden's men have rounded up the assholes who are *visiting*. They've all been zip tied and blindfolded and dumped in an empty room on the ground floor. Anyone who hasn't taken the advice of keeping their mouth shut has duct tape over their mouths.

Downstairs consists of a kitchen, a large room that has some couches, a table with a poker game set up but no one playing and a TV hanging off the wall at an odd angle, like whoever set it up couldn't take the time to do it properly. Everything in here is brown and smells like stale cigarette smoke and sweat.

The last room is being used for storage, like a hotel supply room. Bed sheets, and giant bottles of cleaning products are what get to me the most.

There are three floors and each one has been adapted to fit as many rooms in as possible. As I round the stairs to the first floor, I cover my mouth. It smells really bad. Like drains, vomit and semen. Whoever the fuck thinks there is anything sexy about coming here...

There is no point following that thought. The kind of men who come here are sick fucks who need their brains fumigating and locking the fuck up.

Each door is opened as I walk by, Camden's men doing a full sweep to make sure no one is hiding. Some of the rooms are empty. Most of them aren't.

My head tells my heart not to get involved in this but how the fuck can I not?

There are women in various states in the rooms. I think it's the ones who are more alert and sobbing at being found that hurt more than the ones who are completely out of it on drugs.

Camden comes up behind me when I get to a room with a girl who looks to be in her late teens, she's sitting on the bed, staring out of the window, like she doesn't even know we're here. Her arms and legs are covered in bruises, her hair looks like it hasn't been washed in weeks.

The trauma these women have dealt with fucks with my head.

"We'll get them help," Camden says, drawing my attention. He leans in close. "I fucking swear it Callum. Not a single one of these women will know pain like this again."

"Easier said than done," I murmur.

He knows what I mean, they won't get over this any time soon, if they ever do. He leads me away from the room and doesn't pause to let me check anywhere else, saying everything has been cleared and Sheridan is on the third floor.

When I get to her room, Martinez is standing just inside the doorway with a man on his knees, his hands tied but up over the back of his head, not at his lower back. Martinez has hold of the ties and a gun pointed at the back of his head.

I take all of that in before looking at Sheridan. I don't know her, I've never met her, but I'm pretty sure even Speedway wouldn't recognize her now.

She's way too skinny, the same bruises mar her skin and track marks line her inner elbow. She too is staring into space.

"She's okay now," Xavier says and I turn to see him behind the door, he's holding up a needle and everything you need to inject heroin is behind him.

"What is that?"

"Narcan," he says. "She was OD'ing when we came in here."

"Fuck." I run a hand over my head and turn away from her.

"This piece of shit was shooting her up. Like he knew who we were here for."

Martinez kicks the man in the kidneys but keeps tight hold of his wrists so he can't get away. He is wearing steel toe boots as well and we all hear the crack of his ribs.

"She's okay, she's going to get through this?"

"The medics are on the way up. They'll make sure she is okay before we move her," Camden says from the doorway. Then he looks at Martinez. "Take him next door, the room is empty."

Martinez doesn't pick the asshole up, he grabs his long greasy hair and drags him out. Behind me, Xavier is kneeling beside Sheridan talking quietly to her. He has a wet cloth and is wiping her face.

"His sister was in a place like this once," Camden says quietly. "Come on. Once the medics stabilize her, they'll get her out, then we'll call in the cops."

"This is fucked up Cam. I've heard of these places, but shit. The people behind this-"

"We're on it, Cal," he pats my shoulder. "They're not getting away with this. Come on, we don't have much time."

I take a last look at Sheridan and know she is in safe hands. We are not going to get anything coherent out of her, at least not for a while.

The only person who can tell me anything about what I want to know is currently crying out in agony. It becomes obvious why when we enter and close the door.

Martinez has done some serious damage in the two minutes it took us to follow them in here. I harden my resolve and force out the panic and fear I feel for Sheridan, and any thoughts of people back home. This piece of shit is going to die, how slow or fast depends on him.

"Get him up," I tell Martinez. Even though he was salty outside, he doesn't question me now and drags the man up. "Who brought that woman to you?"

He snarls but doesn't answer. Fairs fair, he manages a place like this, doesn't care what happens to the women that are dragged in here, it's time he feels even an ounce of their pain.

I kick him right between his legs, so hard he throws up all down the front of his shirt. Behind me I hear Camden curse and Martinez laugh.

"Why did you bring that woman here? Who told you to take her?" I shout.

No reply, so I punch him in the gut. It goes on for a full five minutes of me asking and him not replying. Each time I hit him harder. He is coughing up blood before he finally begs me to stop.

"Did you or any of the sick mother fuckers you brought in here stop when they begged?" I scream in his face. "Did you ever give them mercy when they cried and screamed and asked for it to end?"

He shakes, snot, blood and tears running down his ruined face.

"This is your last chance. Who told you to bring her here?"

He pants and says something. I glance back when Martinez pats my shoulder. He holds out a knife. It's a serrated hunting knife with a well-worn handle. Knives aren't my thing but I take it and turn back to the sniveling piece of shit.

"Name."

"Storm... stor...." His head hangs.

"Where is he?"

"I don't know."

"Don't fucking lie to me," I shout and stab the end of the knife into the meat of his thigh, making him scream. "Where the fuck is he?"

"Wes...west Virginia."

"That's a pretty big fucking place, right?" I look at Martinez.

"Really big," he agrees.

Pulling out the knife, I stab it into his other leg and he screams again. "Where?"

"He'll kill me."

"Hate to break it to you," I cock my head. "He isn't going to get the chance. This can be quick, or it can go on for hours. My friend here will tie you up, drive you somewhere nice and quiet and slice you apart, piece by fucking piece, slowly, painfully and you will fucking wish I showed you mercy here."

I've no clue if Martinez would do that. He strikes me as a hard ass, but I don't think he would enjoy something like that. Even Stryker has his limits.

"Romney," he chokes out.

I've never heard of it. Camden pulls out his phone, holds it up when he has a map of West Virginia. It looks to be a couple hundred miles away from Baltimore.

"That's all I know... I swear to God. I don't know where, just the town," he gasps as I rip the knife out of his leg. "I swear, I swear, fuck just, believe me... He told me to bring her here and mess her up. When I asked how long, he said... he said keep her.... He didn't care if," he chokes on some blood.

"Go on," I encourage him.

"If she died. He didn't care."

"Well, I guess that is something we have in common," I snarl, then push the knife into his stomach right up to the hilt. His mouth drops open, and he tries to scream but he doesn't have the breath to do it. "Burn in hell you piece of shit," I twist the knife and drag it upwards. He jerks and drops to the floor, I still have hold of the knife and my hand is covered in blood.

My chest is heaving, my heart pounding so fast I feel like I might fall over. The knife is taken from me and my brother grabs my shoulder and steers me out of the room. I barely hear anything going on around me, my vision has tunneled and it no longer feels like I'm in control of my own limbs.

It will pass. I'll move on but right now, I have to feel this, have to sit with what I've done.

I'm not sure how I end up at the back of his car, Camden cleaning me up before getting me inside. The whole time we drive, he keeps casting nervous looks my way.

"Callum," he says after we've driven a while.

"Is she..."

"They've taken her to a private facility. You did it Cal. You got her out. And you have a solid lead on Storm. Remember that."

I turn to look out of the window, still feeling like I'm not in my own body, I don't know who I became in there, but I can't get the images out of my head.

Not what I did to him, that bastard deserved it, and worse. In fact, I wish I had left him to the fate I created to scare him. I'm sure someone would have done it.

It isn't about that at all. It's the women whose lives have been irrevocably damaged.

Camden doesn't say anything, understanding I need to bring myself from the ledge I walked onto back in that house. He does grip the steering wheel tight enough to make the leather creak when I do eventually answer.

"It wasn't enough."

Chapter Seventeen

Charley

Waking up alone in Callum's spare bedroom shouldn't feel as weird as it does. One night with him, in his bed and it's like everything changed. In a way, I'm glad he has gone out of town because my thoughts and feelings about the last twenty-four hours are going to take a lot to unpack.

How did it go from elation about the dance, to being threatened by an asshole, who then got beat up and what went on between Callum and I when we got back here?

When I came to Baltimore, it was to get away from drama and craziness, not swap it for a different brand.

After watching Callum hit that guy and pin him to the wall, it totally threw me how gentle and sweet he was when we had sex. Insatiable yeah, experienced most definitely but not at all like I thought he would be, given he's a big bad scary biker.

He is living proof of stereotyping. My head and body are at war with one another. No one has ever made me feel the way he did when we were together. I don't exactly have much to compare it to but even in my limited experience, what he did to me, each time he did it, was nothing less than perfect.

Callum is the kind of man I wish I met a few years ago. He's someone who will always protect the people he cares about. He wouldn't stand back and watch me be belittled, mentally and occasionally physically abused by people he brought into my life.

He never would have allowed anyone to play pranks on me, or scare me, or drive me to the point of almost losing my mind, then making one of the biggest mistakes of my whole life.

Shaking out of that thought before memory takes hold and panic surges, I get up and go about the routine of washing, dressing, making breakfast, all things that I can deal with. It's just the silence that is unnerving. I've gotten so used to the noise at the last apartment, and at Elegance, it's never quiet there.

Here, it's like the whole world has been shut outside, and nothing can get to me. Another thing Callum has done for me without realizing it. I can't start to depend on him. It's a bad idea. Good sex and a kind heart doesn't make problems vanish.

Beast made me take a couple of nights off, and wouldn't even let me plead my case. It's only the fact that I got paid a lot of money for that dance, and the tips, that I didn't end up in a real argument with my boss. Not that it would have got me anywhere.

If anything, the bikers were doing everything they could to make sure I was okay. Lily called me to tell me how everyone was pissed about what happened.

Which is dangerous... Why can't I let myself to be open to it?

To prove to myself that I'm not falling into a trap of relying on someone else, I start searching for an apartment. I have enough for a security deposit now so it shouldn't be that hard.

My stomach aches and a weird pull in my chest has me setting the phone down and looking around at this gorgeous house. Callum doesn't want a girlfriend, he doesn't want someone like me. He's an amazing person, he could have anyone he wants. I'm just convenient...

Even as I think it, I know it isn't true.

What is he doing right now? Having something to eat with his family, visiting old friends, or just hanging out with one of his brothers? What would it be like to be there with him now?

The doorbell chimes making me jump out of my daydreams. I'm not expecting anyone and Callum would have said if anyone was going to come over.

Oh God, what if it's his president again? What if he is coming to talk to me now Callum is out of the way?

It chimes again. Shit, stop hiding and go open the door.

When I cautiously open it, a woman turns and smiles at me. "Charley?"

"Yes," I say, looking behind her to see a small red car parked on the drive. She's alone, or so it seems.

"I'm Taylor, did Nashville mention I was coming?"

She watches me as I try to come up with words, because this woman is beautiful and happy and I have no idea who she is or why she is here, yet Callum knew she was coming?

"God, I'm so sorry. I've shown up here out of the blue and you're probably wondering who the hell I am. God forbid these men communicate," she brushes some hair over her shoulder and smiles at me. "I'm Noah's girlfriend. Sorry, you probably don't know who I mean. Do you want me to leave because I'm making an absolute mess of this?"

"Um... Maybe let me know who Noah is?"

"Sorry, I call him Noah. I meant Nero, the president."

"Oh," I open the door a little wider.

"If it's a bad time or you're completely freaked out, then I can go."

"No, it's fine. Um, why are you here though?"

"Noah said you might need company. I hope you don't mind, but he mentioned what happened the other night at the club."

"Well, it's his club and..." How much does she know?

"Could I come in, it's getting chilly out here."

"Oh, damn, sorry," I open the door wide and step back and Taylor comes inside.

She looks around, taking it in as she takes off her coat. "I never would have put Nashville in a house like this," she turns back and smiles. "Then again, these guys are all full of surprises."

We stand in the hallway and I glance about. This isn't my house and I also don't ever have visitors, or guests, to anywhere I've lived. Remembering I'm an adult I offer her a coffee, which she gratefully accepts and follows me to the kitchen.

It's been cleaned since Callum threw me down on the counter, but I can still picture it and my cheeks flush. Taylor makes herself comfortable on a stool and waits for me to finish the drinks.

"Noah said you're new to the city?" she asks when I'm facing her across the island.

"He knows a lot."

"Trust me, you don't know the half of it."

"What does that mean?" I ask sharply.

Taylor frowns. I don't have to be polite to someone I don't know or didn't invite around here but she is nonplussed when she replies. "Noah likes to keep people safe."

"Does he think he needs to protect Callum from me?" My brows lift.

"No. Oh God I've got off on the wrong foot totally here. I'm new to all of this as well if I'm being honest. I've only been with Noah for about three months. I was his best friends nurse when we met."

"You're a nurse?"

"I am," she smiles, some of the hesitancy leaving her voice.

"I don't mean to make you uncomfortable," I tell her. "I'm just a very private person and having people asking questions about me or looking me up is a sore spot."

"I totally understand, Charley. And if I gave you that impression I'm sorry. Noah wouldn't have asked me to come round here if he didn't think you were important to Nashville. And if that is true, then he will respect Nashville's privacy. He just thought you might need someone to talk to. My friends say I'm a pretty good listener, but I'm also amazing at small talk or anything to do with the Baltimore Orioles."

"The who?"

"Not into sports," she laughs. "Got it. They're the local baseball team. My dad never missed a game. All I'm trying to say is, if you need someone to talk to, I can do that. Or not."

My lip twitches. It's been a long time since I've had friends. Lily has been getting closer to me. I'm good with that because Lily doesn't ask questions. She works for Elegance, in turn, the MC but she isn't a part of their world. Unlike Taylor.

I get the sense that she isn't someone who would throw a person under the bus. There is something about her that makes me want to trust her, not enough to tell her anything deep. Her suggestion of small talk, or having a living breathing person in the space with me while Callum is gone might be nice.

"Do you work at the hospital?"

"No, a private clinic," she ducks her head, like she's sort of embarrassed by that. "I'm a diabetes nurse."

"You still had to train like every other nurse," I point out.

Taylor smiles at me, gratitude clear on her face.

"Does it bother you what people think?" I ask her.

"Not usually. It's always a bit nerve-wracking telling new people though. Sometimes I am judged."

"I don't judge anyone by what they do. Look at what I do," I roll my eyes. "I wouldn't worry about what other people think. Until they've walked in your shoes, or even your patients shoes, they have no worthwhile opinion on the matter. Anything they have to say about it is their problem, not yours."

"That's true," she smiles. "I'm going to use that line. People are far too quick to judge, I guess I'm sensitive."

We make more small talk and then she asks if I want to talk about what happened at the club. I get the sense it's not about getting intel for Nero, being comfortable with that is hard for me though, so I brush it off. I'm not sure Taylor believes me.

"Coming into this life," she says, after we've finished our coffee and exhausted the conversation. "It's a transition for sure. I never thought I'd fall for the leader of a motorcycle gang," she laughs. "Sorry, that's a joke Noah and I have. I kept calling the club a gang. Lucky for me he found it amusing."

"He seems intense, from what I've seen. I haven't talked to him."

"He's not so bad. He wants to protect his people, and it's a lot on his shoulders so sometimes he can be a bit direct but his heart is in the right place. It's been nice talking to you, Charley. I know it must feel weird having a stranger show up out of the blue, but thank you for the coffee. If you do need anything, I'm always around," she takes a small pad out of her purse with a pen shoved into the wire rings then scribbles out a number. "If you need anything."

I take it, grateful she didn't ask for my number. Taylor is astute, she hasn't pushed me and she can tell I'm not that comfortable with strangers. She made the effort and I am grateful for that.

She reiterates I can call anytime as I see her out and I close the door before she gets to her car.

I'm not one hundred percent capable of taking my own advice. What if she is judging me? What if she thinks I'm weird? Taylor is a good, decent person, she's nothing like me.

Before I second guess myself, I put her number into my phone. I may never use it and can delete it if I move on from Baltimore. Picturing Callum's face, I wonder if that is something I'm ever going to do.

Another night and day pass with no word or sign of Callum. He knows I'm in his house so hasn't forgotten about me. I'm going stir crazy with how quiet it is here and even resorted to pulling up my fake social media profile so I can check on Stephen, Adeline and Blair, something I haven't done in a long time.

There are continuous tribute posts to their mother, along with veiled, obscure comments about retribution, betrayal and cowardly behavior.

All aimed at me. Of course they don't put it on social media but I know what they're doing behind the scenes, it's partly why I ran and kept running.

It hurts to see my father in the photographs. He lost the life in his eyes after mom died. It felt like he was on autopilot and was glad when Helen came into his life and basically took it over. He didn't have to think anymore because she took control over everything.

I lost both my parents the day he married her, and we moved into their huge house in Woodside.

I'm still not sure what she got out of the marriage. Not to be disparaging but we didn't have anywhere near what they did. But what we did have, once upon a time, was love.

One thing that did come out near the end, and made a little more sense about why Helen did it, was that she went to the same middle school as my mom and they were enemies.

Could a grown woman want to get back at an old rival, who was already dead, by marrying their partner? And taking in her daughter and treating her like shit.

Not a normal one. Helen was not normal.

I hate this, sitting here alone in the silence is bringing back too many memories and giving into the temptation to check up on them is proof of that. It doesn't look as if they've traced me here, so I shut the page and lock my phone.

In less than ten minutes I'm behind the wheel of Callum's car and driving toward Elegance. It's the only place I know where I can go and quiet the noise in my head. When I pull up inside the lot Walker and Leo are outside holding the door open, and the dancers are heading out.

"What's going on?" I ask Tami as she passes on the way to her car.

"Beast closed up for the night," she shrugs and walks on.

That's weird. Why would he do that?

"Charley, why are you here, you know Beast told you to take a few days," Lily comes over to me.

"I was bored. Why is the club closing?"

"Do you think they tell us anything? Not that the girls are concerned, we're still getting paid. Plus a bonus for being accommodating," she deepens her voice for that last part. Not sure who she is imitating, but it's kind of funny.

"You drove down here for nothing."

Walker sees me and comes over, asking me if everything is okay. I like Walker, he's good to the dancers, looks out for everyone. He reiterates what Lily said, that the club will be back open as normal tomorrow and we should get ourselves home and enjoy the free night off.

Easy for him to say. Lily is watching me as I turn back to the car. "What?"

"You came here because you're bored," she smirks.

"It's too quiet by myself. I've been going stir crazy."

"It's been two days since that man almost attacked you, Charley."

"Key word *almost.*"

"You shouldn't be so blasé about it. It's a good job Nashville went looking for you. Why is that by the way?" We've walked back to the BMW, and she gives me a knowing grin.

"It's not like that," I lie. "I had some trouble with my car and he helped me out."

"And where you're living?" She leans against the SUV and gives me a look. The kind that says she knows more than I thought she did. "I'm not the only one who noticed."

"What?"

"Relax, Ellie shut everyone down."

"Oh shit," I close my eyes. How does everyone know?

"Don't worry, he's hot," she winks.

"It's not-"

"Like that," she cuts me off. "Yeah, you've said that."

Her laughter should irritate me, but she is such a genuine kind person I can't get mad. She also isn't judging me like some of the other women would. They'd be right, I have had sex with him. It's nothing like what they would think.

Callum is different with me. Or maybe I'm just being a foolish girl. I haven't heard from him in two days. What if he is hoping I leave and isn't coming back till I've gone?

Ellie knows. Jesus.

"The place I was staying before was sketchy and he didn't like me staying there. He did me a favor that's all."

"Is it though?"

"Lily," I unlock the doors and open the driver side. "I'm looking for a new place. In fact, I have a few lined up to check out."

It's not a total lie. I have saved a few places. After this, I'll be contacting them first thing tomorrow.

"Why don't we go get a drink now that we have nothing to do. You can give me a ride in this sexy beamer. I've never put my ass on something so fancy," she winks and opens the door before I can protest.

Given I don't know the area she suggests a bar and gives me directions.

"I'm not going to pry, but Nashville has always seemed like one of the good ones at the club. He's fun and flirty and respectful. What's it like staying with him?"

If only she knew the other side of him, the one that is not fun and respectful, but what most people would consider scary, even if I don't.

"He's a friend helping me out. That is all."

"You've tried to spy on him in the shower though, right?" she laughs.

"Oh my God, shut up," I laugh.

"I would."

"That's kind of pervy, Lily."

"He's seen your tits, why can't you see his ass?"

"Shut up," I repeat, trying not to laugh.

She doesn't have to say anything for me to know exactly what she is thinking. She's not a million miles off the truth.

It's not until we're pulling close and I see all the motorcycles that I realize where we are. I glare at her.

"What? It's a fun place."

"He's out of town," I roll my eyes, suspecting what her plan was bringing me here.

"Who said we were coming for him. Come on, I'm thirsty and look at that guy," she points at one of the men climbing off his motorcycle. He has a helmet on so we can't see his face, but he is tall and stocky and Lily is practically drooling. "Charley… I never get to do anything fun like this. Please come inside."

"Fine, but I'm driving so no alcohol."

She claps her hands and gets out of the car. Despite myself I am kind of looking forward to it. My fake ID is in my purse, but I'm not risking drinking anything while getting behind the wheel of a car.

My heart begins to pound and I suck in a breath as Lily walks around the front of the car and waves at me to hurry.

Lily links my arm as we walk towards the bar. It's busy given it's a Friday night, a few bikes outside and as we step in I notice plenty of men wearing the Blackhawk Disciples vest, but there are a lot of other people here too.

We're heading to the bar when I notice him and come to a halt.

Lily loses her grip on my arm and turns to look at me, then where my focus has gone. I barely hear anything she is saying as she takes my arm again. Snippets of her words breaking through the absolute rage I feel.

At myself, for ever thinking there could be anything more than sex between me and Callum.

Nashville.

He's leaning against the bar, standing between the legs of a beautiful woman who is smiling up at him from her stool. Someone hands him a drink and he smiles, then looks back to the woman.

"Come on," Lily, takes my arm. "We can go somewhere else."

I allow her to lead me back out, all the while the wall I'd been letting down is rebuilding brick my brick inside my chest.

"I knew there was more to this," Lily is still talking as she leads me to the car. "Honey, he's not worth it. Most men are dumb shits."

"I'm fine."

She stops by the car and stares at me. I'm shutting down. It's my own fault. Nashville never said there was anything going on. I was a warm body in his house that he got to play with for a while.

Oh God, how can I go back to his house.

"Let's go get your things and you can come stay with me. I have a roommate but she won't mind."

"I can't."

"Yes you can. You're not going back to that house. You don't have to tell me what happened, but it's clear this hit you hard and I'm not letting you go back there for him to come back after that. I mean, it might not be what it looks like but... even still. Girl code. You said yourself you're looking for a place, a couple of nights with me is no different from a couple more at his. Except you won't feel like shit," she adds. "Charley?"

I break out of my tumbling thoughts and nod at her. Yeah. That sounds like a really good idea.

Chapter Eighteen

Nashville

Nero called Speedway to the office, and they were both waiting when I got back from Kentucky. After spending a little time with Sheridan, assuring her she was safe, I caught a flight back.

I'm still struggling to get her face out of my mind. Once she was lucid enough, the first thing she asked about was Oscar. Her and Nero's kid.

I wasn't sure how much to tell her, that's Nero's business but I did let her know he was safe with Nero and it was him who sent me to find her.

She went quiet after asking how long till she could go home and the doctors said she would need to stay with them at least a week to get her on the right track. It's going to be a long road for her. Those bastards had been shooting her up with heroin for weeks.

And doing God knows what else to her.

Nero is fully up to speed. I video called him from the clinic and surreptitiously showed him Sheridan in the hospital bed. He called me in to speak to Speedway.

All I want to do is go home and fully admit to myself the thought of the person waiting there is fueling that need. But this has to be done and my mood is still dark enough that I wouldn't want to taint Charley with it.

I'm hoping getting it all out and having Speedway take over will lift some of it so I can go to her.

How I've managed to look at Charley that way so quickly is a mystery to me but I do. It's not even about sex, just being with her feels like it might help.

I don't know her story but there is definitely some trauma in her history. I don't want to pile my shit on her but I get the feeling Charley will understand.

Speedway is pacing when I enter the room, Nero is sitting at the table watching him. They both turn when I close the door.

"Is she okay?" Speedway asks.

"No," I say honestly. Nero filled him in on some of it so it's safe to say that without him thinking the real worst scenario. "But she's in the right place."

"Fuck," he grabs his head with both hands.

"Sit down, Shaun," Nero says.

It takes a moment for him to comply and when he does, it's like all the tension drains out of his body, crashing under the weight of knowing his sister is safe now. They both listen as I explain what went down at the house.

Speedway's fists clench and release when I talk about the man I killed. That was all Nero had given me permission to tell him.

"We have a facility all set up and ready to take her," Nero tells Speedway when I've finished relaying what went down. "I've got a flight set up for you to go and be with her, then accompany her back here with the doctors to make sure she is protected."

"Do we need to worry they'll hurt her again?" Speedway asks.

Everyone at the club knows what Storm is doing and the war he is trying to wage against the club. They might not know the details but everyone is aware and on the lookout.

"We won't let him," Nero assures him. "Your flight is in an hour. Blaze has all the information, he's downstairs."

Speedway thanks us and walks out, looking like a broken man. I can't imagine any of my brothers being hurt the way Sheridan has. The lasting effects of what she has been through are not going to be easy to forget.

"Catch me up on what Camden has done."

Nero listens as I talk about the arrests of the men who were there abusing the women, the guards who were killed and taken away before the police got there. All the women are either in hospital or back with their families, all of them had been kidnapped, not a single one of them had been there willingly.

The building had also mysteriously burned to the ground.

"Cam has a lead on the people behind it. He'll keep us posted, but he is working with someone in Kentucky now who handles this kind of shit, they'll make sure they're taken down."

"Where does Storm fit in?"

"The asshole was an old friend, he has no connection to the pricks running the house."

Nero looks away from me and is quiet, so I hold my tongue.

"Razer has been out to Romney to see if he can find anything."

"Any luck?"

"Not yet, but we're closer than we were last week. Thank your brother for everything, if there is anything he needs."

"Thanks. He didn't do this as a favor, once he knew, he wanted to shut it down."

"Fucked up," he sighs. "People can be so fucked up."

"The women are getting the help they need."

Nero turns back and studies my face. The President getting an update and planning his next moves vanishes before my eyes.

"What do you need?"

"I'm good."

"Callum, you saw some seriously bad shit and you've not been yourself. Anyone who witnessed that is going to be affected."

"I'm fine."

He doesn't believe me but he's never been one to push too hard, unless he doesn't think we are coping with something.

"What's the deal with Charley?"

"There is no deal."

His brow lifts and he leans back in his seat. Psychic. He really fucking is.

"It wasn't expected."

"I hear that."

"Jesus, Nero. Don't put that shit on me."

"You've put that shit on yourself," he smirks. "Ellie says she's smart, too good for the club. Which probably means too good for you. Then again, Taylor is definitely too good for me and I'm never letting her go."

"It's new," I say it like I'm unsure.

"Maybe she is what you need right now."

"Using her to make me feel better isn't right."

"You want her there when you've worked through this shit?"

Who knows? One thing Nero does well is get you thinking. Is that what I want? How could we ever work? I'm still hung up on how old she is, but that went right through the fucking window the second she kissed me. Nine years isn't so bad, is it?

"Go over to the bar, talk with the brothers, have a drink, recalibrate to being back here. Then when you're ready, go home." He gives me a pointed look leaving no room for misinterpreting that shit.

"Fuck," I shake my head. "When did you get so fucking in tune with women and relationships?"

"Since Taylor walked into my house and gave me shit for being mean to Jesse."

I can't help but laugh.

"It might not work out," he says, meaning me and Charley. "You'll never know if you bury your head and come up with a million reasons why it won't. If you need it, Blaze will look into her background."

"No," I say immediately. "Anything like that, I will find out from her."

He smirks. The asshole. I get up and push my chair under the table. "What can I do about Storm?"

"Nothing for now. Razer will get back to me and once we know more, I'll call church."

I leave the office and head downstairs. Blaze dips his head so I go over.

"Speedway left for the airport. That shit man," he shakes his head. "You okay?"

They're asking because they care and I'm grateful for that but I just kind of want to forget about it for now.

"Messed up but I'm good. Gonna go grab a drink, then head home."

Blaze nods. I won't invite him and he won't come along. Blaze is an alcoholic who has been dry for eight years. He never puts himself in temptations way. He'll come to parties and gatherings but he doesn't stick around long.

There are a lot of people in the bar tonight and the noise, laughter and alcohol is exactly what I need to get into a better head space. It's going to take a while to get the memory of that house out of my brain but being back here with family will help.

Seeing Charley is in the back of my mind the whole time I'm chatting and laughing. She can never know what went down in Kentucky but it feels like I can tell her some things. She is smarter than a lot of people twice her age, she studies, sees things. I like that about her. Whatever is in her past that haunts her I want to help her.

"Nashville!"

Raven is sitting on a stool at the bar, waving me over.

"What?" I yell across the bar, earning a scowl.

"Come here, asshat."

"With an invitation like that, how can I possibly refuse."

The guys around me laugh as I get up and walk over. I doubt there is a guy at the club who doesn't want a piece of Raven. Everyone knows Rebel will cut off their dick if they ever touch his sister. One guy tried once and ended up with a broken finger and cheekbone.

He's very protective.

Raven can hold her own, growing up around the club and running this bar, she's learned to take no shit and can be as scary as her brother at times.

Her attacks are more mental and physical though. She can having a cutting tongue at times, but she's loyal. We've grown close over the years but my dick has never been interested. We're friends.

I stop by her and smile. "I'm here, what do you want?"

"You know things."

"This is true."

"What's going on with Beast?"

"Uh," I frown. "Not sure why?"

"You realize he has a seventeen-year-old daughter who is sleeping in my spare bedroom right now."

"I'd heard," I smirk.

"Shit, Nash, come on. He hasn't been round to see her. I heard he'd been told to sort his shit out but so far, nothing."

"Cut the guy a break. He didn't know he had a kid."

"Regardless, he can't get away from the flesh and blood person who showed up here. Tink needs him, she's tough and tries not to show it. He needs to grow a pair."

"Why are you giving me shit about it? This is nothing to do with me." I go to walk away but she moves her leg so I can't get away, jerking it so I am shoved back towards the bar. "Jesus, Raven."

"Don't think you can just walk away from me."

"Wouldn't dream of it," I grin. "But I haven't been around so I don't know where he is or what is going on with him. If you let me go and tell me what Tink is like, I might go find him and have a word."

Raven sips her drink and indicates the server to get me another.

"Buckle up," she says. "This girl is a firecracker. I think I'm in love with her."

I throw my head back and laugh. Fuck, Nero was right, this was just what I needed to get my head on straight. I feel better already being around these people. My friends.

She tells me about the kid and how underneath the bravado there is a scared girl who lost her only family and had the courage to walk into an MC to find the man who fathered her, and as far as she was concerned, abandoned her.

I promise to find him tomorrow and talk to him.

"He's so fucked up about it, he even closed Elegance."

"What?" I straighten up off the bar.

"Yeah, tonight he shut it down. That's why I need your help, he's going off the deep end or some shit. And, as much as I like the kid, she can't stay with me forever. I didn't sign on to be a foster mom."

Beast gave Charley a couple of nights off but if I know her, she would have been going stir crazy and wanted to go back to work.

"Does Nero know he shut the club?"

"Why are you asking me that?" she deadpans.

"Fine, fuck," I finish my drink and step away. "Give me a couple of days and we'll get shit sorted with Tink."

I won't admit I'm worried. Beast never shuts the club, especially not on a Friday. The revenue we'll lose is up there in the six-figure range. One good thing about it for me, Charley will be at home.

It takes another half hour to go round everyone saying bye before I'm on my bike riding back home.

My smile grows when I see the BMW parked beside the Shelby. Maybe tomorrow I'll take her out for a spin in it. She ate it up with her eyes when she first saw it. Kind of like I'm hoping she'll look at me when I get inside.

The house is dark and quiet. Not surprising given the hour. I kind of hope she spent the last two nights in my bed. Probably not, Charley has insecurities I want to help her fight.

I never planned to have her stay here as long as she has but knowing she is here is nice. Which is weird as fuck. Knowing she is in my bed waiting for me, now that is a thought I can get behind.

A quick peek inside my room says I'm right, she didn't feel comfortable in there without me. I move down the hall and knock on her door. Why am I knocking?

There is no sound from inside so I push open the door. Light spills in behind me showing me the bed is empty. Where is she? I flip on the light and look around. Something about this feels off.

After searching the house to make sure I didn't walk past her sleeping on the couch, I go back to her room. Something makes me open the closet and I stare at the empty hangers and space where her suitcase was.

"She left?"

My voice sounds loud in the stillness of the house. Where the fuck is she? She wouldn't go back to that house, I've shown her what a hell hole that place is. If she wanted to get a place of her own, she would have talked to me about it first.

Panic starts to set in. I squash it down, her case and things wouldn't be gone if something happened to her. This is all about what goes on in her head. It's been two damn days, and she chose to leave without talking to me? What the fuck?

I have her number but it's late and I don't want to disturb her. Fuck that. I dial and it goes straight to voicemail, the generic robotic kind, not her voice. I'm not leaving a message, I need to talk to her. What caused this?

Maybe she realized this is all wrong for her, that whatever we've had going on is not what she wants. I'm not the kind to let things fester, if there is an issue I want to know what it is and if I can fix it, I will.

It's late but Blaze still answers the call.

"Can you track a phone for me?"

"Who's?" he asks with a yawn.

I don't even feel bad I woke him up. He takes the number and says to give him five. When he calls back with a name and address, I frown but thank him and hang up. Why is she with one of the dancers from Elegance? She'd rather go stay with her than be here?

My own selfish reasons for wanting her to be here shouldn't have any part of this, she obviously left for a reason but I'm irritated and also feeling rejected and like pure shit. Which is why I get on the bike and head for the address, not giving one flying fuck that it's nearly two in the morning.

Nero is right, if I want to see if this thing can work then I'm not gonna sit back and let her slip away from me with no explanation. Rationally it can wait till tomorrow, but I'm committed now.

She can come home, explain herself and we'll figure this out. In that order.

Chapter Nineteen

Charley

THE INSULTS HAVE FINALLY stopped. There is no point lying here calling myself stupid and delusional that someone like Callum could want me. If anyone deserves the name calling its him. In my limited experience, men are all assholes. No one is different. It says everything that someone like Callum who is sweet and protective and generous turns out to be an ass.

Lily's roommate was okay with me crashing here tonight, and maybe tomorrow but I get the feeling any longer than that and I'd be unwelcome. Which is why I'm sitting up on the makeshift bed on the couch, wrapped in a fluffy blanket, filling in applications for apartments that no one will see till tomorrow.

At least I'm ahead of the game. If I can't get a place in the next couple of days, I'll stay in a hotel till I can. I have the money now to afford a fairly decent one. It will eat my money but I'd rather be there than another place I'm not wanted.

Lily sat up with me for a while and we had a few drinks commiserating and berating men. It slipped out that I did in fact sleep with Nashville.

She congratulated me despite calling him a dirty name telling me that some of the girls had been trying to get with Nashville for years.

She'd drank a little too much that her filter slipped, and she told me Tami was the one who gave him a blow job in the back room the night I first laid eyes on him. She apologized straight away, and I waved it off, but shit... of all the women there it had to be Tami, who has made no secret of not liking me.

Maybe that makes more sense now. Because apparently everyone knows I was staying with him and driving his car.

Being alone, having no friends, no ties was good for me. I don't like this feeling I'm experiencing now, or the re-runs my brain keeps showing me of Nashville standing between that woman's spread legs, smiling at her like she was the only thing making him happy.

The door buzzer scares the shit out of me and I drop my phone into the pile of blankets.

"What is it with me and doorbells," I mutter.

It sounds again and I get up. It's got to be someone for Lily or her roommate but it's really late. It's probably someone who is drunk and pressing the wrong buzzer. As I head to the hallway, I trip over a shoe and kick the table leg and curse, swearing whoever this is will get a mouthful.

I slap the intercom button and snap, "who is this?" It's silent, spiking my anger. "This isn't funny, do you have nothing better to do than ring random apartments? Get a life asshole."

"Charley?"

I pause with my finger on the button, my breath catching.

"Charley?" he repeats my name.

"Go away Nashville."

"Nashville?" he asks, sounding hurt.

That only makes me madder. "Go home, I'm fine, not your problem anymore."

"What? Charley, you're not my problem. I was worried sick about you."

"Right okay."

"What is wrong? What's going on. Can you let me up so we don't have to talk through an intercom?"

"No."

"Seriously?"

"It's two in the morning, I'd like to go to sleep and not disturb my roommate."

"I'm not leaving. If you hang up, I'll just keep buzzing."

"Why?"

"What do you mean why?" he asks, the exasperation clear. "I came home to find you gone, all your things gone. No explanation."

"You did me a favor and now you don't need to. I have somewhere else to stay. Goodnight."

His voice cuts off and I step back, leaning against the wall opposite the intercom. How could he sound so shocked and concerned? Wow, men are really good at manipulation.

It buzzes again, and again, to the point I'm sure Lily's roommate is going to come out and kick me out. I answer again and whisper shout at him to go away.

"Not happening, Charley. I'm getting pissed now. Let me in so we can talk."

God. Fine. I can tell him to his face what an ass he is. "I'll be down in two minutes, do not leave the lobby." I open the door and step back again.

A light has come on in the hallway to the bedrooms. Lily is standing there squinting at me.

"What's going on?" she mumbles.

"Nothing, go back to bed."

"Was that the buzzer?"

"It was prank callers, ringing bells."

"Fucking idiots got nothing better to do," she rubs her eyes. "Sorry it disturbed you."

"Don't worry, just go back to bed."

Luckily she is too sleepy to question my frantic pulse and panicked movements. Get a grip, Charley, just go down and tell him to leave you alone. Maybe throw in he is a bastard... Or maybe just pretend you never saw what he did and let him stew.

I dress quickly, grab a coat, the keys to the apartment and my phone and head out to the elevator. The lights are motion detection in the hallway and are already on when I step outside. I about jump out of my skin when Nashville rounds a corner and walks toward me.

"I told you to wait downstairs," I hiss, pulling the door closed.

"I'm not big on being told what to do, Charley." He looks me up and down and eyes the door behind me.

Lily's apartment is the last on the hallway so I walk away from the door to the window at the end of the hall. I can feel him behind me even though he's keeping his distance.

"What are you doing here?" I ask.

"I could ask you the same thing," he puts his hands on his hips, his face a mixture of confusion and irritation. "Why'd you leave?"

"Because I am getting my own place." He frowns and looks at Lily's door. "How did you even know where I am?"

"That's not important."

"It kind of is," I snap. "Are you spying on me?"

"No, fuck. If I was spying, I would have known you left the house, but I had to track you down."

I cross my arms and glare at him. He stares right back and my eyes are drawn to the pulse in his neck which is beating fast. I take a moment to study him.

How can he look that concerned about me, when he was standing between another woman's legs just a couple of hours ago?

My heart hardens. We owe each other nothing, I barely know this man.

"Charley?" he takes a step closer, his eyes softening. "Tell me what happened? Why did you leave?"

He doesn't get to make me feel bad about this. I'm also not going to make myself look foolish by saying what I saw.

"She saw you at the bar with the woman in the red leather pants."

We both turn to see Lily in the doorway to her apartment. She has a robe on this time over her tiny pajama shorts, and the fluffy white socks on her feet.

"The what?" Nashville looks at her, then back at me.

I refuse to make eye contact with him, or Lily. How could she do this to me? I've never been more embarrassed.

"The Disciples bar, earlier. We came for a drink and saw you all over some other woman."

"Lily," I hold up a hand to her. "Don't try to help."

"He should know."

"Thanks for telling me," Nashville says, then stares at her until she gets the picture and goes back inside. He heaves out a long breath then looks at me. "Get your things."

"Excuse me."

"We're going to talk about this but not in the hallway of some random apartment building. It's late, we're both tired but we can figure this out."

"I'm not going back with you. I'm moving into my own place. Soon."

"Nice try," he smirks. "Come on, get your things."

"You might get other people to do what you want but I'm not one of them."

"I was talking to Raven, the owner of the bar, sister of my Vice President," He moves right up to me, and I take a step back. "He will cut off my balls if I even dared try to touch his sister. We've been friends for years and I value my balls, so I won't ever go there. Now get your things, stop talking about finding somewhere else to go and just come back to the house."

"No thank you. I'm sorting out my own place."

"Charley," he backs me into the wall and moves his mouth close to my ear. "I'm not leaving here without you."

"You'll be hanging out in the hallway all night because I'm not-"

He moves so fast I barely have time to react, leaning forward, pushing his shoulder into my stomach and lifting me right off my feet, throwing me over his shoulder like I weigh nothing at all.

"Callum!" I shriek. "Put me down."

"You're going to wake the neighbors," he turns and walks back toward the door where Lily is wide-eyed.

"Good, maybe they'll call the police," I snap back, arching my back so I can straighten up but he clamps a hand on my ass and turns so I have to lean back down and grab onto his cut.

"I'm not going to drop you," he reassures. "But we are going to talk about this. At my house."

"Nashville," Lily says, sounding unsure but also amused.

If I could see her, I'd give her a stern look too. Is she really going to stand there and watch him kidnap me?

"I'll be by to get her stuff tomorrow," he tells her, gripping the back of my thighs to stop me wriggling out of his grasp.

I damn well am not leaving here without a fight, even if I have to grab the doorframe and cling on. He moves away from it as if he can read my mind and starts toward the elevator. I lift my head as I pass and Lily holds out her hands as if to say, 'what am I supposed to do?'

"Girl code," I grunt at her.

"It's kind of hot," she says.

Nashville laughs and doesn't look back, and he is nonplussed when I bang my fists on his back. I am mindful of the neighbors which says a lot about me right now. If I really wanted out of this, I could get out of it by calling for help.

"Put me down," I say when he enters the elevator.

"Nope."

"I swear to God, if you don't put me down right now I'm going to claw my way through this leather vest."

In answer to that he bites my ass. Literally just sinks his teeth into it, fabric and all and I let out another squeal. He kisses it straight after, then lightly rubs it.

It was not hard enough to leave teeth marks. It also kind of did something to my insides, the kind of thing I shouldn't be feeling when he is stealing me away in the middle of the night wearing nothing but a pair of thin cotton shorts, and a sweatshirt, with no bra underneath.

"Fine," I mumble. "I'll come back with you but put me down."

"I like you where you are," he rubs my ass again as the elevator reaches the lobby.

Fortunately, there is no one around to witness the humiliation but there is a camera in the corner. God knows what they will think when they look back over that footage. Outside, Callum walks to his bike and finally sets me on my feet.

He holds his arms around me to keep me steady as the blood that rushed to my head from being upside down starts to run back to where it's supposed to be.

"You good?"

"No I'm not," I huff, turning my head carefully to stop the woozy feeling.

"Good."

He plonks a helmet on my head before I can say anything else and grabs a leather jacket from one of the bags at the side of his bike. He wraps it around me, helping guide my arms into the sleeves like I'm a small child.

It's kind of sweet he is thinking about protecting me. *What am I thinking?* He is blatantly kidnapping me. He takes my hips in his big strong hands and lifts, setting me down on the back seat of his bike, and grins at my narrowed eyes, the only part of my face he can see.

Taking his place in front of me, he reaches back and grabs my legs and lifts them, I almost tip backwards and have to grab his shoulders. His laughter rings out and I smack his shoulder while trying to move but he has literally crossed my legs across his lap, one of his hands running over my inner thigh.

This shit shouldn't be turning me on. I'm mad at him and he will be getting an earful when I manage to get off this bike.

"Hold on, Charley."

"No."

"I might be acting playful now, but when it comes to your safety, I'm not screwing around," he says over his shoulder. "Hold on."

When the bike rumbles to life beneath us I do as I'm told, tucking my arms under his and clutching them together over his chest. I cannot believe I am wrapped around him like some kind of deranged limpet. He's right, and I grip tight as the bike takes off and he turns it around heading to his place.

Part of me is impressed. He didn't back down, but he is also proving once again that my safety comes first. That protective streak of his hasn't gone away, even when he is snatching me like a god damn thief in the night. I'm going to kill Lily tomorrow, how could she let him take me like this?

All the way back to the house I argue with myself. The devil on my shoulder is trying to convince the angel that this is a good thing. Having someone want me this much is kind of exciting and not something I've felt for a long time. I still need to be mad about it, and about what I saw and about my own stupid feelings for a man I barely know.

He uses the fob to open the garage as we get near the driveway so he doesn't have to stop. I don't try to untangle myself until we're moving toward the space beside the Shelby. Callum's fingers grip my ankles to stop me and he steers one handed into the space and stops the bike.

His shoulders rise and fall like he is taking a deep breath, and he looks down at his lap where my legs are still locked around him. Now we're just sitting here, the silence of the garage after the shutter goes back down, and the engine has stopped running is suddenly deafening.

I was expecting him to jump off the bike and give a repeat performance of the firefighter lift, some dark part of me hoping he'd carry me up to his bed.

He doesn't move. Not even when I uncross my legs and lower them so they're wrapped around the outside of his thighs instead of his waist. I glide my hands up to his shoulders and am shocked by how tense they are.

Is he regretting coming to get me?

The helmet is in the way, so I unclip it and pull it off, setting it on the counter that is just within reach, I push my messy hair back and touch his shoulder again, surprised when he reaches up and hooks our fingers together, resting there on his shoulder.

"Are you okay?" I ask, keeping my voice low because talking loud seems wrong.

"Yeah," he replies, squeezing my fingers.

Something happens to break him out of whatever this is, because he straightens up and lets go of my hand to get off the bike. His gaze falls to my legs, and the tiny cotton shorts I sleep in and his expression changes. My throat dries up as I watch him reach forward and take my ankle so he can turn me to face him.

Jump down, go inside, lock myself in my room and do not talk to him until he apologizes for his neanderthal show at controlling me.

However, my body is not responding to the signals my brain is trying to send. Once I'm facing him, my feet dangling because I'm too short to reach the floor, he touches the pads of his fingers to the inner part of my knees and gently pushes so they spread out, allowing him to step closer. He places his hands on either side of my thighs and leans in close.

"I don't screw around, Charley."

My throat tightens at the rumble of his voice. I want to clench my thighs together but that would only trap him between them. My neck tilts when he reaches one hand up and touches his thumb to my chin, making sure that our eyes meet.

"And if you ever have doubts, you only need to ask me. I will never lie."

"You say that like this is something more," I avert my eyes, my words a mere whisper.

"I don't know what it is," Callum palms my cheek and makes me look at him. "All I know is, you disappearing on me was not a good feeling."

"We barely know each other."

"That is easy to fix."

"I'm not even sure I'm staying."

"Then let me convince you."

Chapter Twenty

Nashville

Charley's mouth opens as I press mine against hers and I sweep my tongue inside, rolling it against hers as I straighten up, still holding her face in my palms. Her back arches and she clutches my waist, her neck tilted back far enough that it may not be comfortable but she doesn't complain as she kisses me back.

The last thing I want is for her to be in any discomfort, so I scoop my hands under her ass and lift her, encouraging her to wrap her legs back around my waist.

I'd expected a harder fight to get her back here. Despite her insecurities and secrets, Charley is a woman who knows what she wants, and she isn't afraid to work for it.

She clings to me as I turn around, all ready to head into the house and take her to my bed but I glance at the Shelby instead. The thought of laying her out on the hood of this classic car has my dick hardening to the point of being painful.

She makes a small sound of surprise when I set her down.

"I might dent it," she says.

"Don't care," I move back far enough to pull down her shorts.

She's wearing a pair of pink cotton panties that sit low on her hips with a heart right over her clit. Using my thumb I press against it, making her gasp as I lower onto my knees, looking up the length of her body. Charley watches me slip my hands beneath the waist of her panties and drag them down.

"I've been dying to fuck you with my tongue."

She lets out a small moan as I nuzzle against her pubic bone. Nudging her clit with my nose, I push my tongue inside of her, gripping her calves and putting them over my shoulder. She rocks back and forth on the hood of the Shelby as I use my thighs to push up and down, pressing further inside of her and licking up and down inside her lips.

She tastes fucking amazing and cries out as I move my head from side to side, my tongue rigid moving in and out of her. Her hands grab onto my hair and I welcome the sting as she tugs on it, pressing me against her. Moisture is running down my chin and I use my fingers to catch it and push them inside of her as I lathe over her clit.

Charley is writhing harder and arches her back when I push my hand under her top, finding a bare breast that makes me almost lose my shit. I roll her nipple between my thumb and forefinger, pinching and tugging on it until she gasps and pushes up her hips.

"Callum," she moans out my name, and it drives me fucking insane.

"Come baby, come on my face. I want all of it."

She doesn't disappoint, my mouth fills with moisture and she gasps and clenches around my fingers. Fuck I've never made a woman squirt before. If she's embarrassed she doesn't show it, too lost in the sensation of the climax tearing through her.

I swallow and pull back, watching as it pours all over the Shelby and I go feral.

Before now I've been gentle with her, I've made it good for her, took my time and made sure not to hurt her but seeing how she is gushing for me is something new and beautiful and fucking sexy as shit.

I get up and unbuckle my belt, yanking down the zipper. Charley is half lidded, almost delirious with the pleasure, her mouth falls open as I push into her without any warning, the warmth and wetness of her draws me in and clamps down, her ankles locking over my ass.

Banging both palms down on either side of her shoulders, I fuck into her, hard enough that the car starts to rock and she jolts with each thrust. She moves enough to get her shirt over her head and my gaze fixates on her tits as they bounce up and down.

Again, I love the fact that she is all natural, and I lean down and bite her nipple, trying to put as much of her tit into my mouth. Charley grips the back of my head and lets out a long gasping cry as I bite down again, all the while fucking into her.

Shit, this is fucking amazing, the tightening in my balls means I'm about to lose it and I thrust harder, gritting my teeth as I try to hold off long enough. Fortunately, Charley goes over the edge again and I pump in and out, pushing upright so I can look down at her.

"Say my name," I grunt.

"Callum."

"Tell me what I'm doing to you."

"You're... fucking me," she whispers.

I grab her hips, my fingers digging into the flesh. "Like you mean it, Charley."

"Fucking me," she cries out. "Fuck me, Callum."

I arch up and roar as I come, my dick pulsing for what feels like forever as I fill her with my cum. The thought of it mingling with hers sets off another shudder and pulse and little pin pricks of light dot my vision as I completely lose control of my body, like I'm going to black out.

My eyes squeeze tight as I lean down and kiss her through our aftershocks, my hips still thrusting, never wanting to leave her tight, perfect pussy.

Her body collapses into a boneless heap, her eyes shut, chest heaving up and down. My gaze rakes over her, the flush on her chest, the redness around her nipples where my stubble has rubbed against the delicate skin. I push up and look down at where we remain joined.

My head is telling me I should have pulled out, coming inside of her is dangerous and stupid but nothing can make me regret it.

She's fucking perfect, and after tonight, the thought of letting her go makes me angry. Forcing her to stay is wrong but I'll damn well make sure she knows I want it.

I'll be fucked if I ever admit to Nero he is right about this, but I'm not opposed to the idea of it being more.

She sleeps in my bed again and I wake her up with my tongue inside her, leaving her replete but furious because I denied her my dick. I had to ride to Lily's and get her stuff.

Shit, it wasn't easy for me to do either but this isn't about sex, this is about showing her she doesn't need to run away from me.

Lily is dying to ask questions as she hands over Charley's things but she knows better than to quiz an officer of the Blackhawk Disciples.

Charley can fill her in, if she wants to. I'm not averse to her talking about us, keeping this a secret isn't necessary for me, but I understand if she wants to. Although carrying her away from one of the dancers last night means news is going to spread fast.

After dropping the stuff back at home and telling Charley in no uncertain terms, I will come and get her again if she leaves, it's only when she swears and pushes me out the door that I set out to find Beast.

Blaze kindly helps out giving me his tracker location and I head to the old bar where he used to hang out a lot. He's with Fury, I'm not surprised to find the two of them there together shooting pool.

People look over when I enter. If I was anyone else, I'd be intimidated but these guys don't scare me, and once they see the cut, they go back to what they were doing.

This place was a favorite with Crash, our previous president. It's dingy as shit in here and although smoking has been banned indoors for a while there still seems to be a layer of smoke floating just below the ceiling.

Iron Maiden is playing on the beat up old jukebox in the corner. Funny thing is, the damn thing still works and is probably older than most people in here.

When I stop by the table, Fury looks over and lifts his chin, eyeing Beast who is lining up a shot on the eight ball to win the game.

Just for funsies, and because he needs to lighten the fuck up and deal with his shit, I move into his line of sight and shout 'hey' as he takes the shot.

Jokes on me, the fucker still slots it into the center pocket without breaking concentration.

"Appreciate the lame ass attempt at an assist," Fury smirks.

"You think I didn't see you the second you walked in the door?" Beast straightens and sets his cue on the felt while Fury starts collecting the balls to wrack them up again. "Who sent you? This asshole said he came off his own back."

"Raven sent me," I shrug, not wanting to lie about it. "You know the woman who has taken in your daughter."

Beast flinches as he picks up the beer behind him on the shelf, he takes a few long gulps without saying anything. Fury is setting up the balls in the triangle behind me.

"I've already had the third degree from him and Nero."

"And still it's not sinking in?"

"You don't get it."

"Of course I don't. I'm not even going to pretend I do. Doesn't mean you're doing the right thing running away from it. Raven's patience won't last much longer, then what will happen to her?"

"I'll take care of it."

"It?"

Fury smirks at me. Yeah okay, fucker has probably already said all of this to him and he's still here in this bar, playing pool, drinking watered down beer and listening to late seventies heavy metal.

"Shit," he puts the beer down and turns to face us both. "Who am I beating next?"

"No one. You're lucky it's us who showed up and not Nero."

"Or Raven," Fury laughs.

"Which will happen if you don't get your shit together," I point out, taking a cue from the stand on the wall. "And no one wants to see her pissed enough to come looking for one of us. That will only rile up Rebel and then Nero will get involved."

"I get it, fuck off," Beast grabs the cue off the table and bends over.

"Hey, my break."

"Get fucked."

He hits the cue ball so hard two of the balls bounce off the table.

"Not it," I cross my ankles and watch the balls rolling in different directions.

Beast drops the stick on the table and walks away. Not to pick up the balls, for the door.

"Good job," Fury laughs.

"He needs to get his head out of his ass. Razer is in Romney tracking down Storm, he could call us down there at any time. Nero is not going to want to deal with this."

"I've told him all of that," he shrugs.

Shaking my head, I walk out of the bar after Beast and find him hunched over his bike. Fury doesn't follow so I head over and lean against the wall by where Beast is breathing heavily.

"Don't have a fucking heart attack on me," I mutter.

There is no quip back, enough that my heart thumps a little but Beast straightens up and looks out across the parking lot.

"Everyone thinks this is about me not stepping up and taking care of my shit," he says.

"It's not?" I ask with less sarcasm or amusement in my tone.

"Her mom... She looks just like her mom."

That is not something I've thought about a lot. The kid's mom died, which was why she showed up here and Beast never knew she was pregnant when he left. That's got to mess with his head. The way he is looking off into the distance is about more than the shock of it. It's grief.

"She meant a lot to you?"

He sniffs and turns to face me. "No bullshit?"

"No," I straighten up.

"She's the only woman I've ever loved."

There is no point asking why he left, that will just open up more wounds. "Then do right by her kid. By your kid. Do you think she would want you to run away and bury your head in the sand? Or be the only person Tink can turn to. She has nowhere else to go, Derek."

"Isabella."

"What?"

"That's her real name. Found out when I did the paternity test. Not sure why she goes by Tink."

"Well, we know more than most about nicknames," I point out.

"I don't... I just... How do I do it?"

"Start by introducing yourself, maybe?"

He rolls his eyes.

"It's gonna take a while for both of you to get your heads around this. Sometimes baby steps is the only way to go. Raven will help. She's all salty asking me to get you to get your head out of your ass but she would never toss the kid out. She likes her."

"She does?" he looks up.

"Not sure that's a good thing, man. I think she might be on Raven's wavelength and that means trouble."

"If you're trying to make me feel better, you're shit at it."

"Making you feel better isn't what is important. Tink is."

He heaves out a heavy breath and nods. "She showed up at the wrong time."

"There is never a right time for shit like this."

"I mean with the whole shit show with Storm. Look what happened to Sheridan."

"That won't happen to Tink."

"How do you know? He went after her to get to Nero's kid."

"We protect our own. We didn't let him get to Oscar. Taylor and Jesse were okay. Sheridan," I heave out my own heavy sigh. "We missed that but we have her now."

All the council know what state she was found in and where she was being held. The thought of Charley ending up somewhere like that raises an instant red hot rage in my veins. I'd tear through the whole fucking place if anyone laid a hand on her like that.

I'm not going to talk about my problems and how I'm dealing with the fall out of all that, this is about getting Beast around to the idea of having a kid who needs him.

The door opens and a blast of AC/DC follows Fury out of the bar. He holds up his phone.

"Razer called."

Beast and I exchange a look. Anything else is going to have to wait. We get on our bikes and head to the clubhouse.

Things are tense when we arrive but no one says anything as we walk up the stairs.

Everyone except Razer is here now. Nero's gaze flicks to Beast as he takes his seat. He waits until we're all sitting down then pushes his cell phone onto the table and hits the speaker button.

"Everyone is here. What have you got?" Nero gets straight to the point.

"This whole town is smaller than Locust Point," he starts out, sounding frustrated. "Keeping a low profile is not easy."

"Is this the part where you tell us your job is hard, or you get to the fucking point?"

Nero frowns at Rebel but doesn't say anything. Everyone is on edge over Storm. Not knowing where the fucker is makes us all frustrated and anxious.

"The surrounding area is owned by a group called the Kivisto's. They're a mobbed up family out of Finland."

"Finland?" Blaze asks, grabbing hold of his beard, a habit he has when he is thinking.

"Second generation but from what I've seen, it's slick."

"Storm is working with them?" Nero asks, looking pissed.

I get it, how the fuck does he keep landing on his feet? Everything went to shit with his last collaboration. Cannon and his crew are likely to be locked up for the next ten to twenty years.

"Trying to. Remember Kirk Wallen? I saw him having a meeting with two of the Kivisto's. We can't get close enough to see what is going down."

"You still haven't had eyes on Storm?" Rebel asks.

"No," Razer says, the frustration clear in his voice.

"I thought Kirk Wallen was in prison," Fury says.

"He got out a year ago," Blaze said, his face a mask of anger.

"That is a piece of information we could have used. We can't afford to let anything slip by us."

"That's on me, Prez," Blaze shakes his head.

"Go find out everything you can about the Kivisto family," Nero says and we all watch Blaze as he stands, his chair pushing back a lot harder than necessary, almost toppling over as he leaves the room.

No one will judge him as harshly as he will judge himself.

"How do you want me to play it?" Razer asks.

"We get intel on this family, you keep watching Wallen. Storm might be making some good moves, but bringing in Wallen isn't one of them. Fresh out of prison and not having anywhere to turn means he could be swayed."

"You want me to try that?"

“Not yet, let Blaze get what he can on this family. I want to know if they’re smart enough to see through Wallen or if they’re just going for whatever Storm is promising them. Hold tight for a couple more days.”

“Got it.”

Razer hangs up and Nero tucks his phone back in his pocket.

“How does he keep evading us?” Stryker asks. “He wasn’t this smart before. Maybe we should have kept Chains alive longer.”

“Chains didn’t know anything else,” Nero cuts that line of thought off.

Chains was a brother and a traitor, feeding Storm information that almost got most of the officers at the club killed. He was also Stryker’s cousin, who he tortured for days to get information out of.

“Storm had him on the hook for what he wanted, not because he was bringing Chains into the inner circle, it was a way to keep track of our movements.”

“Are you suggesting Storm might have someone else behind him?” Rebel asks Stryker, picking up on his comment when everyone else thought back on Chains’ involvement in this whole mess. “Have you heard anything else at the Battleground?”

“No.”

Stryker asking questions would stick out like a sore thumb, he works best in the shadows, watching and listening.

“Fury go to Stryker’s next fight and see if you can find anything out. What Storm was up to all started at the Battlegrounds. Everyone else, keep doing what you’re doing. We’ll get to the fucker one way or another. And no one lets their guard down. Nashville, make sure everyone knows we’re still on full alert.”

There isn’t much more to say so church breaks up.

This limbo we’re in is getting to all of us. No one wants to sit back and wait to see what Storm’s next move is, but the fucker is doing a really good job of staying a few steps ahead of us. I trust my brothers, we will find out what the asshole is planning.

Preferably without anyone else getting hurt.

Chapter Twenty One

Charley

THE RUMBLE OF THE motorcycle engine sends a shiver racing through me and I get up from my seat on the sofa and walk into the hallway where the garage door opens out. It takes longer than I expect but when the door opens, Callum comes in holding my bag. He's been gone for hours, but I'm starting to learn that is what it's like with him.

He pauses when he sees me, his eyes moving up and down my body.

"What else was I supposed to do?" I ask arching a brow.

"Should have left this at your friend's." He drops the bag and walks over to me, backing me up against the wall. "This is really dangerous, Charley."

"Would you have preferred I sat here naked?"

He lifts the hem of his T-shirt and glides his fingers up my thigh, sliding them around to my center, finding me bare. He groans, closing his eyes.

"Truthfully," he laughs as he teases my opening. "This is way sexier, its almost like I have to work to find the treasure. What were you thinking about while you sat here waiting for me?"

He swirls the wetness around my clit and I press my back against the wall.

"To be this wet for me already? Were you imagining me coming in here and doing this," he pushes three fingers inside of me and I gasp at the intrusion, welcome though it is.

With his other hand he unbuckles his belt and draws down his zipper, lowering his jeans enough that his bare cock presses against my thigh.

"Or this," he suddenly turns me around so I'm flat against the wall and tilts my hips back, then lets out a low groan as he slowly pushes into me.

"Either is fine," I manage to breathe out as he fills me, my whole body welcoming him.

Callum laughs and pushes his hand between the wall and my body and strums my clit as he thrusts into me. "So long as you're getting pleasure?" he questions and I nod, rolling my head back so he can kiss my throat. "Cock or fingers, it's all the same?" he teases.

"Cock is better," I push back.

"My fingers and tongue are offended, Charley." He bites the point between my neck and shoulder as he pushes into me harder. "But my cock is really fucking happy to be the winner right now."

Then he stops talking and fucks me until I'm crying out and grasping at the wall, finding nothing to get hold of. He pulls out, turns me around and lifts me, impaling me again and proceeds to fuck into me until he groans and spills inside of me.

I'm not sure when I decided foregoing condoms was a good idea but nothing feels as good as having the hot, hard length of him inside me.

Luckily Helen made me get the implant when I was eighteen. She was convinced I was sleeping around by her daughters who would do anything to make me look bad. What no one, except for Stephen realized, I'd only ever had sex with one person.

I push thoughts of them out of my head as Callum carefully lowers me to the ground, holding my arms so they're around his neck. His t-shirt falls back around my thighs as he watches me, staring into my eyes like he is trying to see beyond the image everyone else sees.

"Are you okay?" he asks. I nod in response. He touches the wetness between my thighs and frowns. "I should have asked."

"I'm not going to get pregnant."

His brow furrows by how easily I say it but there is something unreadable in his eyes too, an intensity I've not seen on his face before.

He doesn't ask any more questions just nods, then scoops me up before I can ask what that was about. Not firefighter style this time, his arm is under my thighs, the other holding me around the middle of my back so I'm cradled into his chest.

I don't ask where we're going because I've already come to learn how Callum takes care of me after sex.

We shower together and he washes my hair for me, massaging my scalp to the point of me almost having another orgasm, which he finds endlessly amusing.

"Fingers win this one," he laughs.

I need to get ready for work soon but he strips off my towel and encourages me into the bed.

"What are we doing?" I ask as he shuffles down the bed and lifts my arm so it's over his shoulders, then he kisses the side of my breast. My heart skips a beat, but he doesn't take it any further than that, resting his cheek on my stomach.

"Things have been shit lately," he sighs.

Both Lily and Taylor have told me how secretive the men in the club can be. Callum has told me himself he can't talk about what he's involved in, even when I saw firsthand how they reacted to the asshole at Elegance.

Asking him a question I know he won't answer is pointless, so I run my fingers through his hair and wait to see if he will elaborate.

"Sometimes you need to switch off, or do something you wouldn't normally do."

"What wouldn't you normally do?"

"Stay in bed in the middle of the afternoon with a beautiful woman I never expected to come into my life."

That was a moment of completely raw honesty. My pulse rate picks up and my anxiety spikes, does he want me to reciprocate?

"I've seen some bad things, been through a lot of bad situations, things I would never want you to know about," he tilts his head to meet my gaze. "It's part of who I am and I've always figured it meant having this kind of thing was impossible."

"What kind of thing?" My voice is a mere whisper.

His lip tilts in a tender smile but he makes the moment lighter by rubbing his palm over my breast, giving it a squeeze.

"Wanting to stay here and find out everything there is to know about you. I'm not blind, Charley, there is something you're hiding from me. I'd be the biggest hypocrite to ask you to tell me, but it's hard not being able to help."

"I don't need you to help me, Callum. Not in the way you're thinking. The last couple of weeks have been the first time I've felt safe."

He shifts and props himself up on his elbow. "That's the kind of thing that worries me, Charley."

"I'm not in any danger, Callum. Maybe safe is the wrong word." God, I'm messing this up. "I've been on my own for a year, moving around, trying to find my place. Baltimore wasn't my final destination, given the shit hole I was living in."

His expression darkens at the memory of that place. He is desperate to ask questions about my past and maybe that is why I finally feel like I want to tell him.

His gaze never wavers from mine, even as he places his palm between my breasts where my heart is beating wildly.

"If ever you want to tell me, I'll listen. You know I won't judge, given the surface details you know about my life."

"I'm not afraid of you Callum," I shift so his hand falls away but roll onto my side and face him. He drops his elbow so his head is resting in front of mine on the same pillow.

"Good. Because I will never hurt you. And I'll never let anyone else hurt you."

"You proved that," I smirk.

"Fucker," he grumbles, like he wishes he'd been able to do more than knock him unconscious and run out of town.

That thought should scare me, but coming from him, oddly it doesn't. We stare at each other for a few moments until I work up the courage to tell him.

"I killed someone."

Inside I cringe, waiting for him to recoil or the way he looks at me to change. None of that happens, what he says shocks me for a moment.

"Did they deserve it?"

"Probably not..." He waits me out, sensing this is only going to come out on my terms and in my own way.

People in my hometown know all about it but outside of that, I've never spoken to a soul about what happened that night.

"My mom died when I was young," I say, looking down at his collar bone.

He doesn't try to make me look at him.

"Dad remarried after six months to a woman that my mom hated. I only found out about that later. I was just a kid and didn't realize the relationship history. She had three kids of her own, two daughters who were a couple of years older and a son the same age. I couldn't understand why she was so cold to me, especially the older I got.

"It was because I looked like my mom. And every passing year all she could see was the rival she hated so much. I still believe she only married my dad as a fuck you to mom."

Callum's brow furrows at the absurdity of that. He still keeps quiet.

"It bled into her daughters, or she told them to do it, who knows. They started treating me like shit, embarrassing me in school, bullying me, getting other kids to bully me."

"Fuck," he shakes his head angrily.

"I dealt with it," I told him. "The wicked stepsisters," I laugh a little. "That is what me and my friends called them. Like I was some kind of Cinderella. They didn't make me clean the house or anything, we had maids for that."

"What did your dad do?"

"Nothing."

"What the fuck?"

"Yeah, I don't like to think about him anymore. He shut down, he let Helen take the lead, and she got to do whatever she wanted. The only person who helped me in that house was Stephen. He kept his sisters at bay, when he could. They hated that we got close, and it really pissed Helen off, but he made life bearable."

"I don't know whether I like him yet."

"Probably hate him. Turned out he was a part of it, he wanted to break me in other ways."

"What the fuck did he do to you," Callum's hand moves up to the back of my neck.

"Nothing I didn't want at the time," I reassure him. "Even if it was all a lie."

"Jesus, Charley. They sound like fucking assholes."

"I hate them all, especially my dad because he never looked out for me."

I don't want to go into any deeper detail than that. Callum doesn't need to know every shitty thing they did to me. I don't want him to feel sorry for me.

"The night it happened, Helen was being an extra special bitch. There was this gala, and they wanted a united front but I refused to go. So to force me, she contacted the college I'd been accepted into, a million miles away from them, and pulled my application."

"What? Can she do that?"

"She was my legal guardian. The one thing I'd been counting on to move away and have a better life, and she made one phone call to a guy her dead husband had connections to and tore that away from me."

"What happened?"

Taking a shaky breath, I focus on not picturing that night but telling it, like it's someone else's story, not a memory.

"I was furious and just wanted to get the hell away from them. There was a huge row, and I ran out to get in the car and just drive away but she got in the car with me, still telling me what a bad person I was, how everyone hates me, so I floored it, went straight through the gate. I genuinely don't know what came over me, I was just so mad.

"There was no plan to hurt anyone, Callum."

He sits up and pulls me into his chest, resting his cheek on the top of my head.

"Stephen and one of the witches chased after us. That just panicked me even more. Helen was screaming at me, trying to get me to stop the car and go back, so I did. I spun around and headed back to the house because I wanted her out of the car.

"Only we were going really fast, and so was Stephen. I swerved to try not to hit them but wasn't... I didn't..."

"Hey, you don't have to go on," he wipes at the tears on my cheeks.

"They ran off the road into a ditch but our car flipped, went down the side of an embankment and hit a tree. In all the chaos, Helen hadn't put her seatbelt on."

My eyes close as I picture her body. Callum stays stock still as I continue telling him what happened.

At first not comprehending that she was halfway through the broken windshield, blood everywhere. Then the engine caught fire. I was screaming the others were screaming as they tried to get to us. It's as clear as if I'm there in the moment, fighting to get out of the car, stumbling and falling on the floor as the whole front of the car went up in flames, and Helen too.

Stephen tried desperately to get to his mom and his clothes caught fire too. He managed to put the flames out, but he was badly burned up one side of his body.

There was nothing more any of us could do. He collapsed and passed out while I stood there, watching my stepmother burn.

"I'll never forget the smell."

Callum hugs me tighter to him. "It was an accident."

"I was the one driving, I was the one who got behind the wheel of the car and was out of control."

"They pushed you to it, Charley, they have to take most of the blame, the rest of it was an accident."

"Do you really think they saw it that way? I was questioned at the hospital, but never arrested. The investigators could see what happened and put it down as a terrible tragedy. That was how the news reported it too.

"My so-called family never stopped trying to make me take the blame, they called me a murderer and worse. I had to go back to that house, where they blamed me for her death."

"Did they hurt you?" he asks, the rage back.

"I fell down the stairs one time," I say with a mock laugh. "My room was trashed while I was out, a lot of my belongings were burned. Things of my mom's. I'd had my college pulled out from under me, so there was no hope of getting away. I had to do it myself. So one night when they were all out, I grabbed what I could, and I left."

"How did you end up at Elegance?" he asks.

"Mom was a dancer, I used to love watching her and I'd trained for years. Helen tried to get me to stop my lessons, but I never did. I had dreams," I pull away and sit up facing him, drawing the sheet over me.

"They took that away too, because I know they're still trying to find me, so the only way I can dance..."

Callum nods as he understands what I'm getting at. The only way I can dance is in a place where they would never think to come looking. They'd be disgusted if they saw me up on a stage at Elegance. It was the only option I had. I never expected I'd grow to love it there, or that the people around me are some of the nicest I've met...

And then there is Callum, he's facing me, trying to contain the rage rippling under his skin at what they did to me.

"I've managed to get far enough away that I don't think they'll come looking."

"Is that your way of telling me not to give them what they deserve for hurting you?"

"That is me letting you know I got myself out of it. The sacrifices I've made along the way brought me here. And I'm... happy."

"You sound surprised."

"Is dancing at a strip club and sleeping with a member of a motorcycle club normal to most people?"

"Probably not."

"I don't care if people judge me for that. I've been welcomed here without question, no one has tried to hurt me." I scrunch up my nose. "Apart from that one guy." Callum grunts but holds his tongue. "It finally feels like I can slow down, stop running."

Callum shifts under the covers, sitting up the same way I am, except the sheet isn't covering him and I can't help running my eyes over his body, the muscles, tattoos, the light layer of hair on his sculpted chest and the prize resting on his thigh. Makes my mouth water.

"As much as I would happily love to put you on your knees, I don't think that is what needs to happen right now."

I bite my lip and he groans again but pulls the sheet over his lap. My brow arches at him hiding away from me but he is right. I just spilled a lot of traumas. Fucking to take that pain away cheapens what we have.

"For what it's worth," he reaches over and brushes some hair over my shoulder. "I'm glad you showed up here too. And I want you to stay."

I want to ask if he means in Baltimore, or with him but I bite my tongue. My body is drained from telling my story, from remembering all the shit I was put through for years. And memories of Helen on the hood of my car.

"I'm gonna go make us something to eat before your shift." He sits forward and kisses my forehead. "I'll drive you in."

"How will I get back?"

"I'll pick you up," he says and hops off the bed.

"You don't need to baby me."

"What I want to do with you has fuck all to do with babying, Charley."

I watch his taut ass muscles as he steps into some sweatpants, turns to wink at me, then walk out of the bedroom. For a long time, I sit in the center of the bed, the sheet tucked under my arms as I try to imagine my life here, if I choose to stay.

Who am I kidding? The thought of leaving makes me want to tear out my own hair. It is time to stop running, and I can't think of a better place to end up in.

CHAPTER TWENTY TWO

Nashville

BLAZE PULLS UP THE news reports about Helen Barton's death. It was ruled an accident like Charley said. There are pictures of the family in the papers, Charley is standing off to the side in most of them. I glare at the image of her father and wish I could go over there and beat the shit out of him.

He let her down. Charley didn't mention him much, she didn't need to. His lack of action is what caused his daughter to be in that situation.

They were your typical well-to-do, rich family who cared more about reputation than being decent fucking human beings.

Her step-siblings have all gone on to college, the bastards. I take some great pleasure in seeing pictures of Stephen before and after the accident. He has burns all down one side of his neck and arm, his hand doesn't work the way it used to, putting an end to his lacrosse career.

"Lacrosse," I mutter. "Isn't that a girl's game?"

"It's a competitive sport," Blaze says, sees my face and smirks. "But yeah, most self-respecting guys wouldn't be caught dead playing that shit."

He nods. Blaze didn't ask any questions when I showed up at his place wanting him to look these people up for me. Now that I'm sitting here staring at their picture, I raise my eyes to him. He stares back.

"When did he ask you?"

"When she started working at Elegance. We do it for all employees."

"The deep dive."

"Rebel asked me."

Rebel? I thought it would have been Nero.

"He said you got one of the dancers out of the Pembroke House, you seemed pissed off enough that he wanted to know everything he could about her."

"Nosey fucker."

Blaze doesn't bother answering that. It's the way the club works. Even more so now. We can't risk any strangers getting close and turning out to be on Storm's payroll. Chains was bad enough.

"No one ever thought she was into anything she shouldn't be," he assures me.

"Of course she isn't."

"I'm glad I don't drink the water at the clubhouse."

"What the fuck does that mean?"

"You and Nero."

I'm really fucking confused then remember what Nero keeps on saying to me about how he fell for Taylor without expecting or planning it.

"If you think it has anything to do with the water we're drinking, then we need to have a chat about the rules of attraction."

"I'm good."

I hate that he only says what he has carefully thought about saying. He's not the type to have an open conversation with. Not that I need to be talking to him about my feelings for Charley.

Which have only gotten stronger, and harder to ignore after hearing what she went through to get here. Other people have had it harder, and that is bad for them, but this is what *she* went through, her trauma is valid.

Blaze drinks coffee like it's his lifeline. Sometimes I think he's traded in one vice for another but he told me a while ago he only drinks de-caf, he doesn't like plain water or soda, so coffee is his go to. No one ever questions him sitting in bars with a mug in his hand. Not that he frequents them often.

"Any word on the Kivisto's?"

"I have some intel, they're second generation American. They're firmly established in Savonlinna where their family originates. It's bordered with Russia."

"Don't tell me they work with the Russians?" My body tenses up.

"Not found any ties yet, serious at least. Maybe a few deals back before the war. Like most people they seem to steer clear of the Russians."

"Good, we don't want to have to deal with that too."

"Even Storm knows better than to get into bed with the Russians."

"You think he's that clever?"

"He's got to have some brain cells to be able to keep hidden from us."

He means him. Blaze is getting more pissed every day that passes where he hasn't managed to track down Storm.

"They're not big players," he goes on about the Kivisto's. "My guess is Storm is trying to link them up with another player. One we don't know about."

"Well, that's worrying as shit."

"I'm surmising."

"Blaze, you don't surmise. You don't verbalize shit if you don't think there is a legit reason to say it."

"Yeah, well until I know for sure, I'm not spreading it around. Nero will bring it to church when I have more news."

He is saying keep this to myself until Nero is ready to share. As the sergeant-at-arms for the club, he isn't in the wrong for filling me in. Nero won't be pissed at Blaze for that.

"You want me to do anything else with this stuff?" he points to the pictures of the Barton's.

Maybe I can't go there and kick their asses, but I can mess with them. I grin at Blaze and he lets out a heavy sigh.

"Maybe Stephen is about to have a bad run at his finals."

"Maybe," he shakes his head and turns back to his computers.

"Or their bank might make some bad investments for them."

"You gotta keep an eye on your portfolio," Blaze calls over his shoulder. He gets what I'm saying.

Those fuckers deserve it. It's the least I can do for Charley, even if it is more about my own personal satisfaction than her getting her vengeance.

Hitting them where it hurts the most is the best way to deal with bastards like that. I leave his house whistling a happy little tune.

I still have four hours before Charley gets off shift, but I don't mind going and hanging at Elegance to watch her in those tiny little shorts and heels.

Most guys would get pissed at the thought of their woman dressing like that, having men stare at them, not me. Charley is her own woman who knows what she wants.

Having a deeper understanding of her reasons for wanting to dance at Elegance also means I will never ask her to stop.

The dancers at Elegance are treated well and always protected. People can look, but anyone who dares to touch I will personally shoot their dick off.

My woman. Sounds weird to think that, but it isn't freaking me out anymore. The problem is, I don't know if she will react the same.

Fury calls as I'm about leave and asks if I want to go to the Battleground with him. Stryker isn't fighting, but another brother is, so it gives us a reason to be there. What the hell, I have some time, so tell him I'll meet him there.

The Battleground isn't too far from the clubhouse by Penn Mary Yard, the large rail yard that has warehouses all around. It's a protected set up but is classed as neutral ground between any factions within the city. People who like to watch and take part in fights go there knowing if there is any trouble, they'll end up under the old rail lines.

Stryker is with Fury when I arrive and I greet them with a chin dip.

"Opponent next week is fighting tonight," Stryker confirms his presence.

"Excellent opportunity to observe then," I slap his shoulder. Not many people can get away with that. I'm not worried.

We head inside. It's busy because it's a Saturday night, and from the board there are a lot of fights on the roster. Stryker knows his way around so we follow him to the heavyweight rings. Fury heads to the bar to grab us some beers and I stand beside Stryker and watch the two men in the ring beating the shit out of each other.

It's bare knuckle, violent and bloody. I've watched a few fights in my time but never really enjoyed it as a sport. Stryker has yet to be beaten in any weight class.

Nero said a while back that scouts on the professional circuit have tried to entice him away but Stryker is the furthest thing from corporate you can get. He'd never let any big agent or sponsor tell him what to do.

He also does this for a reason. It's not out of enjoyment for the sport either. If he isn't breaking faces for the club, he uses this as an outlet for whatever rage he is holding under his skin.

"That the guy?" I ask, pointing at the man walking around the ring holding his arms up. He hasn't won yet, he's just showboating.

Stryker nods. "He's from out of town."

"What a fucking dick," I say, watching him bob back and forth, shadow boxing while his opponent is given a medical assessment.

"Sometimes cockiness isn't just for show," Stryker says. "Sometimes its to hide a deeper issue."

"Which one is it?"

"I think he is dangerous."

"You scared he'll take you?" I quip.

His dark eyes turn to me, and I hold up my hands.

"I'm not invincible," he says, looking back at the fighter.

I'm about to tell him I never expected to hear him say shit like that but he beats me to it.

"I can kick his ass."

My laughter draws attention to us and Stryker scowls at me. People are suddenly more interested in him than the fight. Before anyone can approach him, Stryker turns and vanishes into the crowd. Even I lose sight of him in less than five seconds.

The asshole in the ring was watching too, but he's drawn back into the round and before the three minutes are up, he's KO'd his opponent. He looks around to see if Stryker is anywhere to be seen but he's long gone.

Fury comes over with a bottle of beer for me and him, guess he knew Stryker would disappear.

"Seen anything?" he asks.

"Just this dickhead," I lift my chin at the fighter who just did a back flip in the ring.

Fury pulls a face, but he too laughs when I say it's Stryker's next fight.

A couple of people approach us as we move around, mostly just greeting us, or checking in because we're wearing our cuts. One guy starts asking about Stryker, but I reckon he's already left. He saw what he needed to, and didn't want any further attention.

We make another circuit, convinced there is nothing happening when Fury pauses, peering up at one of the balconies. There is a man leaning over watching one of the women's fights beneath him. I have to squint but finally see what Fury has.

After setting our drinks down we separate and circle around to the metal staircases on opposite sides of the room, giving him no way to get down if he sees one of us first. I text Stryker on the off-chance he hasn't left and give a grin and a wink to a woman who tries to stop me because we need to get to this guy at the same time.

Fury does manage to get to him first and as soon as Venom sees him, he turns to hurry away but walks right into my fist straight into his stomach. Fury grabs the back of his shirt to hold him upright so people around can't see what is going on. We get on either side of him and walk towards the back wall, chatting to one another about nothing to further disguise what is happening.

"What is this about? I haven't done anything to the Disciples," Venom says, looking from me to Fury, now that he has his breath back.

"Shut up," I tell him.

There are large columns up to the ceiling that hide us from everyone. Once we're out of sight, Fury grabs him by the throat and pushes him back against the wall. I make sure no one is watching.

"We think you might know something we want to know," Fury says, squeezing his throat.

He claws at his hands. "No, I don't know anything."

"Where is your boyfriend?" Fury snarls at him.

"Fuck you," he spits and gets a fist to the kidney for his trouble.

"Come on, are you saying you don't know where the guy you're fucking is?"

"I'm not fucking anyone, let alone a guy," he snaps.

"We have pictures that say otherwise," I lean in closer.

Venom glares at me.

"We can send them to your boss if it makes this any easier for you."

"Fuck you," he repeats, this time with less effort. "And I don't know where he is. I haven't seen him since we... since things stopped."

"Aw, he didn't want your cock anymore?"

"Shut the fuck up," he says, even more dejected.

Now that I know what it's like to have someone you care for, it's obvious what is going on here. But I have no fucks to give about how this guy feels. The man he's fucking, or was, is one of Storm's friends.

"Leave him out of this. Whatever shit is going on with Storm, he has nothing to do with it."

"What makes you think there is shit going on with Storm?" I ask, all casual as Fury holds him so tight he can't barely move.

"Because there is always shit going on with Storm," he grits out. "Jake hasn't seen him in months and doesn't want anything to do with him, he's getting out of the life."

"Is that why he's walked away from you?"

His eyes lower and I kind of feel bad for him.

"Where is he?"

"I don't know. He left town."

Fury and I exchange a look. Does that mean he's gone to Romney too? We question him for a little longer and Fury gives him enough punches to know he's telling us all he knows. He gives him one last punch to the jaw, and he slumps to the floor.

That was a waste of time but we at least have something to give to Razer, to be on the look out for someone else in Romney.

"What do you want to do?" Fury asks as we head back downstairs. If anything the place is busier.

"I'm going to Elegance," I say, watching everyone around us.

"Might as well come along," he shrugs, he takes out his phone to text Razer.

Outside Stryker is standing by the bikes talking on the phone. He looks up when he sees us coming and instantly my hackles go up. He is rounding to the side of his bike as he hangs up.

"Elegance. Now."

He doesn't have to say anything else. The last time I jumped on my bike and raced somewhere was to Nero's house. Storm and his men were going for Nero's son.

All I can see in my head is Charley sitting on my bed, looking at me as she tells me all of her truths, smiling at my promise to always keep her safe.

I've never got on my bike so goddamn fast in my life.

Chapter Twenty Three

Charley

Being back on wait staff duty is not what I was expecting, but that is where I find myself while the others are up dancing or doing whatever else in the back rooms. I've avoided being questioned by anyone about Callum by staying out of the dressing room. Lily keeps trying to get my attention, but I have avoided her as well.

I'm not mad, especially given what happened between me and Callum and he told me he didn't speak to her much, just grabbed my things and left. I just want her to stew a little because she gave me up way too easy. In all likelihood it won't be long before we're talking again.

I meant what I said to Callum, it feels like I've found the place where I'm supposed to be, where I can be happy.

It's Saturday night, and after the unexpected closure of the club yesterday, we're at capacity tonight so I'm run off my feet.

Ellie has been walking the floor talking to people and making sure everyone has what they need. I notice her talking to a couple of men in suits who remind me of the asshole who tried to assault me at the private party.

It amazes me how she handles people, when one of them puts his hand on her lower back, two of his fingers grazing down between the crack of her ass. She bats her lashes and laughs at whatever they're saying while twisting herself away, but taking hold of his other hand so he doesn't feel rejected.

"She's a master at the art of get the fuck off me." A voice says from behind me.

My guard immediately goes up but when I see the cut, I relax. Marginally. He's eyeing me in much the same way the suited guy was to Ellie.

"I've been watching you," he says, leaning one elbow against the bar where I'm waiting to collect a drink order.

"Did you need to order a drink?" I ask, not looking at him.

"Not like that sweetheart," he leans forward to get my attention on him.

I give him a cursory look and a small smile then turn back to Max loading drinks onto my tray. He drops a couple of straws into the tall glasses and looks at the man. He can't say anything because Max is an employee, and this guy is in the Disciples.

"It's really busy, I have to get these drinks out, can I catch you later?"

He looks disappointed, but he nods and I lift the tray and walk away. It's heavier than normal but I've got this down to a fine art now and move like a pro through the tables, delivering drinks to booths in my section.

Lily is on the stage when I set down my last drink and I glance up at her. She winks as she turns around and looks over her shoulder at me, wiggling her ass. It makes me laugh and I take one of my twenty-dollar tips out of my apron and slot the bill under the waist of her G-string, making her laugh too.

"That was hot," the guy at the table next to me says. "Why aren't you up there?"

"Who would bring your drinks if I was up there," I smile and walk away before he starts any more conversation.

I glance around my area to see if anyone is waiting for a drink and notice Ellie with that same man from before. He's standing quite close to her and I'm about to turn away because Ellie is good at getting rid of men but he pulls her into him.

Ellie's back arches in a way that makes me think something must have bashed into her stomach. The guy must be drunk. Looking around, I spot Walker and wave a hand to get his attention, but he doesn't see me. When I glance back, the man is helping Ellie into an empty booth.

Shit, is she sick? I start towards them as the man backs up, and that is when I see what is in his hand. At first it looks like a trick of the light but I got used to carrying a knife when I lived at that house. I watch in horror as he slams it into her again.

I scream as loud as I can, startling the people around me, and the man looks over at me.

I don't think, I just react and throw my tray at his head. I'm close enough that the impact is hard, and he stumbles backward, grabbing onto whatever he can to stop himself hitting the ground.

Grabbing a bottle of beer off the nearest table I run at the man and swing it at him, clipping his chin. He thrusts the knife toward me and I use the bottle again, slamming it down on his arm. His fingers open and he drops it, yelling out in pain. Before I can hit him again, he turns and runs away.

The commotion has finally got the attention of Walker and some of the other bouncers and people are hurrying over. Leo reaches me first.

"That man, he attacked Ellie, grab him!"

"What? I just watched you assault a customer."

"Walker!" I scream, frustrated at Leo for not listening. "Grab him!" I point at the fleeing man.

Walker doesn't question me the way this other asshole is and I elbow my way past Leo, falling to my knees at the booth where Ellie is now slumped to the side. Her eyes open as I touch her.

"Ellie," I reach for her trying to pull her up. "Are you okay?"

"He..." her hands drop to her waist and when the red lights above flash blue I can see the blood.

"Call 911!" I scream at Leo, who is finally fucking realizing something is wrong.

I jump up and tug the cloth off the table, bottles and glasses flying everywhere, then press it to her waist.

"You're going to be okay, I promise," I tell her. "Try not to move okay. An ambulance is coming."

Behind me I can hear Leo calling for help. People still don't know what is happening but the girls on the stage have all stopped dancing and are looking over at me. The men who work here are running around, starting to clear people away.

"Charley," Lily comes up behind me, takes one look at Ellie and her mouth drops open.

"Don't panic," I tell her. "Move that chair, help me keep her upright, push here." I take her hands and press them down on the cloth over Ellie's wounds.

Everything I say, she does and the other girls come over and form a barricade around Ellie. She might be hard and aloof but she loves this club, and she loves the dancers. She would fight to the ends of the earth for any one of us.

The girls get the table out of the way and I move around to Ellie's side and sit down, taking her hand, and helping Lily keep the cloth in place to try to stop the bleeding.

"Stay with me Ellie, okay, open your eyes."

Her lids flutter but the pain is clear all over her face. She tilts her head toward me and opens her eyes, trying to speak.

"Don't talk," I tell her, putting my arm around her and holding her tight.

"Have... to," she whispers, a groan following.

Even with stab wounds she is being stoic. She is one of the strongest people I've ever met in my life. Her elbow nudges my side as she tries to lift her arm. There is a card between her fingers. It's covered in blood. I'll worry about it later, but she pushes it at me.

"Tell Beast... tell him... it's about storm."

"Storm? What storm? Ellie, please don't talk."

Two men run up and move the dancers out of the way. One has a first aid bag, but they're not paramedics. The lights go up and I notice the club has been cleared of everyone but staff and members of the MC.

Lily backs up and lets one of the men kneel down by Ellie. I lift the tablecloth, and she cries out as he touches her.

"Be careful!" I yell at him.

"I need to find the wound," he says, not in the least bit concerned about me shouting at him.

Ellie winces and I stroke her hair, squeezing her hand. A tear squeezes from one eye and runs down her perfectly made up cheek.

"Ellie, you can't let this asshole beat you," I tell her. "Fuck him for thinking he can take you down. You're not going to let him do this. You fight. Okay, you fight, don't stop fighting, promise me."

"You think... I'm going to... let that loser..." she closes her eyes.

"Ellie," I turn and touch her face as the man cuts her dress. There is blood everywhere. It takes great effort not to show the horror on my face.

"Paramedics are here."

"Walker," I look up at him, my nose and eyes are burning as I fight tears.

"She's gonna be fine," he assures me, then turns to clear the way for the paramedics.

They take over and ask me to move.

A roar from behind me makes me jump and I turn to see Beast storming across the room. Walker jumps in the way to hold him back so the medics can get Ellie on the stretcher and get her out to the ambulance.

"Let them do their job."

"Get the fuck off me!"

"Beast, fucking calm down."

"Who the fuck did this?" he screams.

That's when I remember the card in my hand. I walk over and grab Walker's arm. He moves back as if he is about to tell whoever it is to fuck off but he frowns when he sees me. Beast's eyes are wild, I can finally see what Callum means when he says he lives up to his name when he has to.

"Beast."

He turns to me and looks down at my clothes, his eyes full of horror. I'm covered in Ellie's blood so I get why but I don't have time to worry about it.

"No offence Charley but you need to get out of the way."

"I saw him."

He pauses and looks at me again. Walker explains that it was me who raised the alarm and that I'd interacted with the guy. Beast shoves Walker off and steps right up close to me. If I didn't know him, or if I hadn't seen him with Ellie, I'd be terrified of the way he is looking at me.

"What did he say to you?"

Looking around, I see everyone is watching, all of them looking shocked, scared or angry.

"Clear them out," Beast says to Walker, then holds out his hand to me. He starts walking to the exit, following after the medics who are rushing out to the waiting ambulance. "What did he say?"

"He didn't say anything, but I saw him... stab her. I tried to stop him but he ran."

He winces when I say *stab* but he doesn't lose the intensity in his eyes. We walk out into the dark night, punctuated by the red and blue flashes of the ambulance.

"He gave her this," I hold out the card. Beast takes it and turns it over. It's hard to read the writing, so he pockets it and goes to walk away but I grab his arm. "She told me something."

"What?" he takes my arm, squeezing tighter than he needs to but I don't try to pull free.

"She said there was a storm, or it had to do with the storm."

His face changes immediately, his whole body goes tense. I have no idea what is going on but whatever the message Ellie was trying to give him, has made his whole body lock up and his eyes go cold. He turns to the ambulance and looks torn. Before they can close the doors, he pulls me over to them.

"She goes with her," he tells the man who has just loaded her into the back and he looks down at me. "Stay with her, Charley. There will be men following and they'll meet you there. Only men in Disciples cuts get near her. Keep her..." he chokes up then sucks in a breath. "Don't leave her alone."

He doesn't mean he wants me there to protect her. He means she needs someone there that she knows, someone that can give her comfort. I haven't been around here long and am sure one of the other girls would be better to go along but Beast doesn't hesitate to guide me nearer. I glance down at my outfit, the paramedic is staring too, wide-eyed.

"Get her a coat," Beast snarls at him.

The man opens a cupboard in the ambulance and hands over a padded red jacket that says BCFD on the back and sleeves. I'm grateful for it, it's cold out here. Not that it does much to cover my legs, but it helps with my top half which is only covered by the apron, I haven't bothered with the nipple covers since I did the dance with the other girls.

Beast helps me into the ambulance and glares at the paramedic.

"Do not let her die," he threatens.

Fair play to the guy, he doesn't make any promises that he can't keep which only worries me more. Beast steps back and slams the door, shutting us inside.

I stay out of the way as the man gets back to doing what he can to stabilize Ellie. I notice her eyes are open and she blinks at me. An oxygen mask covers the lower half of her face.

"You're going to be okay Ellie," I reach over and touch her shoulder.

It takes a little over five minutes to get to the hospital and I hang back when they pull her out and wheel her through the ER doors.

The rumble of bikes alerts me to the Disciples arriving. No one can stop them going inside, ushering me along with them. They form a barrier around the bay where Ellie is taken, not getting in the way of the doctors, but not allowing anyone else to get near her either.

Almost immediately they come out saying she needs to be taken to surgery. One of the men talks to a nurse and after Ellie has been wheeled out, we follow along, one man going with them after some low and persistent conversation.

Another nurse takes us to a waiting area where we're left. The third man who went with Ellie arrives a few minutes later and says she has gone into theater, where he can't follow.

And now we wait. They don't introduce themselves to me but one of them gets me a coffee, while another produces a blanket to wrap around my legs. My phone is still in my bag in the dressing room at Elegance so I have no way of getting in touch with anyone.

My mind is on Callum. I'm sure he knows what has happened by now, I just don't know if the man in charge of his club is going to let him come here, or they're going to be looking for the man who hurt Ellie.

Chapter Twenty Four

Nashville

When we first arrive at Elegance, everyone is in panic mode. Nero is climbing off his bike as Fury and I get to the door and we stop to wait for him.

"What happened?" Fury asks.

"Ellie's hurt. Not sure how bad, she's on her way to the hospital."

He walks into the club and we follow. There are a few people still here but they're all related to the MC. Over in the corner the dancers are huddled together but the one person I want to see isn't among them.

Nero walks through the room without looking at anyone and heads for the security room. I don't see Charley when we get inside.

Beast is in there with Walker and a couple of other brothers, all of them staring at one particular screen. All I want is to go find her, but until I know what we're dealing with, I have to stay here. Nero would have told me if Charley was hurt.

Beast points at the screen as we come to a stop beside him.

"Freeze it there," he snaps. Blaze does as he's told and looks up at the screen.

My jaw tenses as I figure out what I'm looking at. A man is standing with Ellie, her mouth is hanging open, her back bent forward, the man looks like he's hugging her. His face is clear in the shot and as we stare, Blaze gets out a laptop and starts transferring the images.

"Is she alright?" I ask.

"Don't know," Beast snaps.

"How bad is it?"

"I said I don't fucking know," Beast snaps at Nero. He closes his eyes for a second when he realizes who he just yelled at, but Nero doesn't say anything. "She's alive. For now."

Nero nods. There is nothing we can do for Ellie, but we can figure out who the fuck this guy is and why he went after her.

"How the fuck did he get a knife past security?" Fury comes into the room and looks at the screen.

"Play it," Nero says. "From the start."

Beast takes a few steps back and folds his arms across his expansive chest. He never takes his eyes off the screen. For a moment I watch him, but I need to see what happened too.

I'm not sure how deep he is in with Ellie, or if what Charley and I witnessed was a one-off ,but from his reaction, this is hitting him hard. He's really scared for her.

My attention is caught on the blonde hair and sleek back of the woman I'm worried about as she walks on to the screen, moving through the tables carrying a tray. She stops at a booth just out of shot of the camera. This is about watching Ellie, not Charley.

We all stand still and watch what looks like the man hugging her and helping her into a seat but the knife is plain as fucking day before he has a chance to put it away.

"Fuck," Nero curses under his breath as Ellie slumps into the chair.

He is about to say something else when a tray comes sailing out of shot and hits the man right in the side of his head almost knocking him on his ass. He grabs his head and stumbles just as a little spitfire brandishing a bottle comes running onto the screen.

I stare wide-eyed as Charley launches herself at the man hitting him with the bottle enough that he drops the knife and runs away. It's clear she is caught in two minds about what to do but I'm pretty fucking pleased to see she signals someone then runs to Ellie and does not chase the madman.

"Did she just throw her tray at his head?"

"Yeah," Fury answers Stryker's question. Despite the situation there is a hint of amusement in his voice. "Managed to disarm him too."

Nero casts a look at me, then goes back to the tape. We all watch as Charley helps Ellie, Walker coming into the shot, then the dancers show up and start moving things, gathering around Ellie, doing what they can to help.

"There, that's when she does it." Beast points.

We all see Ellie passing Charley something. My heart starts pounding. Did Charley withhold something?

"I don't know how she got it, but Ellie somehow managed to get this off the asshole." He holds out a bloody card. Nero takes it carefully and flips it over. "Blaze is working on the number."

"Getting this facial recognition sorted first," he says, not looking up from his laptop.

"She also told Charley it was about a storm."

We all look at Beast. I'm not sure if any of us are really surprised but we're all really fucking pissed.

"Those were the words she used?" Nero asks.

"Charley didn't know what she meant, but it's pretty fucking clear to us."

Ellie knows what is going on with Storm because she has been helping Nero try to find him. I watch my president as everyone talks around us. His head is lost deep in thought. He cares about Ellie, we all do but he's slept with her more than a few times, before Taylor came into the picture.

We all have a soft spot for her. She is as loyal to the club as any brother.

"Where is Charley?" Nero asks.

"She went to the hospital with Ellie. I sent three guys with them and told them not to let either one of them out of their sight."

She's not even here? Fucking hell. I pace back and forth until Nero gives me a look. If it was Taylor, he'd want to leave too but he wouldn't, and he expects that I will be the same. We know she's okay, she's safe, but that isn't helping right now.

"Got it," Blaze leans back in his chair. Nero bends down to look at the laptop screen. "Timo Kivisto. He flew into Baltimore last night, got a reservation at the Woodland under one of his aliases."

I'm not surprised Blaze knows as much as he does already, since we walked in he's been sat there working on his laptop.

"I want men there, now. Fury, Stryker."

Fury heads out without question, Stryker has a dark look on his face that would scare the ever living shit out of even the hardest of men as he nods and follows.

"What the fuck is going on?" Nero turns and looks at us. None of us answer, because none of us can. "They're going after our people. Not the club, not the ones that can protect themselves. Innocent people."

Rebel comes into the room and sees what we're all looking at. "Fucking knife is ceramic. That's how he got it past the metal wands. Who is he?"

"A Kivisto. Working for Storm."

"Fucking hell," he snarls. "We need to get a handle on this shit."

"You think I don't know that?" Nero turns on Rebel. "You think I'm happy about this shit? That Storm is coming at us from every direction and angle and we can't figure out where the fuck he is?"

Rebel doesn't answer him. That is the most animated I've seen Nero since the night we stormed his house to protect his family. He doesn't usually get rattled easily, but he's right. There are too many variables. It's like Storm has contacted every bad person he can find to send after us. It makes no sense.

"We find this guy and we bring him in. Blaze keep looking into these guys I want to know everything about them. Beast, Elegance is shut down for now until we know what we're dealing with. Make sure the girls get home and reassure them they're still getting paid. Once we're done, we go the hospital."

"Everyone?" Rebel asks.

"Ellie is one of us," Nero says. "Anyone not doing something to track down these assholes goes to the hospital. Until we know she is out of the woods, we stand by her."

"I'll stay here, keep working on this," Blaze says.

We leave him and head outside. I go with Beast to talk with the dancers. Some of the brothers, Walker and Leo will see them all home. Except Lily, I call her over.

"Is Ellie okay?" she asks straight away.

"Not sure. I need Charley's things."

"I'm coming with you."

"Not happening."

She looks like she is about to lose her shit, her fists clenching.

"Charley might be with you, and you may think you're the only thing she needs right now, but Nashville, she is my friend and so is Ellie. I want to be there for them, both of them. Please." She adds on.

Maybe she's right. "Fine, get her things, you have a car?" She nods. "I'll follow you."

Lily runs off to the dressing room to get Charley's clothes and I let Beast know what's going on. For a brief moment I think about asking how he is but his expression tells me not to even try. He doesn't know I saw him and Ellie together.

Once Lily is back Beast goes out front to let them know I'll be escorting Lily and we all set off to the hospital. People watch us, staring open-mouthed or backing up as we enter the hospital but that is nothing new, it happens wherever we go. None of us give a shit about it as we get on the elevator.

Lily stands right at the front by the doors, not in least perturbed about being surrounded by bikers. When the elevator doors open, we step straight out into a waiting area. Rebel goes ahead to talk to the nurse at the station who looked up as we all walked out. Lily is heading for the people sitting in the small alcove but I move faster.

My vision has tunneled onto the one person I needed to see more than anything. The relief that floods me at seeing she is safe almost makes my knees buckle. I knew she was, everyone said she was fine, I've even watched the replay of the videos on the security cameras at Elegance but nothing compares to having her in my arms, seeing for myself that she is safe and unhurt.

I don't give a shit about anything else, or what people are going to say or even think, I scoop her up and Charley wraps her legs around me as I walk away from everyone into the first empty room I see, and kick the door closed behind me.

"Callum, I'm okay," she says, stroking her fingers through the back of my hair.

I stop her from saying anything more by covering her mouth with mine. After a few seconds of hesitation, probably thinking this is not the time or place for this, she kisses me back, lifting up by pushing her hips against me and gripping the back of my neck tighter.

Until this very moment, I haven't been able to relax. The rest of the shit can be worried about later, all that matters now is the woman in my arms.

I set her down on a counter by the window but don't back up. She's wearing a big red coat that looks as if it belongs to a firefighter which pisses me off, and I open it to get her out of it, thinking I should have brought the bag off Lily but I pause when I look down.

She is wearing the tiny little apron and shorts that she wears at Elegance and my blood boils at the thought of her being out there like that in front of my brothers and all those strangers.

All of that rage dampens when I see the blood. Ellie's blood. She has sat here this whole time with blood drying on her. Most of it is on the clothes but her hands have crusts of dried blood on them.

There is a bathroom beside me, so I grab what I need, then come back and help her out of the coat and clean her off, the whole time Charley is silent watching me. Once I've done the best I can with the paper towels, I take off my cut and unbutton the shirt I'm wearing over a T-shirt.

No one can see her here, but I stand in front of her shielding her in case anyone comes in, as I untie the apron at her neck and peel it down. It's natural instinct to look down at her bare tits, at how her nipples pebble in the chilly air. She wraps her arms around me again when I pull her against me, stroking my fingertips up and down her spine.

"Fuck, Charley," I press my forehead against hers. "I'm mad at you."

"Why?" she tries to pull back but I grip her neck to keep her there.

"You tried to fight him."

"He hurt Ellie."

"I don't care."

"If you think I was going to stand there and watch-"

I cut her off again with another kiss, because she is right, Charley did just enough to make that asshole back off, God knows what else he would have done if she hadn't.

Chapter Twenty Five

Nashville

She's here, she's safe, she's in my arms and I can't go another fucking second without telling her how I feel, except Charley isn't giving me the chance, she is clawing at me, pulling on my shoulders and gripping me tight to her with her thighs.

Her breasts are rubbing against the thin fabric of my T-shirt which she clearly doesn't like because she rips it over my head. Whatever she needs to make her feel safe, to know that she has me and I will always be here for her, then I'm going to give it.

I shift backwards and grab her shorts, taking them off and I throw them on the floor as she opens my jeans and takes out my very hard cock.

"Callum," she whispers.

"I'm here," I take her cheek in my hand and hold my cock with the other, guiding it inside of her. "I'll always be here," I kiss her again as I push all the way inside.

Our bodies move together like we were made to be joined. I swallow all of her little gasps and moans as I give her what she needs, letting her know she got through this horrible thing.

"I'm never going to let you go, Charley," I grip her chin and make sure she is looking at me. "You mean too much to me. I was scared shitless when I thought you were hurt. I can't feel like that again. Not without letting you know what this means to me."

She arches her back, clamping down tight on me and I groan but I have to tell her.

"Fuck Charley. I've never loved anyone before, but I know," I groan again and thrust deeper. "I know with you, you're the only woman I want."

"Callum," she moans again and pushes against me, rolling her hips back and forth.

Between us, I watch my cock going in and out of her and grit my teeth against the need to fill her. She cries out when I cup her ass cheeks and pull her hard against me, pumping into her. Her mouth drops open, and she lets out another cry, which I smother again so no one can hear as my girl comes all over my cock.

Charley is panting and gasping as I keep thrusting in and out, chasing my own release. It doesn't take long before I'm filling her up and I clutch her to me by the back of her neck and her lower spine. Her head lolls to the side as I kiss her throat, lightly sucking on her perfect skin.

This is probably very wrong given where we are, and what is going on, but Charley needed it. Not the sex. The closeness, the knowledge that even though something awful has happened, she is alive, here with me.

She lets me kiss her all over her neck and throat, then palms my cheek and pulls me up so she can kiss me, long and deep. It's a life altering kiss, which I will never recover from, this woman owns me.

It'll fucking kill me if she walks away from me again, even if the last time was only a few hours and I dragged her ass back, that feeling of her being gone slayed me.

"Do you mean it?"

"Yeah," I grin. "I didn't say it very well."

"You said it perfectly," she smiles back at me. "You said it like only you could."

"Like an ass," I laugh but she frowns so I straighten my face and be serious about it, because this is what I want, and I never say anything I don't mean. "I will never stop showing you that you belong here with me."

Her eyes soften as she leans back and stares at me. "I want that too," she whispers, then frowns at her words, as if they're not enough.

I'm about to tell her that is good enough, but she says the words that make my heart soar with more conviction. She leans in and brushes her lips against mine, the gentlest of touches but it holds so much promise. This woman will bring me to my knees, I can already see it and I'll gratefully go there if she agrees to be mine.

"I love you too, Callum."

Her little smile has me wanting to throw my head back and scream at the fucking ceiling but I finally remember where we are and why, and having her sitting here naked is not the greatest of ideas.

There is just one more thing I want to say and this might not be the right time either but I can't go another minute without her knowing.

"I know you don't know how things work in motorcycle clubs. This is one of the things I don't know much about either. What I do know, with you I want to try. I can't imagine you not being in my life Charley."

"What are you saying?"

"I want you to be my old lady."

Her eyes widen. Guess she knows what that means.

"It's a little more than a girlfriend, not quite a wife but either way, it means you're mine. And I'm yours."

Her throat works as she swallows and we stare at one another. "You really want me?"

"I want every single fucking part of you Charley. No matter what you think you've done, no matter what happened in the past, none of that matters. You're the only thing that matters."

Charley leans forward and wraps her arms around me. Her words are a whisper by my ear. "I never thought anyone would want me like this."

"No one else gets to want you like this. Or have you. This," I lean back and look at her. "Is real. I fucking love you and I might sound like an asshole but I'm not letting you go," I grin at her and she laughs.

"Well," she tilts her head. "I'm okay with that."

"Good. Now get down and put some clothes on before I do something reckless like bend you over."

"This is really bad of us."

"No," I stroke her cheek. "You needed this. After what you just went through, it's perfectly normal to reach out for human touch, Charley.

Maybe the kind I gave you was inappropriate for the location," I duck my head. "I will always give you what you need. Mind, body and soul. And jokes, and kisses and all the good shit."

"Okay," she pushes me back and hops down off the counter, looking around at the discarded Elegance uniform. "We need to check on Ellie," she bites her lip.

Charley lets me help her into my shirt and I button it up for her, then grab her shorts and panties to throw in the garbage.

"Stay here," I tell her. "Lily has your clothes." She grips my arm before I turn. "What?"

"You've made this place my home, Callum. You've made me want to stop running."

"I'll spend the rest of my life making sure you always feel that way," I smirk and lean in to kiss her. "I'll be back."

A few of the men look up when I walk over. Nero checks behind me to see I'm alone and arches a brow but doesn't say anything. Lily stands and looks between me and Nero, she is holding Charley's bag. When I ask her to take the clothes to her, she hurries away.

I turn back to my brothers. The whole council isn't here but I don't care.

Nero is staring at me, to most people he's unreadable but I've known him a long time, he understands what this moment is. I indicate for the ranked members to step away from the other brothers, which they do without question.

"I know it's meant to be discussed and agreed by everyone," I tell them. "But I'm telling you all right here, right now, she is mine."

"Who?" Rebel asks.

"Fuck off," I glare even, though he was taking the piss out of me. "I want Charley to be my old lady."

"You know the council votes unanimously on that," Nero tells me.

"Like we did when you claimed Taylor," Rebel scoffs.

"Yeah well, that was different," Nero shrugs. "Plus I'm President, I don't ask permission."

"By that logic neither does Nashville," Rebel says. "Does that mean we start breaking all the rules?"

"It's not like this is something we're used to," Beast says, for a moment not lost in his own head over Ellie. "Until Taylor."

He's right. When Nero took over, he appointed a whole new council to work alongside him. None of us had an old lady or expressed any interest in getting one.

"That's true," Rebel agrees. "Still, it's protocol."

"Fuck protocol," I keep my eyes on Nero. "She stepped up for the club tonight, Nero. She put herself in danger to protect Ellie."

He glances toward the door where Charley is, then looks around at us all. "We can vote here and get the others approval after," he says.

"Fine by me," Rebel says. "If it's what you want," he looks to me and I nod.

"Be careful with her," Beast tells me. "Ellie thinks she's special." He swallows hard. "I'm good with it too."

I dip my chin in thanks and look at Nero.

"Told you." He says it with a smirk. "Make sure she knows how things work."

"She already does," I reassure him.

He looks over my shoulder and I turn around to see Charley and Lily coming back into the waiting room. She is wearing her own clothes but still has my shirt on over her top. Nero walks over to her, and she looks at him without any fear, making my heart swell.

"You protected the club tonight, Charley," Nero says to her.

"I had to stop him hurting Ellie." She says it like she doesn't want any praise for what she did.

Charley looks at me with a question in her eyes.

"You're staying right here, where I can see you," I tell her.

"I was going to anyway," she says. "I want to be here when Ellie wakes up."

"Me too," Lily says.

Nero eyes the two women in turn and I see the smile he's trying to hide.

I kiss Charley's temple. "Why don't you both go sit down, I'll see if I can find you some coffee."

While the women go sit down, I hand over a bunch of cash to Wheeler to get drinks. We could all do with it, given Ellie is in surgery for God knows how long.

Nero has taken a call but hangs up when I go back over.

"I've just called Jesse to get Taylor and Oscar to his place." Jesse lives in a penthouse at the top of one of the most expensive and secure buildings in the city. "With a Kivisto in Baltimore I want everyone safe," he glances at Charley, he knows why I'm keeping her close. "I'm even considering a lockdown," he adds as Rebel comes over.

"You think it's that bad?" Rebel asks.

"I think too many of what Storm sees as our weaknesses are getting hurt."

He's right and now I'm even more concerned.

"Lockdown is a big call," Rebel says, rubbing his chin.

"And one I will not make lightly," Nero tells him. "The last thing I want is Storm thinking he has us on the back foot. Risking our families isn't an option."

"Raven will tell me to eat a bag of dicks if I try to make her hide," Rebel grunts out.

"Raven will fall in line if she has to," Nero says, an amused half smile on his lips despite the seriousness of the conversation.

"You can be the one to tell her then."

Raven will listen to him over her brother, even if she doesn't like it.

"I've told Fury and Stryker to take him to the warehouse when they find him," Nero says. "It doesn't take all of us to question him. I'm going to call Razer, I want the council all here for this. Nashville, sort out some guys to go down there and take his place, people Storm won't recognize. I don't like all these new players coming out of the woodwork. We need to find out everything we can and fast."

I move away to make the calls, keeping an eye on Charley the whole time. She has a coffee and is chatting with Lily, both of them looking anxious but now and then she seeks me out and that anxiety lessens just a little when our eyes meet.

Nero is right about the people we care about being targets. It might not have been as obvious with Sheridan because she was never a major part of Nero's life, but their son is. And Storm knows how important Ellie is to the Disciples and the things she has done for the club. She can get even the strongest of men to break down and feed her information and has done numerous times in the past.

It's worrying that Storm made a play to take her out of things. We have at least one advantage now. This Kivisto guy was not meant to be seen.

The way he attacked Ellie, his plan was that she was supposed to be found after he got out.

It was only that Charley saw him and stopped him part way through that we know someone from their family is in Baltimore.

I was scared as fuck when I saw her go after him in that video but looking at her now, I see the strength in her.

She is so fucking scared of what happened with her family she doesn't realize how strong she is. I'm going to make sure that is all she sees from now on.

We finally have something that Storm is not aware we know. We have to figure out how to make this turn to our advantage. I'm not sure how, but finding the bastard who tried to kill Ellie is our first move.

Beast is leaning against the wall staring at nothing. Grabbing two coffees I go over and stand beside him, handing one to him. He takes it but doesn't say anything.

"She's gonna pull through."

He's quiet for a long time, then looks at me. "You didn't see what he did to her."

"Ellie won't go out like this, Derek."

He shakes his head slowly, not that he is disagreeing, He's just finding it hard to believe.

"You and Charley," he says after a while and a few sips of the coffee. "Should have seen that coming."

"Yeah? How's that?"

"You couldn't take your eyes off her. Every time she smashed the shit out of more of my glassware and expensive champagne bottles, you didn't think it was amusing or get angry, you thought it was fucking endearing."

"I thought I had a better poker face than that."

"Women can make us stupid, Callum. Showing that you care is what can get them hurt."

Well, if that isn't a telling fucking statement, and not about me and Charley. I don't agree with him. I don't think we should sacrifice our happiness and be afraid of what might happen, when we can be happy and be there and protect them.

"No, they make us stronger. When you find the right one."

"Now you sound like Nero," he scoffs, but he looks away.

If I was going to bring it up, now would probably be the time, but it's not my business to step into whatever is going on between him and Ellie.

As long as Ellie does what we all need her to do. And I'm really beginning to worry that hoping and praying is not going to get her through this.

I slap Beast's shoulder then head over to Charley and sit down. She reaches for my hand. Beast really is wrong. Nothing could make me feel stronger than having this woman at my side.

I just hope he gets the chance to experience it too.

EPILOGUE

Rebel

THE DOOR SLAMS BEHIND me as I walk into the clubhouse. Nero is gonna give me shit because I'm not sticking to his plan, but what fucking good am I standing around in a hospital waiting room. He has Beast and Nashville there, as well as three other brothers and the two strippers from the club.

I don't think Ellie will give one shit either way if I'm there or not. Especially given she is in surgery for God knows how long anyway. We could all up and leave, and she wouldn't know.

Ellie is great, she does good work for the club, not just running Elegance, our strip club, but she does side work for us too. We've never been close, I don't know her like some of the other guys do.

My cell rings as I head to a small back room where we keep an armory in case we need something close in an emergency. Only myself, Nero and Fury have a key to this room. Taking out the phone, I see my sister is calling and decline it, pushing it back into my pocket. A normal person might be concerned that their sister is calling in the middle of the night. Not me, Raven is a night person, she's always been the same and knows I'm often up late.

Fury and Stryker have gone out looking for the man who stabbed Ellie. After scouring facial recognition after the attack, Blaze figured out he is a low-level mafia member from a Finnish family in West Virginia. Coincidentally, where our arch fucking nemesis is currently hiding. I'm doing my part to find this bastard too, I will not stand around waiting for others to do it first.

Checking the clips in the two Glocks are loaded, I put one in each holster under my cut.

Nero isn't acting fast enough for my liking. It's been the same for the last few weeks now. We've argued back and forth when no one else is around about how we are going after Storm. With each attempt Storm makes to harm the club, I get more and more pissed off.

I want to be out on the streets, find the bastard and end this once and for all. Nero wants to be careful, take his time, and do it right.

And I was all for that, because Nero is the brains and heart of this club. No one doubts that, even if some of the other brothers whisper that he is getting soft because he's taken an old lady. I know him better than that. The rage rippling under his skin is as clear as if he were throwing chairs and shooting up places he knows Storm frequents to find him.

If anything, having Storm go after his best friend, son and old lady has made him more determined to find and end the bastard. He just wants to do it carefully. And when we strike, we do it in a way he never sees coming. We have to make sure it takes out not just him, but anyone working with him. Leaving people out there with a grudge against us is what caused this whole mess in the first place.

It's the right way to do it, but I'm sick of sitting on our asses, watching and waiting for Storm to make his next move. Nero and I are almost always in complete agreement, but with this, we're beginning to veer off on how it should be handled, which is causing some strain between us. Above all, Nero is the President and what he says goes. Usually, he is fair, he hears us out.

Somewhere, deep down, I know he is right, but I've always been reactive. I want to end this now, not after a tactical battle where more people get hurt.

My phone rings as I lock the door, and again, it's my sister. She's probably heard about Ellie. Raven is going to keep calling until I answer because she is that level of annoying and petty. She is my sister and I love her, but the club comes above everything else. She will have to wait, but I tap out a quick text saying I'm in the middle of something and only to call or message me back if it's an emergency. When nothing comes back, I put away the phone and get back on mission.

This Kivisto asshole isn't at the hotel Blaze tracked him to. If he's got any sense, he'd have figured out we'll find him and he has gone somewhere else to lie low after failing his mission.

I've already put out calls to at least six guys I have around the city who, in turn, have put out feelers to their networks. If this prick raises his head, one of my guys will find him.

The clubhouse is still empty when I walk back across the main room to the front door, I didn't bother parking the bike out of sight in the warehouse and the bar has been closed for a few hours now so it's dark in there too when I step outside.

With only streetlights guiding me back to where my bike is parked, I move fast, antsy to get out looking. I know this place as if it were a part of me, and I know everything around it and what should be here and what shouldn't.

When something moves out of the corner of my eye over by the church across the street, I reach for my gun and crouch down behind by bike. Everyone says I'm a little reckless, hence the road name. I've been taking care of myself and my sister for years, been a part of this club, playing my part to protect. I'm more than capable of handling whatever this is.

Provided it's not more than a couple of people. Storm has never been the same as the rest of us. He uses pack mentality, never going after anyone himself. Tonight is a perfect example of that. Fucker sending someone else in to hurt a woman. My heart is pounding in my ears and my adrenaline is skyrocketing, but all of my focus is on one dark corner to the side of the church.

Holding my breath, I keep watching, wondering if my eyes were playing tricks on me, until I see it again. There is someone there. Someone who shouldn't be sneaking around out here at this time of night. My head is telling me to call for backup, but even if I needed to, I don't have time for that. This threat is imminent.

What the fuck would Storm come here for anyway? The pumping of my heart gets harder, I can feel the violence burning in my veins at the thought of him using Ellie as a distraction. There is nothing here. Unless there is... something we don't know about? Is that why Storm did this? He wants something out of the clubhouse... Or he wants to destroy it.

Fuck. Weighing up my options quickly is something I'm adept at. I pull out the phone, ready to send a message to Blaze. He is the one person who is guaranteed to check his phone instantly.

A shadow stretches across the sidewalk as the person moves out of the darkness. My eyes move quickly, taking in the surroundings, checking for anyone else.

They're not hiding, walking into the circle of light of a streetlamp, passing through at a normal pace. It doesn't look like they're trying to hide, apart from the dark clothes, hood drawn up and a bag over their shoulder. He's small, kind of wiry. Definitely not Storm. From what I saw of Kivisto on the cameras, though, it could be him. Maybe. The shadows cast around his face make it difficult to identify him.

He stops, looks around, not toward the clubhouse but at the church, then he sets down the pack and bends over. Whoever it is, he's alone. I lock the phone and push it back into my pocket, my other hand tightening around the gun.

It's now or never. My head is running in a million different directions of what could be in the bag he is pulling something out of. What the fuck is he doing?

Not to my goddamn clubhouse. I don't give a fuck what he's planning. I'm ending this.

On silent feet I move around the bike and between two parked vehicles, keeping low, watching as he sets something down beside the bag. Then he straightens, his back to me, and I make my move. At the same time, he lowers the hood, and long dark hair spills out. All I see is an assailant, someone who doesn't belong here, wanting to attack my club, my heart, my fucking world.

The only reason I haven't already fired a shot is because I don't have a silencer, and if I can take this guy out without a sound, even better.

I'm two steps away when he turns, but I'm moving too fast to stop the collision. The hoodie is unzipped, dark hair spilling over the white low-cut shirt with a strange logo I don't recognize, barely covering a body that I am unprepared for.

Even in the dark, moving as I am, I see the cut of high cheekbones, the long lashes, and full lips, and the terrified gaze of a woman, just as I slam into her and we hit the church wall. Without thinking about it, I grab the front of her shirt and pull her toward me to prevent her head from smacking into the bricks.

All without losing my grip on the gun. It's not Kivisto, but that is no reason to get complacent. Women can be the enemy too. Her eyes are wide, her body shaking as her head comes up and our eyes lock.

Fuck. That one moment is all it takes for her to get her wits about her, and she pushes back, opening her mouth to scream. Or so I thought.

What happens is so fast, I barely comprehend it until she has grabbed my arm, slipped one leg around the outside of mine and shoved her hip into my side, knocking me off balance.

She doesn't let go, spinning us with the momentum of her hip movement so my back is against the wall.

"Back the fuck up, asshole, before I fill your face with-"

She might have got the drop on me and spun me against the wall, but I still have my gun and when I point it at her chest, her eyes get even wider and she freezes.

"With what?" I snarl.

"Jesus, what the hell?" she gasps.

She holds up her hands, in one palm there is a small bottle, and I have the good sense to turn my head enough that when she sprays it, the stream goes behind the back of my head and misses my eyes. Jesus, she was going to mace me?

I grab her hand, twisting it so she drops the can. She stumbles back, but I fist her hoodie and turn her back into the wall, this time so she is facing it and I step up close so she can't move. She's tall for a woman, her baggy clothes and the darkness hid a lot, but it hides nothing now that I'm close. The scent of her is undeniably all woman.

"Who the hell are you?" I grunt out.

"Fuck you," she yells back. "I don't have any money, I have nothing worth stealing. If you think I'm going to stand here and not fight back, you're dead wrong."

"What?"

"You heard me, you fucking pervert."

She telegraphs her next move, so I'm able to back up by bending at the waist and avoiding her back kick, which was aiming between my open legs.

The fuck? "Why are you here?"

"I'm going to scream bloody murder if you don't let me go right now!"

"Go ahead, no one will come. No one will step in if they do. You messed with the wrong person tonight, sweetheart."

"Don't sweetheart me, you asshole." She fights against my hold on her again.

"You've got five seconds to tell me what the fuck you're doing sneaking around out here..." I don't know how to finish that sentence.

Shit, I don't hurt women. I've had to restrain a few. Drunk ones, handsy ones, and a few who've tried to attack the brothers or other club girls at parties, but never with violence.

"My cousin works here," she snaps, wriggling her shoulders.

"Wrong answer. I know everyone who works here. They're all my brothers."

"Your what?" She shakes her head, turning and straining to see me, but I keep my face away from her view. "Your brothers? That's bullshit. There are like three people who work here and only one of them is a man, and he is my fucking cousin."

What the fuck is she talking about? I glance up at the spire of the church I've got her pressed against. Shit, is she talking about the pastor?

"Explain this to me."

"Because you're stupid?" She asks in a mocking voice.

If I weren't so wired on adrenaline, I'd smirk at that, but I'm still not convinced this isn't to do with Storm.

"Who is your cousin?" I snap, pressing the barrel of the gun into her spine. It's enough to stop her wriggling.

"Look, I... we got off on the wrong foot here. I'm pretty sure neither of us is who the other is thinking we are."

"I don't hear a fucking explanation."

"Maybe take the gun out of my back and we can talk like civilized people."

"Honey, you're getting on my last nerve."

"Oh, I'm sorry, sweetheart. I didn't realize being held at gunpoint makes people unreasonable."

Jesus Christ. I glance down at the bag off to the side. It's open and some things inside spilled out when I collided with her. Are they... spray cans and a torch?

"You're going to graffiti this fucking church?"

I take the gun away, but keep a hand in the center of her back so she can't move, slipping it back into my holster.

"No," she grunts. "I told you, my cousin works here."

Tugging her hoodie, I twist her around so she is facing me again. Immediately she checks my hands and sees the gun is gone. Her body relaxes, but her shoulders are still back and she looks like she is one wrong move on my part from kicking me in the balls.

"Then what the fuck is this?" I indicate the bag.

"That's my supplies."

"God damn it, woman, just tell me who you are and why you're sneaking around in the middle of the night."

"You could do the same."

I've never met a more infuriating woman in my entire life. "You don't know how to answer a simple fucking question, do you?"

"Neither do you," she scoffs.

Then she folds her arms, and my eyes lower to where the movement has pushed her tits together. Luckily, I'm far enough out of reach for her to hit or kick me, and she doesn't try, which is surprising.

"Look, whatever the fuck it is you thought you were about to do to this church, it's not happening. And this is not the right place for you to be sneaking around in the dark. So do yourself a favor and get out of here, go back to wherever you came from, take your paint cans and your attitude and stay the fuck away from this neighborhood."

"Are you gonna make me?" She cocks her head.

If I'm not mistaken, there is a fucking glint of amusement in her eyes. She is enjoying this?

"Yeah, if I have to," I lean on the last two words, saying them quietly but in a tone that most of my brothers know it's time to quit messing around.

Her eyes flick back and forth on mine, and for the first time, with the dim light of early morning starting, I can see it's not a trick of the darkness and shadows, her irises are steel gray. She has some dark blue glittery shit on her eyelids but no other make-up. Not that she needs it.

"What's it gonna be," I fold my arms too and we stare at each other. Neither one of us is about to back down.

"When you two have finished comparing dicks, or vaginas, I'm not sure who has what..."

We both jolt at the voice, but where my little villain's eyes go to my sister's, I keep mine locked on her. I'm used to Raven's sarcastic drawl, but I'm not all that happy she crept up on me without me hearing a damn thing.

What is even more shocking, the woman who I've still not taken my eyes off, looks like she knows my sister.

"What are you doing here?"

"I tracked you when you didn't answer my calls," Raven says, walking towards us. I spare her a sarcastic glare.

"Raven? You know this guy?" The woman asks.

"Unfortunately," she gives her a sweet smile, then turns it on me. "Kinsley, this is my brother. River."

"Rebel," I correct her, it's habit. When she is irritated or feeling left out, Raven pulls this petulant shit. She's being a little asshole using my real name.

"River the Rebel?" The woman asks. There is that amusement again, the mischief dancing across her face as she stares, waiting for me to react.

"I've got more important shit to do. You know her," I turn to my sister. "Vouch for her."

Raven's mirth drops as she takes in my stance, my look. The one that says it's time to stop fucking about. She nods, eyeing me more intently now, wanting to question me about what is going on. She won't, not in front of a stranger.

"Do yourself a favor and stay away," I tell the woman before turning away.

"That'll be kind of hard," she says, making me pause and look back at her. She smirks at my annoyance. "Seeing as I'll be living here for the next three months, painting a commissioned mural on my cousin's church."

She wants to get a rise out of me, but it won't work. After tonight, chances are I'll see a lot more of her. I don't even want to unpack what thoughts of that are doing to me. Taking a few paces closer to her, she doesn't back away, she doesn't look scared, she faces me square on, her head tilted so our eyes are locked.

"Then whenever you see me coming," my voice is low so my nosey sister can't hear. "Walk the other way."

"Gladly."

She wants to have the last word. I'll let her. This time. But just to be a jerk and because it will get a rise out of her, I kick her bag as I turn to walk away. Spray paint rolls out across the sidewalk, and she curses after me as I head to my bike.

I spare Raven a quick look, and she follows me.

"What are you doing out here? It's not safe tonight. You need to go home."

"What do you mean?" she asks. "Has something happened?"

"Nero is floating the idea of a lockdown."

It's the only way to get Raven off my back and listen. I'm not explaining anything else.

"Go home. Until you hear otherwise, carry on as normal, but take no chances. I fucking mean it, Raven."

"Okay, I heard you." Her brow creases, then she rolls her eyes, she knows I'm not going anywhere till she is in her car. "I can't just leave her here."

"I don't care what you do with her, just get off the street."

"Do you have to be such an asshole all the time?"

My look tells her to stop asking questions she already knows the answer to.

"Fine. She is staying here, so I'll convince her not to start her art tonight."

Who fucking paints a mural in the dark? I don't understand normal people.

"Be careful," she whispers.

I dip my chin as Raven turns away. She speaks to the little villain for a few moments, who gathers her things and walks towards the rear entrance of the church. Raven walks past me and makes a comment that I don't bother paying attention to as I watch *her*.

Once I hear my sister getting into her car and turning over the engine, my body relaxes. She might be a pain in the ass, but I don't want her around here alone right now. Or this other woman, who is not rushing to do as my sister told her. Probably because the directive came from me.

She has a key to the door, which further confirms her story. I will not leave until both women are away from here.

Pushing the door open, she turns back to me, giving the motorcycle a long look, her eyes running from my feet to my head. That one look has my dick getting into the conversation, which is fucking stupid with a woman like this...

And I'm proven right when she stops eating me up with her eyes, then slowly and deliberately raises her middle finger at me.

The smile on my face is slight and involuntary as she disappears inside the church, which is quickly wiped off when Raven drives by, repeating the gesture.

Fuck, if those two are friends...

My cell rings again, and I check it to see Fury's name.

Fun time is over. We have a motherfucker to find and destroy.

Acknowledgements

THANK YOU SO MUCH for reading. If you have enjoyed Nashville, please consider leaving a review, these really help indie authors.

Since writing Nero, Book 1 of the series, I've found an amazing group of ARC readers and want to thank each of them for taking the time to read these books, it's very much appreciated.

To Finn as always, even though he's going through some tough times, he still keeps me laughing. Big thanks to my family also for their support and helping keep me sane.

Thank you to Sandra and Karen for their amazing Beta reading skills. I'd be lost without you. And to all my indie author friends, particularly SE Robin and Em Solstice who have got me through the writing process and challenged me to keep going.

And as always, to the readers for supporting me and loving these characters, and for being able to spot all the tie ins to my other books, I do weave a tangled web!

Thanks

Love Chris

Also by Chris Reilly

The Devil's Chaos Duet:
Devil's Chaos
Devil's Daughter
Devil's Falling

Novellas:
Devil's Desire
Devil's Kiss

BreakNeck Series:
Sky Full of Stars
Touch in the Dark
The Sounds of Her
Perfect Storm

Spin-Off Novellas:
Standing Still
Fight For Forever

Sports Romance:
Off The Line

Red Alert Series:
Electric Touch
Midnight Heat

Standalone Romance:
Reckless

Christmas Eve, Eve
Undone, Love Times Three

Blackhawk Ink Tattoo Series
Broken

Blackhawk Disciples MC
Nero
Nashville

About The Author

I was born and raised in Liverpool, UK and loved to read from as early as I can remember. Writing came along when I was about 13-14 and English and essay writing (creative obviously) became my favorite lesson! I currently live with my son and two cats.

The majority of my 20's/30's I read thrillers. Both mysteries and detective-based books. I made the switch to romance when I picked up a book called 'Dirty Letters' I loved it and the authors so much, I went looking for more. I then went down the rabbit hole of Indie Romance and was amazed and inspired by these amazing authors.

Happily ever after is always the goal for my characters, but there may be a cliff-hanger or two, and definitely some angsty situations to work through, occasionally a little bit dark, but oh so delicious.

www.ingramcontent.com/pod-product-compliance
Lightning Source LLC
LaVergne TN
LVHW020043110826
845155LV00029B/624

* 9 7 8 1 9 1 9 4 5 4 0 1 6 *